SARINA, SWEETHEART

Sarina, Sweetheart

MEGAN CARNEY

The characters, names, and events as well as all places, incidents, organizations, and dialog in this novel are either the products of the writer's imagination or are used fictitiously.

Megan Carney is also the author of the Navy Trent series:

Trap and Trace, From Hackerville with Love, and *Humans, Practicing .*

Cover art by BeeJavier.

Learn more about Megan Carney at megancarney.com.

ISBN-13: 978-1-7347590-6-8

Dedicated to those who fight for the freedom of the human spirit.

Prologue

My name is Sarina.

My breath is poison.

I was not born out of love.

I'm not sure whether my father named me after the virus or whether he named the virus after me. Some of my father's less accurate biographers claim he gave me a Russian name because the HF186-2A outbreak (think Ebola plus seizures and hallucinations) was part of a Communist plot. They're wrong about my name. The name Sarina is Latin in origin, not Russian. My father isn't even Russian. As for whether my father is a Communist, it's possible.

A biological warfare expert without a conscience would be Putin's best friend. For all I know, he and Putin communicate regularly via letters to and from my father's maximum security prison cell. I only know this from the bits and pieces of my history I've managed to read through Mentor's proxies. The censors at the lab are very careful about what I'm allowed to read otherwise. You probably want to know how Mentor and I were even allowed to start talking. More on that later. In this story, my father is the catalyst. We should start with him.

In the grand tradition of psychopaths, my father has a cult of followers. Even after two decades, many of them still communicate with him in prison. He's convinced them the virus is a test of sorts, in the same way charismatics handle snakes. It's easier than sending them all the vaccine, I guess. The only people my father vaccinated were himself and my mother. I've always wondered how his followers can overlook that.

If you ask one of his groupies, I am my father's crowning achievement. Other people call me an abomination. The more accurate biographers note the root of my name is 'sarin.' As in sarin gas, the poisonous nerve agent used in the Tokyo subway attacks and on Bloody Friday in Iraq. I am the only known person in the world able to carry HF186-2A without dying from it. Sometimes I imagine my breath is green with the poison he taught my lungs to manufacture. The virus I carry is a hemorrhagic fever designed to attack the nervous system. There are no memoirs to record firsthand accounts of what HF186-2A feels like; none of the approximately 300 victims survived. Gruesome videos taken inside the quarantine facility show men and women gone mad, bleeding from every orifice and screaming at the walls. The lucky ones choked on their own tongues before the hallucinations came.

I was born out of desperation 23 years ago. My mother wanted a baby to please my father. My father wanted a child to destroy the world. He told my mother he was infertile— they would need to do IVF. He used the lab at the IVF facility, where he worked as a doctor, to grow embryos and tinker with their genes. Most of his embryos died under the microscope. Of the ones that survived long enough to be implanted, only two pregnancies were carried to term.

The first was stillborn. I was the second.

Afraid that I wouldn't survive, he insisted on a family road trip to the docks in Key West. He was hoping to infect a few cruise ships while he had the chance. Instead, government officials traced the budding pandemic in south Florida to us: the Wocek family, with their adorable 6-week-old daughter, Sarina.

All reports agree that my mother was unaware of my father's plans. She's variously described as "shell-shocked," "despondent," "decimated," and "crushed." They took us to a hazmat building—all plastic and cots and lights—and put my parents in separate rooms. I was kept with my mother because she was still breast-feeding. They questioned her for hours. She refused to let go of me. When they told her I was engineered to be the carrier of a virus that could wipe out half of humanity, she cried. When she realized I would spend the rest of my life in a lab, poked and prodded like a science experiment, she tried to smother me.

She had the right idea.

I have a lot of time on my hands in the lab. I watch more television than is healthy. Most people my age spend their free time going to bars or complaining about the costs of tuition and the crappy food in the cafeteria. I have hobbies. I've mastered a lot of hobbies over the years. Model building. Knitting. Painting. Puzzles. Jewelry making. Sewing. Some hobbies are forbidden: chemistry, electronics, cooking, martial arts. My latest round of hobbies has a higher purpose. To keep my censors in the dark, I limit my official requests to hobbies that seem innocuous. Like beauty makeovers. I use Mentor's proxies to study things that might raise the censors' ire. Like magic tricks. The two hobbies pair nicely. Learning how to use makeup is a great excuse to spend a lot of time in the bathroom with the door half-shut, where I can practice my sleight of hand.

Aside from my doctors, the only person who interacts with me regularly inside the lab is the in-house tutor. She's a relentlessly cheerful woman with blonde hair that naturally curls into spirals. I have received a first-class education in the humanities, sciences and social arts. They spend a lot of energy preparing me for a world I'll never see.

I have contact with exactly four people outside of the lab. Three of them are language tutors who teach me via Skype in carefully monitored sessions. They've been told I'm the mentally disturbed daughter of a rich family, just in case I get any ideas about asking for help escaping. I am fluent in French, Mandarin, and Russian. I'm more than adequate in Italian and Spanish. All of my tutors have been told to make sure my accent sounds as close to a native's as possible. I don't know why the lab cares. I don't dare ask. It's nice to have people to talk to, even if they think I'm deranged, and my French tutor is easy on the eyes.

The fourth person is Mentor. The censors at the lab know him as mentor4923@3Dchess.com. On my 14th birthday, Dr. Choebach gave me Millennium 3D chess. The box contained an ad that offered a free game with a master via email. Dr. Choebach convinced the censors it was safe if the messages were restricted to moves. You're probably surprised the censors would allow even that. The truth is, I didn't even consider escaping before I knew Mentor. When they granted me permission to email him, I was a model prisoner. The lab carefully raised me to believe that I was doing the public a service by allowing myself to be studied. It was Mentor who encouraged me to look further. He sent the message that opened my eyes.

Don't take the pills.

Chapter 1

I like that my French tutor lives in the heart of Paris. He runs our video chats from a sidewalk coffee shop. Behind him, I watch the city of lights change into her evening clothes. It is early afternoon here, and the clock tower in the background puts Paris six hours ahead. I've calculated that the time difference places me somewhere in the Eastern half of the United States. Men and women with frowns and briefcases are swallowed by the underground entrance to the metro, their figures slowly replaced by couples holding hands. A clutch of girlfriends in skin-tight clothing giggle and click their heels as they pass. I know they are cold by the way the huddle together, headed for a fashionable party no doubt.

"Sarina, m'avez-vous entendu?" he asks.

My attention is forced back to his warm green eyes and curly brown hair. "Désolé, quoi?" *Sorry, what?*

"Guy forces us to work, en francais."

"Guy nous a fait travailler."

"Bon travail. Maintenant, we dressed."

Easy. "Nous nous sommes habillé."

He smiles, like it's a trap. "Spell it."

I write the words on a sketchpad. He shakes his head. "Nous nous sommes habillés. In this compound verb construction—"

The screen freezes with those gorgeous lips pursed on the last syllable. I see the wireless signal on my laptop has dropped. The blaring of the fire alarm follows. By the guards' relaxed posture, I know it must be a drill. Figures they would have it during the lesson with the one tutor I like. My Russian tutor is ancient, and my Mandarin tutor barks at me like a drill sergeant.

The loudspeakers crackle to life. "Attention, all personnel. This is scenario three. Assume the sprinklers have failed and the RIC is inoperable. Proceed according to the manual. Non-compliant personnel will be disciplined."

RIC refers to respiratory isolation chamber. It's a plexiglass rectangle just big enough for me to lie down, equipped with an advanced breathing system. The tangle of pumps, tubes, and tanks pulls in air from outside the coffin, then stores and recirculates every exhalation. The batteries will last for eight hours. If I'm not at the auxiliary lab by then, they will let me suffocate. If the RIC is inoperable, they leave me to burn alive.

I get my earplugs out of a drawer to dull the sound of the alarm.

The walls of my cage are transparent. I watch the luckier ones make their escape as I sit at my desk. I know the scientists by their clothes; they are all civilians. My guards are all soldiers. They wear fatigues, as if this were a military base. Which I guess it is, in a way.

The head psychologist, the one I meet with weekly, sees me watching the spectacle and looks annoyed. We'll talk about it in our next session, I'm sure. He's often told me that I should use the distractions available to me to get through fire drills. I think that would make *him* feel better.

My room is filled with distractions that are supposed to make me happy: a nice television and a large, but carefully censored, movie collection; an HD DVR connected to a premium cable package (any show I watch has to be recorded and reviewed by the censors first); the latest version of every video game console ever made (I'm allowed pretty much any video game, except for the realistic ones that might teach me how to drive or how to escape); a large, rotating collection of clothing catalogs and fashion magazines; a shelf of neatly organized clear plastic tubs with my fabric collection and art supplies, everything except scissors, pins and any sharp objects, of course. (Those I'm only allowed to use under the supervision of a guard. Sometimes, for fun, I spill a box of pins on the floor. Then the guard has to pick them up and count them.)

Nurse Rita in her too-tight scrubs marches out from the hallway that holds the operating wing with a purpose. Like she does everyday. Dr. Werham, my anesthesiologist, doesn't even look back before pushing through the swinging doors on the hallway that leads to the lobby. I often wonder why she hasn't arranged a little accident for me yet. My weak heart could easily explain the mistake away. Only Dr. Choebach turns to offer me a sad smile. He'd take me with him if they wouldn't kill him for it. This is his least favorite drill.

I study my 3D chess game in progress to spite them all. The handsome board gleams under the fluorescent lights. It is three glass boards mounted vertically, about seven inches apart on silver posts. White starts on the lower board, black on the upper board. I only know my opponent and teacher by his handle, Mentor. I was 14 when we started playing against each other. Seven years later, I only win about every fifth game, and perhaps only because he lets me. It's hard to say.

We communicate through moves in email. My censors learned just enough about the game to make sure the moves are legal. That's probably why they didn't notice the second year when Mentor's tactics changed from brilliant to average. I started winning every other game, when before I had hardly won any. I had plenty of time to study the board and eventually teased the code out of his moves.

That first message laid out the deal we keep to this day. If I win, he gives me an hour on a proxy that lets me read any page I want on the Internet. If he wins, he names a book or an article I have to read. The list reads like the syllabus of a graduate-level philosophy course, which explains why my censors haven't objected to any of my requests for reading material.

The fire drills are a good time for me to decode the messages, since everyone's distracted. I pull the well-thumbed strategy manual from the shelf above my desk. Every one of Mentor's moves designates a word from the manual; it's the key to the code.

I use my sketchpad and colored pencils to decode Mentor's message. If I write softly, I can cover up the messages with art. The panel of psychologists who pretend to be concerned about me enjoys dissecting the meaning behind my creations. I stick to abstract art so they see whatever they want to see.

On my laptop, I pull up this game's worth of emails with Mentor. First move: his, B2b2. White bishop to second board, file b, row two. Second board means second chapter. The column b converted to a numeral means second paragraph. Row two means the second word. Two, two, two.

B2b2: German

R2a1: philosopher's

N2d1: brilliance

Lots of his messages start out this way lately. The D'Agostino three-move opening is his way of referencing Nietzsche. My current reading assignment is "Thus Spoke Zarathustra," a favorite of anarchists, Nazis, and apparently Mentor.

Truth is, I don't even like talking to Mentor anymore. I need him to get access to the proxies, but his messages are starting to get tiresome.

Q2e2: mythical

B2a3: master

He must be referencing the concept of the Übermensch, the overman. Some people believe that the original—and non-successful—version of the Superman character was a villain modeled on Nietzsche's ideas.

B3h3: above

R2c1: people

B2g4: risks

B1f5: all

B2e4: for

1c3: improvement

Rx2c7: humanity

I'm sure Mentor has better grammar in real life. The limitations imposed by the legal moves in the game make us both sound like stroke victims sometimes.

R3h3: consent

Rx3h7: pawns

B3b2: not

R3h8: required

I write it out as a sentence, adding punctuation and prepositions where it makes sense. *German philosopher's brilliance—mythical master above people. Risks all for improvement of humanity. Consent of pawns not required.*

I want to win this game just to make him eat his words. I think I can set up a fork to threaten both his bishop and his queen. But the move has to make sense in the context of the message I've already spelled out. I check the clock on the wall. It's been five minutes since the drill started. In a real fire, people would scatter to their homes. If someone happened to ask, both the guards and the civilians would deny they knew anything at all. This lab isn't supposed to exist. I'm not supposed to exist.

The guards will be back soon. I reconstruct my own message to figure out my next move.

Am studying the book hard. You have interesting thoughts on pawns and people. Looking forward to

I try to use a lot of filler words. There are lots of places in the manual with 'to,' 'the,' 'it,' etc. It leaves me more options for moves. It also means I have to find fewer things of substance to say to Mentor, which makes my life easier. My messages used to sound more like his, with all the padding left out. He was the first person I'd talked to without the censors standing over my shoulder. I told him about how whole days disappeared in the anesthesia of surgery. How I would wake up with injuries that no one would explain. I told him how much I wished for the childhoods pictured in sitcoms, even for the angst of a college student's identity crisis. I told him about my higher purpose and why I couldn't leave.

I just wanted a friend. Instead, he started lecturing me on his own version of a nihilist paradise.

He hasn't told me anything about himself, but I imagine he's a 42-year old who lives in his parents' basement, reading too many comics and playing too many video games. His interpretation of philosophy is simplistic and self-serving, focused on justifying the use of his brilliance as a weapon. I hope for humanity's sake he never gets access to any sort of lab.

Still, occasionally he makes a good point. There's a balance to be found between Apollonian rationality and Dionysian pleasure. Sacrificing all of your happiness for the sake of others might be noble, but it isn't natural. In my darker moods, his arguments lurk at the edge of my thoughts. I have to remind myself everyday that my desires are unrealistic.

I wanted things. Correction, I want things. I want to walk down a pier and hear the waves crashing beneath my feet. I want to go to a crowded concert and feel the music vibrate in my bones. I want to ride in a convertible with the top down. I want to flirt with a handsome man. I want to go home with one. I want to play chess with friends in a coffee shop while drinking lattes with designs in the crema.

I settle on Q2g7, which codes 'next,' then tap out the one-word email to Mentor on my laptop. When I hit Send, it doesn't actually send, of course. The censors will have to review it first. When they come back, they will move a black queen from 2e7 to 2g7 on the board in their office, completely unaware that they are pawns in our game.

I know I'm a pawn in theirs.

Chapter 2

Day and night in the lab are marked by lights on a timer. I get out of bed when the lights click on because it's expected of me. When I finish my shower, I notice breakfast isn't waiting. Today must be a surgery day. My next meal might be lunch or dinner; I have no idea.

When Mentor told me not to take the pills, he was referring to the pills given to me by my only friend in the world, Dr. Choebach. I can see the good doctor now, approaching through the glass walls of my cage. Behind me, there is a hallway and a fire exit I can't reach. In front of me, there's an observation area, a guard's post, and a hallway that leads to the lobby. To my left is another hallway that leads to the operating wing. I live in a fish tank. The only room in my cage where I have any privacy is the bathroom that doesn't have a lock.

Today, like many other days, I will be going into surgery. That's why Dr. Choebach is bringing the pre-op pills and a stretcher. He punches a code into the door and holds his face in front of the retinal scanner. There's a soft beep before the heavy deadbolts on the door slide open.

"Good morning, sweetheart." He doesn't need a mask or anything around me because everyone here gets the vaccine developed at the lab.

I don't mind that he calls me sweetheart. He has handsome dark blue eyes, a square jaw and a kind smile. His wife, Dr. Werham, works here too. Dr. Werham always shoots dirty looks at Nurse Rita when she tries to flirt with her husband.

He sets the plastic cup of pills on my desk. "Your pre-op pills." The sedative in the IV line would be enough to put me to sleep for the operation. They prefer that I don't see the operating room at all. "And your sterilized outfit." He puts the ridiculous operating gown on the desk, and the package crinkles.

I know the gown's ridiculous because I made it. I make earrings, too. The panel of psychologists that pretends to be concerned with my well-being was cheered by my sudden interest in the creative arts several years ago. They took it as a sign I had accepted my confinement and was making the best of it. They recommended I be allowed to wear my outfits "whenever possible," including into surgery. The only downside is I'm obligated to wear my designs outside of surgery too, to make the ruse convincing. Clowns would be offended by my style.

"Today is just—well—it's just a nerve block instead of general anesthesia," he says. "We're only operating on your legs." He wants to tell me more, but it's not allowed. He's already been disciplined once for telling me that I was in pain because they took a bone marrow sample. Around here, you only get one warning. I don't know what happens on the second warning. All I know is I never see that person again.

"I'll go change," I say.

The bathroom is meticulously clean. It's not about my comfort; it's about making sure I don't keep anything hidden. I'm allowed to keep my earrings in here because they don't know their real purpose. I change into the gown. The sleeves are long and flared and nearly cover my hand. The fabric of the sleeves is layered so it flares out like a skirt. Inside the innermost layer, there is a pocket that runs the length of my wrist. I stuff the pocket with cotton cosmetic pads. I'm allowed nearly unlimited quantities of these for my makeovers.

My earrings are mostly a series of dangling, oddly shaped pipes. I couldn't care less about the shapes. But they might get suspicious about my motives if I made 10 pairs of the exact same design. Each earring has one sharp end and one open end. The sharp end will pierce the IV line. All of them are filled with a mixture of sugar and water that dries to form a cap. The cap gradually dissolves under the pressure of the liquid in the IV line; it keeps air from being introduced into the line. In the sleeve of my gown, I have created a tiny pocket just above the larger pocket with the cotton pads. This tiny pocket is for the earring.

I hear the harsh buzz that signals I've had the bathroom door closed too long. In 10 seconds, the door will open automatically. I have one more thing to do. Behind the mirror, they keep small quantities of acetaminophen for me. The pills look just like the pre-op pills. I open one of the packages and hide the contents in my hand.

Dr. Choebach is waiting for me, fidgeting uncomfortably on the small couch next to my desk. The stretcher waits for me, too.

"Can I have a small glass of water?" I could have filled one of the paper cups myself. But I like that Dr. Choebach will get a glass of water for me. And I need the distraction to pull off my magic trick.

"Sure," he says.

I take the cup of pre-op pills in my left hand and pretend to dump them into my right. Dr. Choebach returns with my water. I open my right hand to show Dr. Choebach the acetaminophen I took from the bathroom and set the empty cup on the desk. The actual pre-op pills are now hidden in my left hand. I swallow the acetaminophen with the small glass of water. I open my mouth and lift my tongue so he can see I've taken the pills. It's part of the protocol. I don't want to get him in trouble.

I used to be more difficult. They think I've surrendered; I've just learned new tricks.

Dr. Choebach frowns and sighs. "Lie down, please."

I lie down on the stretcher. I let my head drop to the side. I take this opportunity to slip the pre-op pills into the pocket filled with cotton pads. I can see through the glass wall into my small dance studio, next to the operating wing. Every lab rat needs an exercise wheel; that's why they allow the dance studio. I'm always looking up dance videos. My watchers think dance is innocent. They don't study history. In the 16th century, African slaves in Brazil practiced fighting moves by disguising them as a dance style called capoeira.

Nurse Rita comes out of the operating wing. She could benefit from a makeover; she has blotchy skin and a pug nose. Not that I'd give her makeup tips; she's been nothing but mean to me. She doesn't like me for the same reason Dr. Werham doesn't like me. They think I have designs on their precious doctor. The truth is, I'd be nice to them too if they'd just smile at me once in a while.

Nurse Rita leans into the retinal scanner and unlocks the door with her ugly face. I close my eyes and pretend to be drowsy. It's a good time to review my plan.

There is one good thing my father has done for me. When he was messing around with my genes to create his biological weapon, he weakened my heart. It's too risky to give me general anesthesia for all my operations, so they use nerve blocks when they can. Nothing I can do will let me stay awake during general anesthesia.

A nerve block is a different story. There are three steps in the nerve-block sedation process. The first is the pre-op pills that are supposed to knock me out before I leave my room. These are meant to keep me unconscious until the second step, the intra-operative sedative. That sedative is delivered via an IV. The IV only keeps me unconscious. The actual numbing happens in the third step, the nerve block.

Already, Nurse Rita and Dr. Choebach are talking like I'm asleep.

"You're too kind to her," Nurse Rita says. Even if she didn't stink of it, I can tell by her voice that she smokes. She probably thinks the gravelly voice is sexy.

"A glass of water doesn't cost me anything," he says.

"She doesn't need any more advantages."

I've heard Nurse Rita grumble about my attractiveness before. A young Liv Tyler and I could be sisters, except that I have dark brown hair and dark green eyes. Not that it matters here.

I'm not sure which part of my life she's jealous of: the part where I am forced to be a lab animal, or the part where the lab hides its true plans for me.

In a few minutes they will wheel me into the operating room. Nurse Rita will hook me up to the EKG, leaning over more than necessary to stretch her uniform over her ass. Dr. Werham will put an IV in my left hand. When Dr. Werham is distracted with the nerve block, I will kink the IV line. When the nerve block is in place, I will press the line against the exposed tip of the earring in my sleeve. The liquid will dissolve the hard sugar-water mixture until the sedative flows to the cotton pads.

It's taken years for me to get the process down, but the effort is worth it. The only time they speak honestly around me is when they think I'm not listening. They don't want me to know what they're doing to my body. They don't want me to know they have a cure. The first time I tried to escape, I just wanted out. My second attempt will be for very different reasons.

I've overheard a lot since I figured out how to stay awake during minor surgeries. Engineering a child to be a weapon of mass destruction, that's unethical. Refining a weapon of mass destruction that someone else created? That's just being clever.

Chapter 3

Faking sedation is tricky. Sedated patients aren't stiff like mannequins or relaxed like in sleep. I pretend I'm a doll with loose joints, posable as they see fit. Nurse Rita takes the head of the stretcher and wheels me toward the operating wing. She slams the stretcher through the swinging doors harder than necessary. I let the impact slide my arm off the edge, and it swings against the cold metal frame. Dr. Choebach stops the stretcher, then lifts my arm back onto the warm sheets.

"Rita," he says firmly.

"Fine," she snaps. "I'll be more careful."

I don't believe her.

Dr. Choebach's weight presses against my arm as he leans over the gurney. "It's not her fault," he whispers to Nurse Rita. "She's a victim here, too."

I've spent my entire life suffering for my father's crimes. I don't think I can carry more blame than that.

"They're going to let her go," Nurse Rita is whispering too, almost frantically. "Once she's gone, what will they need us for?"

It occurs to me that Nurse Rita's blotchy skin could be from crying, not genetics. If so, she's cried a lot over the years. My newfound sympathy for her is uncomfortable and impractical. I don't want to see Dr. Choebach, or even Nurse Rita, hurt on my account, but there's nothing I can do to protect them. If they're letting me go, it means they've decided how to weaponize me. It means I have less time to escape than I thought.

Nurse Rita hits the swinging doors into the operating room a little less forcefully than before.

"Rita," I hear Dr. Werham say. She's the anesthesiologist and Dr. Choebach's wife. There's no welcome in her greeting.

"Jennifer," the nurse replies.

"Girls," Dr. Choebach says.

Nurse Rita pushes aside the ruffled collar of my outfit to attach small plastic circles to my chest and shoulders, muttering about how my fashions make her life harder. The circles connect me to the EKG that monitors my heart rate. A little lotion wouldn't kill her; maybe then her hands wouldn't feel like sandpaper.

Now it's Dr. Werham's turn.

She stands on my left side, like she always does. It's why I let my head drop to the right. Despite my long history with needles, I can't help but wince when she places the IV. The sedative is a cold trickle in my veins. It will put me to sleep if I can't kink the IV line in time. But I can't move just yet. She presses a sheet of sticky plastic—it's like a bandage—over the IV. The plastic will hold the IV in place during surgery. There's no way to disconnect the IV from my hand. The cold trickle has reached my shoulder. It's my imagination, I know. The liquid would have warmed to my body temperature by now. The wooziness will start soon. Sometimes Dr. Werharm moves quickly enough that I can kink the IV line before I pass out. Sometimes she doesn't.

When Dr. Werham is satisfied with the IV, she tells her husband to lift me up. The nerve block requires access to my spinal column. He threads his arms underneath mine and gently lifts me. I slump against his chest. Sometimes at this point he whispers, "I'm sorry" very softly. He does today. He smells like mint and lemon.

I know Nurse Rita isn't close because I can't smell her perfume. It's like roses dipped in disinfectant. With Nurse Rita elsewhere and Dr. Werham distracted by the nerve block, I can finally kink the IV line. My fingers seem fat and clumsy from the sedative, but I hold on. I feel the cool sting of alcohol along my spine then the prick of a small needle. The alcohol is to disinfect the skin, and the needle is a local anesthetic. I won't feel the big needle she uses to pierce the spinal column, or the very thin catheter that follows it.

I can hear the soft hiss of the pump Dr. Werham connects to the catheter. It will deliver the trickle of liquid that blocks nerve signals from moving up the spinal column. They don't just want to dull the pain; they don't want me to feel anything at all. My legs are being erased. I'm a torso.

Knowing I can't run or kick or even move my hips makes me want to swear at them in all the languages I know. I have to fight to keep my breathing even or the EKG will betray my ruse. For a while, they tried to use a brain wave monitor to make sure I was actually asleep during surgery. But the technology was experimental, and they never could get a clean reading. They thought it was due to interference from the other machines in the operating room. Turns out brain wave monitors are also sensitive to the iPod minis I hid in my sleeves.

"Lower her down, please," says Dr. Werham.

He lowers me carefully back to the stretcher. My chest feels like it's attached to a sack of meat.

There's no danger of me passing out, but until I can bypass the IV line there's a risk that someone will notice the level isn't going down. I can't do anything but listen very carefully. It will be safe to bypass the IV line when I hear two things: Nurse Rita pushing the tray of surgical instruments, and the squeak of the wheels on Dr. Werham's stool. That means Nurse Rita will be busy assisting Dr. Choebach with surgery, and Dr. Werham will be busy monitoring my vital signals.

I hear steel knives sliding on the green paper napkin in the surgical tray. I hear the cart being pushed by Nurse Rita. One long second after that, I hear Dr. Werham's stool squeak. It's time.

I press the IV line kinked in my hand against the pointy end of the earring hidden in my sleeve. The fabric pocket that holds the earring in place stretches, but my stitches hold. I wait for the slight give as the plastic line is breached, then quickly release the pressure. The damage to the IV line must not be noticeable. Now I just have to wait until the sugar plug in the earring dissolves. I'm not worried about bubbles in the IV line. The system has worked so far. And anyway, it would be only too kind of them to let me die.

The cotton pads hidden in my sleeve are wet. That means the sedative is flowing in the IV line again, just not into my arm.

"Scalpel," Dr. Choebach says.

"Here it is," Nurse Rita says. Her voice is missing the usual singsong flirt. I wonder how much time she has before she's irrelevant. Before I have to escape.

"Making the first incision," he says. His stiff paper mask rustles. I only know he's cut me because I hear the hiss of the suction machine change to a gurgle.

"The tracker," Nurse Rita says.

That's new. A tracker seems overly paranoid, even for my watchers. My keepers would never let me walk around unsupervised outside a cage. *They're going to let her go.* Did Nurse Rita mean I would actually be let go? Not just moved to a different sort of cage?

Surgical gowns rustle again, and I assume the tracker is implanted. "Second incision," he says. He seems more upset than usual today. If I were waxing poetic, I would say he is profoundly sad.

"The capsule," says Nurse Rita.

Containing what? If it were another tracker, wouldn't she just say so? Dr. Choebach is still. I know because his surgical gown crackles with every move. "We could cure her completely," he says.

Dr. Werham's stool squeaks again. She must have turned around. "She'll never know," she says brusquely. "Just put the damn thing in. She'll get out of this place and she'll never know." There's no kindness in her tone; she's too pragmatic for that. I am an assignment she was ready to be done with a long time ago.

But never mind all that. Did Dr. Choebach mean I'm partially cured right now? That I won't have to live the life of a hermit after I escape?

My first attempt was just after my 16th birthday. I made it as far as the hallway leading to the front door. I failed because I hesitated. I was so focused on getting past security that I hadn't planned much beyond that. When I saw the first bar of sunlight —real sunlight—under the door, I realized how ridiculous I'd been. If I had walked out onto a city street, infecting everyone I passed, could I live with myself? Back then, I wouldn't have fared any better in a rural area.

I'm smarter now. Faking sedation has allowed me to learn a lot more about the lab. We're near a state forest that includes mountains. Where there are mountains, there are caves. I have spent years carefully watching every entertainment show that includes survival tips. Like *Survivorman* and *Man vs Wild*. Now I know all sorts of tricks for how to find water, how to trap game, how to build a fire without matches. They might not work, of course. I haven't exactly had a chance to practice.

But I would gladly die shivering and hungry on the hard floor of a cave if it meant I could spend my last nights outside of a cage.

Something beeps in the lab.

"Her heart rate is spiking," Dr. Werham says. "Are you done?"

"Rita, clear the incisions, please," he says, the professional again.

I hear more rustling; she's checking to make sure nothing is left in the wounds before Dr. Choebach stitches me up. Nothing, that is, except what they deliberately implanted. "Incisions are clear," Nurse Rita says.

"Closing the incisions now," he says. I try to imagine his hands on my skin, pulling needle through flesh. Dr. Werham's touch is cold. And Nurse Rita is the one who does my annual exams. She has the bedside manner of an irate troll.

I have to unkink the IV line now. Soon, Dr. Werham will come over to remove the epidural. I nudge the earring back in its pocket. The collection of cotton pads is moist against my wrist. I must remember to remove all evidence of my tricks after I wake up in bed. The sedative is starting to work. Dr. Choebach's voice, asking Nurse Rita for something, becomes hard to follow. Like he's talking too fast. The clicking sound of Dr. Werham's heels grows softer as she walks closer. I press my fingers into the mattress so I won't kink the IV line again.

It's my imagination again, this chill spreading all over my body. Like being pulled into icy water. I can't hear any voices now. I can't even feel the sheets against my skin. There's nothing. It's cold and dark, like the bottom of the deepest sea.

Chapter 4

A fire truck speeds down the highway. I know it's a dream because I can see the sky. A gray, hazy sky with clouds locked in combat, trying to swallow each other. It's so hot. I throw off my blankets and sheets. I rub at my eyes to open them, like every morning, but I find my eyes are already open.

I'm not dreaming. It's not a gray, hazy sky; it's smoke. Great, billowing masses of smoke surround my cage. Black snowflakes land on the glass roof. Smaller wisps have invaded my room. I start coughing and can't stop. No matter how much I cough, my throat still burns. The sound of the fire truck in my dreams was only the fire alarm blaring.

I listen hard for the hiss of water and watch for droplets spinning from the ceiling. Flashes of stationary metal wink at me through the gray swirls, the polished steel turned orange by the reflection of the flames. The sprinklers aren't moving. I look at my coffin and see a beam from the ceiling has fallen, cracking the lid. The guard who usually sits outside my cage is gone. Of course he is. Everyone is gone. The sprinklers have failed and my coffin is inoperable. Fire drill scenario number three.

I try to remember where the exits are. The interior of the lab is shaped like an L, with my cage at the corner. The longer hallway leads to the operating wing and the offices. The shorter leads to the lobby. There are only two exits, one directly behind me and one in the lobby. The closest exit, the fire exit the guards usually prop open on their cigarette breaks, is already blocked by flames. The other exit is down the hallway towards the front door. That hallway is nearly blocked by flames, too.

It's an academic exercise anyway. There's no way to unlock my cage from the inside. There's no fire exit for me.

The laminated wood of the guard's desk blisters then ignites. The monitors and the control panel blacken, and the acrid stench of burning plastic reaches me. I have considered many times how I would die. A botched medical procedure. My weak heart finally giving out under anesthesia. Killed by a guard while trying to escape. There were times when dying seemed like an acceptable ending. But now, coughing up smoke and dripping with sweat, all I can think of is how agonizing it must be to burn to death.

I run to my desk and pick up the chair. I hit the metal legs against the glass until the smoky air forces me to my knees. The glass isn't even scratched. Orange, ghostly flames flicker in and out of sight in the thick, roaring clouds. Gray, smoky fingers reach under the door and around the side. Around the side of a sealed door. I half-stumble, half-crawl towards the door. It's open, just a sliver. Enough so the lock won't engage, but not enough so someone running from the lab would notice. On the floor in front of my knees are two objects that weren't there last night: a white drawstring bag and a pair of sneakers in my size. I look in the drawstring bag. There is a light jacket, a pair of pants, and a tightly rolled circle of cash, among other things.

I'm meant to escape.

Is this why they installed the tracker? Because they want my release to look like an escape? Sacrificing the lab seems foolish. All of the Sarina vaccine is here, and there are millions of dollars in equipment going up in flames. But maybe it's not a friend of the lab. Maybe it's an enemy. Then why help me escape? So I can run out and get shot by the guards?

I touch the glass on the door. It's warm. The knob is too. Cinders land softly on my skin as I stand in the doorway.. I am a weapon. I didn't plan to escape with so much fanfare. A fire this large might have brought the fire department. Gawkers. By leaving, I could kill thousands.

By staying, I will die.

I think about what Dr. Choebach said during surgery. *We could cure her completely.* I wonder if he meant I'm less contagious. Or not contagious at all. A circle of heat flares painfully at my wrist. I'm wearing a simple metal bracelet. It's not one of my creations. And I wasn't wearing it when I fell asleep. I try to take it off, but it's too small to fit over my hand and I can't find the clasp.

Soon I will be caged by flames in the same way I was caged by glass. I pick up the bag. I step out of my cage and drop to my knees, like all the public safety ads tell you. My palms land on something hot and sharp, burned beyond identification. I shove it away. And that's when I know.

I am just an animal. Wounded now, nearly choking, crawling through ash that chars my hands and my knees, hoping my hair doesn't catch fire before I reach the door.

I should stay, but I will go. I am just an animal.

There are no flames in the hallway to the outside world, just thick smoke. I keep crawling with the roar of the flames behind me. I look back to see the plastic tiles buckling as the flames give chase. I have never, in my memory, been past this point. When I was brought to the lab, I was barely two months old. When I tried to escape, it was here the guards hit me with the tranquilizer gun. Now, getting out is as easy as pushing on a metal bar. I'm in a lobby of some sort. A glass door leads outside. There's nothing but the velvet night beyond it. No fire trucks, no waiting guards.

The smoke is thin enough so that I can stand now. I run the short distance past the white walls, the guard post, the door, and into the fresh air. A free-standing tent the size of small bathroom flaps in the empty parking lot. I wait for my eyes to adjust, breathing in gulps, starved for oxygen. Still, no one. Is it better to run or to check the tent? To run, of course, but my nerves aren't satisfied with that. I crouch by the bottom edge of the fabric, tentatively lift with one finger. There are no feet. The pavement is wet and smells of antiseptic. A decontamination chamber for the fleeing employees. There must be another, more permanent version near the entrance of the lab.

I walk across the parking lot to an open gate. There's a fence surrounding the lab, about 10 feet tall and topped with razor wire. I overheard the guards say once that it's electrified with enough current to kill a human being. By the slight buzzing I hear, I'm guessing it still is.

One tentative step takes me past the gate. The surface beneath my shoes is softer than I'm used to. I kneel down. It's soil. I dig my hands in it. Not just soil like I had during my science unit on seeds, but earth. I feel it under my fingernails. It cools my tender palms. I bring a handful to my nose. Yes, that's the smell in the air. Pine. My breathing slows; I can taste the air. It's richer and deeper than the sterile, carefully filtered air at the lab. I look up to see the trees that have scented the earth, then past them to the sky.

Pine needles prick my hand as I gasp. There are stars. Thousands of them.

The sharp, clean scent of the air reminds me I'm polluting it just by breathing. My escape plans included a facemask made from layers of cloth. They're actually more effective against viruses than the surgical masks that became the latest fashion during the H1N1 scare. I feel around in the bag. The fabric of the jacket isn't breathable enough, so I wrap one leg of the pants around my mouth like a scarf and let the other dangle down my back. I look back at the buzzing fence. I could still do the right thing.

But someone wanted me to leave. The bag of supplies and the open door were acts of kindness. A person who would do that wouldn't let me out if an epidemic was inevitable. At least, that's what I tell myself as I walk into the wilderness.

The sounds become less frightening as I identify their causes, one by one. The rustling all around me is just the leaves submitting to the wind. The skittering shapes along the forest floor are small, nocturnal animals. At first, the chill night is a welcome change from the furnace I just escaped, but soon even walking doesn't keep me warm enough. I pull on the light jacket and continue. When that isn't enough, I have to sacrifice the makeshift mask to stop my violent shivering.

An hour of walking takes me far enough where the flames aren't visible. Another hour passes before the smoke becomes a background scent. I leave the gravel road to take stock of my supplies. Hopefully, my benefactor thought to include a flashlight, or I'll have to make myself a sitting duck on the road. I feel around in the bag. There's metal cylinder that seems promising. Rotating the top illuminates a small circle of the forest.

I carefully examine each item from the bag one by one: a thick roll of cash, a manila envelope, a few energy bars, and a full water bottle. My throat hurts so much that I gulp down the entire bottle before I remember I should ration it. Inside the manila envelope, there's a birth certificate and a passport. I am now Janine Butler, born in Manchester, Vermont.

I know from the conversations at the lab that the gravel road I've been following is a long driveway that heads south. Eventually, the driveway will intersect Route 49. Turning right and traveling east will take me towards the national forest. West would take me into town. My feet hurt, but I can't stop now. I don't know what sort of tracker they put in my leg, whether it's long-range or short-range, but I can't do surgery on myself with rocks and sticks. I need to get to the mountains, to the caves, before they figure out my body is not among the ashes.

I repack the bag and set off again. Finally, I see the wider, paved road. I turn right before I reach it so I can stay among the trees.

To distract myself from the pain in my feet, I set my mind to other problems. I have food. I need water. Streams run down mountains, and there might be maps I can steal from a ranger's station. Until I get to the national forest, I'll lick the dew from the leaves in the morning. Branches scratch my hands and face as I make my way through the thick forest, always keeping the paved road to my right. Gradually the dark forest turns gray and a pale orange circle upstages the glowing orb of the moon.

I can't help myself. I go to the road and sit at the base of a tree, the bark rough against my back.

It's my first sunrise. No movie or show or book has ever done it justice. I understand now why there are a hundred words for orange. Streaks of burnt sienna, apricot, saffron, auburn, chestnut, copper, ochre, peach, gold, and brass radiate along the horizon. I understand why the Mayans would mistake the sun for a god. It's the most beautiful thing I've ever seen.

I eat an energy bar to placate my growling stomach, even though my dry throat makes swallowing painful. That's when I realize how tired I am. I can't say how long I had slept before the fire woke me. My eyes feel like sandpaper now, my legs anchors. The rhythm of my heart is as fragile as tissue paper, like when I push too hard in the dance studio. I'm still not far enough away. But it's all I can do to crawl a few yards into the forest before I curl up, shivering, and fall asleep.

Chapter 5

I am warm. My hip is cradled by a cushion, not pressing into the hard ground. A soft cotton blanket covers me. I smell chicken soup, and I can hear someone moving in another room. I open my eyes slowly, blinking at the sunlight.

They focus on a little girl's face. She was standing so still I didn't even hear her. She is eight, maybe, with dark hair and round eyes and a gap in her front teeth. When I considered the possibility my escape might kill someone, I didn't consider someone like her. I wonder how long she's been standing next to me, inhaling the poison I breathe.

"Hello." She grins. The gap-toothed smile is equal parts innocence and mischief. She skips out of the room, her skirt bouncing at each step. "Mom! Dad! She's awake."

I curse myself for not finding a better place to hide. Was I lying that close to the road? Has the lab tracked me here as well? The bright sun in my eyes tells me I have slept far too long. I look for a clock and find a tall, stately grandfather clock in the corner. It's nearly 2 p.m. I should be halfway to the mountains by now, where there's hope of finding a cave to block the signal of the tracker in my leg.

A classic rock song finishes on the radio, the music crackling from the bent antenna. A DJ interrupts the last guitar chords. "Now that's a trip down memory lane, folks. Time for some more current announcements. The Grafton County police department is glad to report that the fire at Next Squared Industries is nearly contained. Several employees are still missing, however, and the police would love to have good news for their families. So, please, if you see anyone injured along Route 49, call the police immediately."

I shiver under the blanket. The announcement can't be a coincidence. The lab already knows I didn't die in the fire, and they know I had to walk out on Route 49. They could have published my description and my picture, but they haven't. Their weapon won't be a secret if my picture is plastered all over the local news.

The little girl's parents have probably called 911 already. My shoes and bag are on the floor near me. I sit up and reach for the laces.

"You don't need to go." The voice belongs to a man framed in the doorway. He's good-looking, in a bland, vanilla sort of way. The kind of man you might see modeling khakis in a department store catalog. A long-sleeved shirt is bunched at his elbows. The shirt and his jeans are streaked with black dust. Black like the soot that covers me. I look down to see streaks of black on the worn floral pattern of the couch. I've ruined that, too.

He leans against the wall, arms crossed, holding a steaming mug in one hand. "If you're worried about the police, Mandy wouldn't let me call them." His voice isn't exactly unkind; it's a mixture of curiosity and annoyance.

Should I believe him? I shrink away as he comes closer.

"I'm Tom, by the way."

I stare at the hand he holds out in greeting. My curse is airborne. Shaking his hand won't expose him any more than he's already been, and it will help me pass for normal. But, by the time I reach that conclusion, the offer of friendship is retracted.

"I heated up some soup for you," he says. "If you want it."

I consider the possible universes. If he's lying about not calling the police, I need to get out of here as soon as possible. If he's not, I have to stay. It's not just that I want the soup. Partially cured could mean a lot of things, and I don't know if they'll get sick. Three subjects is more than enough to start an epidemic.

The words have to be forced over my dry throat. "How did you find me? When?"

His eyes narrow, and I know I've asked the question in the wrong way. "Two hours ago. We were driving back from our hike when Rose spotted you in the woods." He hands me the mug, and the spoon clinks against the ceramic. "You didn't even wake up when we carried you to the car. You must have had quite a night."

They must not have called the police then because the lab would be here by now. The lab wouldn't wait two hours to reclaim their prize. I have to keep the family here for 24 hours, until the incubation period is over. If they show any symptoms, I'll have to—no, I can't think about that. I just have to keep them here.

The soup smells heavenly. Short noodles and small chunks of meat float in a creamy yellow broth. The first salty sip warms me all the way down to my stomach. I've gobbled half the soup before I look up again. A woman is staring at me; it must be Mandy. She has the same high cheekbones as the little girl. Tom is staring, too.

"Thank you," I say. "It's delicious." It is. My nutritionists never allowed anything with a sodium content this high.

My compliment amuses Mandy. "We only serve the best canned soup here." Her smile is friendly. "This is our week-end place, so we don't have much around." She sets two outfits beside me. "I had these old clothes upstairs. I hope they fit." They're faded and 20 years out of fashion, but at least they don't look like clown clothes.

Two chimes from the clock ring through the room, and I jump in surprise. That means they were exposed around noon. Correction, *I* exposed them around noon.

"The clock belonged to my father," the woman says. "It's an old relic, really. The pipes are out of tune, and we have to reset it every time we come up here. But I can't quite get rid of it."

I imagine turning back the hands on the clock, crawling a little farther into the forest so the little girl wouldn't see me. Tom and Mandy wait for me to speak. A normal person would know what to say. Biohazard issues aside, I haven't had much social interaction besides the stilted, overly formal conversations with my language tutors. This is generally the point in the script where I ask where the train station is.

Mandy presses her hands into her lap. "Well, the bathroom is just down the hall." She looks over my bizarre outfit, then clears her throat. "If you leave your dirty clothes in there when you change, we can wash them for you."

"Don't bother." I'd rather burn them. Yesterday was—I have to think about it—Saturday. That makes today Sunday. Mandy said this was their weekend place. Odds are, they're planning to leave soon.

The little girl reappears in a flurry of steps and jumps on the couch next to me, spilling the pile of clothes and nearly spilling what's left of my soup. She grins again. "I'm Rose."

"Where are our manners?" the woman says. Tom just raises his eyebrows, as if it's not their manners in question here. "I'm Mandy Harris," the woman continues. "And this is my husband—"

"I introduced myself," Tom says. "But she didn't." There's another expectant silence.

I am Sarina Wocek, a 23-year-old living bio-weapon engineered by the infamous Gregory Wocek. I am their prison warden until I know if they're contagious.

"Janine," I finally say. I try to think of the last name on my passport. "Janine Butler."

Tom and Mandy exchange looks.

I need a few minutes to think. I gulp the last of my soup. "I think I'll go shower now."

In the bathroom, I throw my pajamas in the trash. They stink of smoke and sweat and fear. The jacket and pants that were provided in the bag are little better. I throw those away too. As I run the shower, I hear footsteps in the hall. I tiptoe to the door.

It's Mandy and Tom, speaking in hushed voices. There are small paper cups with cartoon designs next to the sink. I hold one up to the door and, sure enough, I can make out what they're saying. Years of practice eavesdropping helps.

"Now can we call the police?" It's Tom voice.

"Don't tell me you believe the news. If she's an employee, why is she dressed like that? And carrying a passport but no driver's license or employee ID?"

They went through my stuff. I guess I would have in their place.

"Maybe she burned the place down. Did you ever think of that? We should let the police sort it out."

Mandy snorts. "You're talking about Deputy Jim. The guy who gets drunk at the bar, then pulls people over for DUIs."

"We have to think of Rose's safety."

"I *am* thinking about Rose." I'm beginning to like Mandy. "We need to set a good example for her. To help someone if she's in trouble."

"Mandy, she's carrying $10,000 in cash. Whatever she's running from, we shouldn't get involved."

During the long silence, a thin sheen of moisture gathers on the cup I'm holding. Mandy speaks next. "No one knows she's here but us. Let's take her back to Claremont, I trust the police there."

"That's a long drive with a stranger."

"You know the rumors about that building," Mandy says.

This time it's Tom who snorts. "You mean the ones about the mansion with the serial killer who skins his victims to make clothing? Or the one about the insane asylum where they perform routine lobotomies? Now who's spinning conspiracy theories?"

"Something not right went on in that building." There's another long pause. The shower's been running so long the humidity makes the air hard to breathe. "She's scared, Tom. I've never seen anyone so scared in my life. There are scars all over her arms and legs. I can't take the risk of handing her back to the people that hurt her."

The cup slips. I look down at my naked, pale skin, crisscrossed with waxy scar tissue. Some are years old, some only weeks old. I didn't stop to think how it would look to someone else. Even if I wanted to answer Mandy's questions, I wouldn't know what to tell her. My body has never been my own. I pick my listening aid up from the floor.

"If she's so helpless, why haven't we heard about any other survivors?" Tom asks.

I hope, for their sake, he listens to Mandy. If they call the police, the lab will find out. The whole family will be killed.

"I just keep thinking that if Rose was hurt and scared and another family found her, what would we want them to do?"

"That's not fair," Tom says in a softer tone. "Fine. We'll do it your way."

"You know this is the right thing to do."

"Remind me of that when we're fighting off the guards from the insane asylum."

I count to 100 without hearing anything. I think they're gone. When I step in the shower, rivulets of black and brown run into the drain. I want to enjoy the first shower in my life that isn't timed, but it's been running for a while. I scrub myself quickly, mindful of the fresh incisions on my thighs. The towel is soft and smells fresh. I wonder if they use one of those fabric softeners I see advertised all the time. The laundry at the lab always smelled like bleach.

The belt has to be cinched tightly on the jeans Mandy gave me, but they'll work. The sweatshirt is baggy and faded. The mirror confirms that the clothes don't flatter me. I look forgettable. Perfect.

When I come out of the bathroom, Rose has a board game laid out on the table. Along the edges, squares are labeled with the names of places I don't recognize. A cheerful man, illustrated in black and white, holds out a top hat. The board reminds me of a cheesy family movie I saw once. The psychologists were always trying to expose me to family values. Everything except a real family, of course.

"You're playing, right?" Rose says.

I can't refuse her smile.

"Just one game, Rose," Mandy says. "Then your father and I need to talk to Janine."

Hopefully, it's a long game. I need to think of a story that will convince Tom and Mandy I'm not a threat. It doesn't have to be plausible. It just has to sound like the kind of thing a girl running scared would make up.

"Two 500 dollar bills." Rose carefully places two dark yellow pieces of paper in front of each of us. "Two 100 dollar bills." These bills are a lighter yellow. The pile grows as she counts out more fake bills. Then she digs in the box and pulls out a handful of mismatched objects.

Mandy offers me a smile. "We lost all the playing pieces a long time ago. We had to make some substitutions."

"You can be the acorn," Rose says.

I balance the object she hands me in the middle of my palm. I've only seen them in pictures. The smooth brown skin comes to a fine point on one end. On the other, there's a rough cap that looks like tree bark. Words from my biology unit come back to me. The cap is a cupule, the outer skin is a pericarp, and inside is the seed coat. Near the fine point is a plumule, a miniature of an oak tree, just waiting for right conditions. All seeds are like that. Their fate is programmed into them from the beginning.

"You're the paperclip, mommy," Rose says. "And you're the bottle cap, daddy."

Tom and Mandy accept their assignments. I have mine. A story that will allay Tom's suspicions. Bonus points if I can think of a story that will delay their return to the city.

"Janine?" a deep voice asks.

I remember that's my name and look up. Three sets of eyes watch me. Rose reaches for me and pries open my hand. I don't remember closing it. Her soft fingers lift the acorn and place it on a square labeled *Go*. She replaces the acorn with two dice.

"House rules. Guests go first," Tom says.

I think I'm supposed to roll, so I do. The game has too much chance for my liking. Chess is all about strategy, dissecting your opponent's intent. In this game, I find my pile of fake cash dwindling on every turn.

With each roll, I create and reject a new story to explain my presence, my outfit, my scars, my stash of money. A 23-year-old runaway? Hardly. A mental patient? Tom would never let me stay. A camper? That might work. National forests mean camp-grounds, right?

I haven't had time to flush out my story before Rose wins. It occurs to me that Rose should be around while I'm trying to explain myself. It'll keep them from asking too many uncomfortable questions.

"I never thanked you for the soup," I say. "And the clothes. You're probably wondering how I got lost."

Mandy clears her throat. "Rose, honey, why don't you—"

"It's okay, she can hear this." I untwist my hands. "I was out camping with friends. I decided to go out to this stargazing spot after dinner. But I got lost on the way back. I walked for hours; I just couldn't find my campsite." None of this will explain why they need to stay here. My words tumble over each other as I improvise. "I left my cell phone in the tent, so I couldn't call anyone. When it got too dark to see anything, I decided to rest. I guess I fell asleep."

Tom looks dubious. "You were covered in soot."

Mandy shoots him a look that tells him to let it be.

"We had to clean out the fire pit. It was messy." My explanations aren't lowering Tom's eyebrows. I have to say something before he thinks of another question. "Maybe I could use your phone to call them and let them know I'm okay."

"The phone's right there." He's pointing to a table in front of a window overlooking the yard.

On the short walk to the phone, I try to think of a phone number—any phone number—to dial. I've watched hours of infomercials in my life and I can't think of one. A notepad by the phone saves me. It says *Hobby Electronics* across the top, with a phone number and an address in Ellsworth, New Hampshire. If I can dial the number without hitting '1,' I'll know where I am.

A male voice answers. "Hobby Electronics, sparking your imagination. This is Victor, how can I help you?"

I can't help but smile a little. Last night, all I knew was the lab was near a national forest and a road called Route 49. For the first time in my life, I know where I am. I say nothing. Maybe this is how I can keep them here, by pretending my friends didn't answer.

"Hello?" Victor asks. "Anyone there?" He sounds more bored than annoyed.

How long does a cell phone ring before it goes to voicemail? I wouldn't know. I've never been allowed to call anyone before.

"You think you're the first prank call I've had today?" My new friend Victor hangs up on me.

Everyone is watching me when I turn around: Mandy with sympathy, Tom with suspicion, and Rose with confusion. The little girl looks between her parents, her protectors, and me, knowing without being told that I am the cause of the troubled vibes in the room.

The phone clicks as I set it on the base. It's the loudest sound in the room. "They didn't answer," I say. "I'll try again later."

Tom crosses his arms. A damsel in distress might soften him. At the lab, every once in a while I could get a special favor from the guards if I played the vulnerable, fragile girl. The key is a soft voice and a sloping back.

"Could I stay here with you until I reach them?" I can call Victor every 10 minutes all night, if that's what it takes.

Mandy opens her mouth to speak, but is cut off by Tom.

"We're going home this afternoon," he says. "We can drop you off at the motel in town on our way out."

Chapter 6

Rose dumps a collection of plastic blocks on the floor at my feet. She has every color and shape under the sun. There are bits of people mixed in too, with sets of legs, smiling heads, and torsos in costumes ranging from emergency workers to business suits to fantasy characters.

"We're going to make a dragon," she announces. I wonder if all children have the ability to be cute and bossy at the same time.

Mandy is somewhere down the hallway, where I can hear a dryer running. Tom is cleaning out the fridge, keeping one eye on Rose and me the whole time. I still have no idea how I'm going to keep them here. I doubt Tom will be talked into anything.

I might as well help Rose with her dragon. We run out of green blocks and move onto pink, then yellow, then blue. It's a dragon with a Technicolor coat. While I search through the bin for pieces that look like claws, Rose searches for wings.

"It's too bad there aren't real dragons," she says.

There are, I want to tell her. Men cold as lizards, with weapons scarier than fire, who really do hold women hostage. I want to tell her that sometimes the people who are supposed to protect you can't or won't, that the fairy tales have it all wrong.

You can't count on anyone else. Princesses have to slay their own dragons.

"There are dragons," I say.

Mandy stops mid-stride, just entering the room. A basket of laundry is tucked against her hip. Tom's look from the kitchen is forbidding. I see in Rose's expression what they're fighting for, her precious innocence. She still has the luxury of only being afraid of the imaginary.

"Except they don't breathe fire," I continue. "And they don't attack humans." I have no idea if that last part is true. "They're called komodo dragons, and they only live on islands in Indonesia."

Rose lights up, and Mandy relaxes.

"Do they look like our dragon?" Rose holds up our motley creation, a pear-shaped creature with two eyes of different sizes and only one wing.

"More like a lizard. They walk on four legs."

"How far away is Indonesia?"

They have a library's worth of *National Geographic* on the shelf. I choose one, figuring there has to be map in it somewhere. "We're here." I point to the Eastern seaboard, still enjoying the novelty of knowing where I am. "And Indonesia is way over here."

"Can they fly?" Rose asks excitedly. "What color are they? How big are they?"

I'm happy to have answers for her. "No, green, and bigger than you."

Rose ticks off my responses to her questions on her fingers, then points to an image on the other page. "What's that?"

"A red panda. They use those long bushy tails as blankets on cold nights." I'm a font of knowledge on all sorts of useless topics. I spent a lot of time reading to pass the time. My censors considered exotic foreign species a safe topic.

"It looks more like a raccoon."

I try to think of how parents in family sitcoms tell children they're wrong. "Sure it does. But it's closest relative is actually the black-and-white panda."

"Like Kung Fu Panda?"

At my blank expression she pulls a movie off the shelf.

"Kung Fu Panda." The cover shows a panda doing a karate kick at the top of a mountain. I wonder how many other pop culture references I don't know about. I can't even hold a sane conversation with an eight-year old. From there our conversation jumps to another animal that doesn't look like its species, the flying squirrel, to how trees grow, to how you can tell how old a tree is, to how a bird builds its nest, to why birds fly differently from squirrels, and then somehow to a discussion of tornados.

Mandy interrupts us with a smile, tousling Rose's hair. "Okay, future biologist. Go upstairs and get your stuff together please." Her phone chirps in her pocket. "My battery's nearly dead. Someone was playing Angry Birds on it all morning."

Rose dodges her mother's good-natured tickle and skips upstairs. She never walks.

"Mine needs charging too," Tom says, entering the room. "Someone ran down the battery playing Fruit Ninja." He takes her phone and his to the table where I used the landline earlier.

After plugging the phones in, he disappears upstairs with Mandy. To pack, or talk about me, I guess.

I stare at their cell phones, a plan forming. I'll do to them what the lab did to me. Cut them off from all forms of transportation and communication. That way they won't be able to call the mechanic until I let them.

The only hiding places in the living room are inside board games. But that's the first thing Rose will open when they find out they're stuck here. In the kitchen above the refrigerator, I find a small cabinet with a thick layer of dust along the bottom. It seems like a good place. I turn both phones off and put them in, shutting the cabinet doors slowly. For a wasted second, I watch the carpeted stairs. How much time can I spend in the garage? Two minutes? 10?

I force the question to the back of my mind. I open the pantry door first, then find the door to an attached garage. The car is unlocked. I can see a booster seat in back for Rose. Disabling the car is easier said then done. The complicated tangle of belts, pipes, and wires under the hood is a foreign landscape. My knowledge of car mechanics is limited to what I could pick up from action movies and buddy cop flicks. I could take the distributor cap. Isn't that what always happens in the movies? Except that there are lots of things that look like caps. I'm not willing to guess. Sabotaging the wrong part might mean the car breaking down on the side of the road. Or causing an accident.

I'll have to be less subtle.

A workbench, with an open toolbox, catches my eye. Grit covers my hands as I search for any tool that will give me an idea. Near the bottom, I find a utility knife that flips open. The outside is dirty, but the blade is fresh. The wicked sharp edge glints in the meager light of the garage.

My knee bumps into the pedal of a bike as I kneel beside the car. A cut on the outside of the tire will be obvious. I reach into the shadows underneath the car and stab. The blade ricochets off the rim, slamming my wrist into something hard and greasy underneath the car. I adjust the angle of my hand to be flatter and stab again. This time I manage to bury the tip of the knife, but I don't hear any hiss of air.

It's not just my life at stake here, I remind myself. It's theirs. The lab must never know that I was here. I tighten my grip on the handle. On my third attempt, the knife sinks into a deep groove. A slow hiss of air tickles and chills my wrist. My hand is sweating so much it's hard to get the knife out. I'm about to go inside when I remember there's always a spare in the trunk. I puncture a second tire, then put the knife back where I found it.

Now there's only the landline to worry about. *Only.* As if I know how to sabotage a phone without cutting the line.

As I gingerly close the door to the garage behind me, I hear Mandy's voice upstairs. "Rose, I told you to pack. Stop playing and open up your suitcase."

In the living room, I examine the phone. There are four screws along the bottom. I could get a screwdriver from the garage, destroy the guts then—

"Are you done, Rose?" It's Tom, still upstairs.

"Almost, daddy."

There's no time to do surgery on the phone. I did see some small tubes of superglue while I was searching for a good place to hide the cell phones. Superglue isn't conductive, so a thin layer should be enough to disable the jack. As I grab the tube from the kitchen, a suitcase appears at the top of the stairs. I stick the narrow tip of the superglue into the jack and squeeze just a little bit where the copper wires shimmer. The directions say it takes 90 seconds to set. I listen to the unreliable grandfather clock tick off one minute, wondering if it loses time or creates it. There are more sounds of movement upstairs. I angle my shoulders so I can fit underneath the narrow table and blow into the jack.

I bet Nurse Rita would love to see me now.

When I hear footsteps on the stairs, I stick the phone line back into the wall, hoping the glue had enough time to dry. I have just enough time to stick the capped tube in my pocket and grab a copy of *National Geographic* from the shelf so I can pretend I was reading the whole time.

"We're leaving in a few minutes." Mandy appears and points to my white bag, still on the floor near the couch, with a rueful smile. "Not that you have much to get together."

I nod and force a smile in return.

She glances upstairs, where I can hear Tom's deep laughter mixing with Rose's giggles.

"You know, if you want our help, all you have to do is ask. We have a guest room at our house in Claremont."

My hand freezes on a picture of a rainforest. I wonder how Tom would feel about Mandy offering their guest room to me.

"I know someone hurt you. You're safe with us, I promise."

I want to laugh. My father turned me into a freak. My mother tried to kill me. And the government has been using me as a lab rat ever since. "I just got lost, like I said. That's all."

"Not even Rose believes that story."

The picture of the rainforest blurs into a watercolor of green and brown. I haven't cried in a long time; I won't cry in front of her.

"You've just met us. It must be difficult to trust anyone after whatever you've been through. I know Tom can be… difficult. But he'll help if you're honest with us."

I drop the magazine on the coffee table with a slap. "I'm going to use the bathroom."

Mandy shakes her head sadly. I leave the room before I tell her my real name.

When I come back into the living room, I find a very angry Tom. He takes a threatening step in my direction. "There are two flat tires on the car. Two. An hour ago, all the tires were fine."

Mandy gently pulls him away. "Calm down, sweetheart. I'm sure it's just a coincidence. We'll just call the garage in town."

That's when they discover their cell phones are missing. Mandy tries the landline and then finds the phone is dead. She tries another cord, another phone. Luckily, Rose has roped me into building a city for our dragon to destroy while her parents argue about who had their cell phones last. They search for a good half hour before giving up. I disguise my sigh of relief as a breath of fire from the dragon. Rose's giggle is heartening. Still, the worse Tom's mood gets, the less I want to be stuck with him in a cabin for the next 18 hours.

His face is a mottled red when he interrupts our game. "Rose. Go upstairs. Now."

"Tom—" Mandy puts a hand on his shoulder, but he shakes it off.

"Now, Rose."

Rose, frightened, goes upstairs with her head hanging. I hate that it's my fault.

"You have five minutes to explain yourself," Tom says, "before I tie you up and bike into town to call the cops."

Mandy tries for a kinder tone. "If you'll just be honest with us, we can help you."

No, you can't. I'll have to think of a new story. Something that takes advantage of the rumors they've heard without living up to them. A plausible reason there would be a secure, nondescript building housing scared young adults in rural New Hampshire.

I can't tell them the truth. Knowing what actually went on at the lab will kill them, if the virus I carry doesn't. And I don't think I could bear to see Mandy's face if I told her I was selfish enough to escape without being sure I was no longer contagious.

"This is my family." Tom's hands are balled into fists. "If you do anything that puts Rose in danger—"

"Rose is perfectly safe," Mandy says, but she doesn't seem sure.

I wonder if my father got angry when I was taken from him. I wonder if, in all his years writing and reading letters in that tiny cell, he ever thought of his daughter as anything more than the vehicle of his self-destructive vision.

"Four minutes, Janine," Tom growls.

I've been lying for the past nine years. I managed to convince a panel of psychologists that I was a cooperative prisoner. Surely I can convince a nice suburban couple that I'm no threat to them. The damsel in distress bit didn't trigger his protective instincts earlier, but then I was only a lost college girl. A daughter in distress will remind him of Rose. I need to think of something that will garner their sympathy without threatening them.

I take a deliberate breath, then let it out slowly. "Okay, fine." My hands twist in my lap. "The building that burned down is a rehab center focused on college students. I was a patient there for alcoholism. When my parents and I toured the place, we were shown all the nice rooms. The attendants we met were nice too. But when you're locked in there as a patient, every-thing's different. The building is falling apart, and the director hires the cheapest attendants he can find. They just keep the good rooms for show."

I look up from my lap to judge Tom's reaction, careful to keep a vulnerable express on my face. His arms are crossed over his stomach, but the glare is gone.

"The director skims off the tuition. My room is near his office. I heard him talking about it when he thought I was asleep." The last line is close enough to the truth that it makes me shiver. I can hear the scrape of scalpels again, feel the cold-ness of anesthesia creeping up my spine.

Where was I? The director of the imaginary treatment center. A reason to be on the run.

"One of the attendants forced my roommate, Gretchen, to sleep with him to get her methadone. She tried to blackmail the director, threatened to tell her parents unless they found her a real fix. Then last week she died, just before her parents were supposed to visit. The center claims it was an overdose and that she snuck in the drugs on her own." I think back to Mandy and Tom's conversation. "The director even paid Deputy Jim to backup the story."

I risk a sideways glance toward Tom. He's softening. Mandy's eyes are wet. The pang of guilt I feel is unexpected. I never felt bad about lying to my keepers at the lab.

"Gretchen's parents hired a PI out of Claremont. He came out a couple days ago to talk to me. I didn't see anything the night Gretchen died, I swear. But the center thinks I did." I stare down at my lap, trying to work out the rest of my story. "The other patients were scared too. Lots of rotten stuff happened there."

"What about the scars, sweetie?" Mandy asks. "Did they hurt you?"

I hug myself before I can think better of it. But then that's how a scared runaway patient would react, right? Mandy seems to have already filled in this part for herself. I might as well go with it. "I couldn't tell anyone. All of our phone calls are monitored, and they read our emails before we send them. They have cameras in all the rooms." The truth in my story disarms me. I stare at the shelf to avoid their eyes. There's a black and red chessboard just below the Monopoly game. For a second, I wish I could talk to Mentor. He's a scheming bastard, but he wouldn't get distracted by sentimentality.

Tom's expression hovers between skepticism and sympathy. I almost have him.

I take a deep breath to steady myself. "A few of my friends and I decided to escape by starting a fire. The night attendant just left when he heard the alarm. We knew he would." I can see the laminate on the guard's desk blistering outside my cage and smell burning plastic again. Think like Mentor, I tell myself. The consent of pawns is not required. "We broke into the director's office and found his stash of tuition money. Once we got out of the building, we divided the money and scattered. We thought it would make us harder to find."

"Oh, honey," Mandy says.

There's a hand on my shoulder. For a second, I mistake its warmth for Dr. Choebach's, but when I look up it's Tom. "We can help you, but we'll need our phones," he says. "We can take you to the PI that came to see you. There's a route to Claremont that doesn't go through Ellsworth. No one has to know you were here."

There's no way I can let them leave the cabin. "I stole one of the attendant's phones and tried to call the PI before we escaped. His secretary said he was traveling and won't be back until Monday afternoon."

Tom and Mandy exchange a look, like I'm missing something obvious. "What about your parents?" Mandy asks. "We could call them."

Right. Normal children have parents who care where they are. "My parents don't much care what I do. The day I started at the center, they left for Rio de Janeiro."

For once, neither of them jumps in immediately with a practical suggestion. The silence leaves me with my regrets. I should have let myself burn in my cage. I should have thrown myself on the electric fence. If they are not infected, I promise myself I will make sure I'm never a threat to anyone else again. But even as I make the promise, an animal stirs within me. The one who made me crawl across the floor of the lab. It's a promise I can't keep.

If they are not infected, I will find myself a cave in the mountains where no one will ever see me. No one will ever serve me chicken soup or play board games with me again. And I'll carry a knife, just in case. To defend others from myself. That's a compromise the animal will accept, I think.

"I'm sorry I slashed your tires," I say. "I didn't think you'd believe me."

"The police in Claremont will protect you after we explain everything," Mandy says.

Always with the police, these people. It must be nice to trust the people who watch you. I shake my head. "I'm guilty of arson and theft now. They'd make me spend the night in jail until they talk to the PI."

Mandy sighs. "Okay, Janine, if that's what you want. We won't call the police until tomorrow. I promise."

I look at Tom, to see if he agrees.

Tom nods. "Now can we have our phones back?"

"I'll give your phones back Monday. When I can call the PI. He'll know what to do."

"No," says Tom emphatically. "If you want us to trust you, you'll have to trust us."

Fair is fair, I suppose. But I can't hover over both of them to make sure they keep their promise. In their minds, they'd be helping me. "You'll call the mechanic. It's a small town. The l— center will figure out I'm here."

Tom throws up his hands and swears under his breath. "Janine, look at the time."

I can read the clock as well as he can. I don't understand why it matters that it's past seven.

"The garage in town closed four hours ago," Mandy explains. "Emergency service this far out practically costs an arm and a leg. We'll wait until tomorrow."

The floral pattern on the couch mocks me as I stall, trying to think of another excuse. Can I trust them? How do people in the real world figure this out? There's no background music, no soundtrack, to give me a clue.

"You have to give us our phones back at some point, sweetheart," Mandy says. The endearment makes me think of Dr. Choebach. He's probably the only one who even cares if I'm all right. "We're both due back at work Monday, and Rose has school. Someone will call the police to report us missing. Everyone knows we have a weekend place here. The police will be sent out to check on us."

I hadn't considered that. No one else can show up before the quarantine period is over. "You won't call the mechanic until I can talk to the PI?" As if I'll know for sure if they're lying.

Mandy sits down next to me and puts her arm around my shoulders. A muscle in my core shakes. It's grief, cornered, trying to kick its way out. I won't break down. I won't.

"We won't call the mechanic until you talk to the PI," she says softly.

I'll have to trust them. I have no choice. "In the cabinet above the fridge," I say, not looking at either of them.

Tom returns from the kitchen with the cell phones, then plugs them in to charge. He gives me a smile that's half an apology, half a joke. "For dinner, we have gourmet mac and cheese from a box and canned green beans. You know, you could have slashed our tires after we went to the grocery store."

60 – MEGAN CARNEY

Chapter 7

Night at the Harris' cabin is wonderfully noisy. The sounds of chirping crickets and throaty frogs punctuate the long, low hoots of owls. Last night, the new cacophony was frightening. Tonight, when I'm warm, fed, and relatively safe, the sounds are almost comforting. What worries I have are concentrated on the bodies inside the house. Beyond the chirps and hoots and croaks, I listen for coughs from the family. I watch for the sudden sweats or chills, the moments of dizziness and disorientation that come with a high fever. The victims of my father's masterpiece get harder to handle the sicker they get.

I won't know anything about Rose until morning; she has been tucked into bed for hours. It's midnight now. I am on the couch, pretending to read. Tom is replacing the jack I ruined with my superglue trick, swearing under his breath. Mandy disappeared into a room down the hallway an hour ago. I should go check on her.

Shelves filled to bursting with board games, toys, tools and home repair manuals clutter the room. I peer around a shelf with four kinds of Monopoly games and see Mandy, intently hunched over a workbench in the corner. She's concentrating too hard to hear me enter. In one hand she has a small teddy bear, and in the other she has a box cutter. She slits the back of the teddy bear open with one smooth stroke. It's a jarring image for such a sweet, caring woman.

My shoulder brushes the corner of a puzzle. The creaking shelf startles Mandy. "Oh, hello, Janine." She motions me over. "Come see."

On the workbench there are two small circuit boards, a speaker, spools of wire, and lots of tools I don't recognize. The project doesn't make any more sense when I'm standing right in front of it. Learning about circuits was strictly forbidden at the lab.

"It's an RFID teddy bear," Mandy explains. "I'm making it as a birthday present for Rose. Once I finish testing the circuit, it goes inside the teddy bear. I thought I wouldn't get to finish it this weekend. I guess I should thank you for delaying us." Her smile seems genuine. Part of me is still expecting the cops to show up.

I suppose there are lots of people like Mandy in the world—kind, generous, pleasant people who have children who love them, hobbies for their weekends, and jobs for their weeks. I just don't have much experience with them. Everyone I knew at the lab was either spiteful and mean, like Nurse Rita, or unhappy but kind, like Dr. Choebach. I don't know how to react when I don't need to play games. "How do you know about all this stuff?"

"Oh, I'm an electrical engineer. At work, I design industrial control systems. But I enjoy making toys for Rose when I can."

Under the harsh lamp on her workbench, her skin seems paler. I scan her arms for the sores characteristic of HF186-2A. "What does an RFID teddy bear do?"

Her face lights up. "It works like a jukebox, except instead of triggering sounds with buttons, you use RFID cards."

The cards scattered on the workbench look similar to the ones I always saw the employees at the lab carrying. "Are these the same sorts of cards used for access to buildings?"

"An RFID chip can trigger anything you can connect the reader to. Here, I'll show you." She holds up a plastic card with a picture of a birthday card on it, and I see her arms are clear of any sores. Her neck, too. Perhaps I'm imagining things.

Mandy frowns at the circuit. "That's odd. The red light shouldn't be on. The card has to be closer to trigger the circuit."

I shake my head blankly. "It isn't triggering the circuit. Nothing is happening."

She points to a small red LED on the circuit board. "See that light? It means the circuit is getting an RFID signal. But all of the cards are too far away. The circuit was fine 10 seconds ago." She sets down the card and picks up two probes with sharp ends, one black and one red. They're connected to a yellow meter with a large knob and lots of markings. She uses the probes to touch different parts of the circuit. "A beep, that's connected, that's good. No beep, that's not connected, that's correct..." She tests the circuit several times before putting the tool down, confused. "Everything's wired as it should be. I don't understand."

She's embarrassed. I want to give her time to fix it. My bracelet snags on the corner of the workbench as I back away.

"Do you have any tools in here?" I ask. "It's this jewelry. I want to take it off." I'm not sure if it was given to me by the person who helped me escape or by the lab itself, but it reminds me of my captivity. I want it gone.

Mandy takes my hand to examine the silver circle. "It has no clasp. What kind of bracelet has no clasp?"

"Costume jewelry," I say hastily, reclaiming my hand. I try to laugh, but it comes out more like a hiccup. "I don't even remember how I got it on. It's too small to fit over my hand."

"It's from the same attendant who abused your roommate, isn't it?"

She takes my hesitation as a confirmation of her suspicions, and folds me into a fierce hug. "You're safe here."

I can't remember being hugged before. I guess you could count the time my mom tried to smother me, if I remembered that. I start to hug back, and that's when I feel like I'm about to cry. I untangle myself from her as casually as I can. "The tools?" I manage.

Mandy lets me back away. "The shelf by the door has a tool-box. Careful you don't pull anything down on yourself."

The tools are rusty but serviceable. I even find a pink princess flashlight to examine the bracelet for weak points. The only interruptions in the sleek metal circle are a small hole the size of a pin and a panel an inch long. Maybe the clasp is under the panel. I dig the flat edge of a screwdriver into one of the visible lines. At first all I do is leave scratch marks, but then a rectangular panel falls away. The opening is lined by a rubber gasket. There's no hidden clasp. Just a row of tiny, flat batteries, like the ones used for watches.

Another mystery to solve. Tired as I am, it's tempting to wait until tomorrow. No, I can't afford to be lazy. Think of it like a chess game, I tell myself. Each move narrows the possible universes. Everything you need to know about your opponent is on the board. If the bracelet were sending out some sort of signal, the lab would have found me already. And they wouldn't need a second tracker, right? They already put one in my leg. I remove one of the batteries to see what happens.

Nothing.

"Happy birthday!" says a cheerful, recorded voice. "Dad and I want to sing you a song."

"There, fixed it," Mandy says. "Come see."

I walk back to the bench, battery warm in my hand. Mandy waves the birthday cake card over her circuit board. The red light blinks, and the speaker comes to life with Tom and Mandy singing *Happy Birthday*.

Envious. That's how I feel. Rose has a mother and a father who love her enough to make fools of themselves. I know without asking that there is a bulletin board at home full of Rose's artwork. That every Mother's day, Tom makes sure Mandy has a card signed by Rose. If I wanted to send a Mother's Day card, I'd have to address it to a federal prison. And I don't think Hallmark has anything that says *Kill me faster next time and save us both some trouble.*

"I can program the teddy bear to trigger any audio file for any card," Mandy says. "I'm going to make a whole library of sounds for her language flash cards. She's studying Spanish in school."

"Rose will love it." And I think she will. Not because her parents are great singers, but because someone spent hours hunched over a workbench just to make her a stupid teddy bear that sings. I never was much for stuffed animals. It wasn't that they were forbidden. I just never asked for them. I learned from books and TV that stuffed animals are tokens of affection, gifts from someone who loves you. Picking one out for myself didn't seem right.

I slip the battery back into my bracelet to see what happens. Nothing. I run my fingers along the edge to find another weak point to attack.

Mandy waves a card with a picture of a cat over the RFID sensor. The speaker stays silent. I'm beginning to think I'm jinxed when I remember I just replaced the battery. I remove it again.

The frown is back on Mandy's face.

"Maybe it's the card," I say. "Try a different one."

"It worked before…" She tries a card with a picture of a dog.

"Perro," says the speaker.

She tries the cat card again; this time it works. "Huh. That's odd."

My bracelet jams RFID signals. That's why the red light is always on when the bracelet is powered. It must have come from the person who helped me escape.

Questions pile on top of each other in my brain. Could the tracker they implanted be an RFID tracker? What's the range on a tracker like that? Why not use GPS? Mandy said she was an electrical engineer. Maybe she knows.

"Are RFID chips ever used in tracking devices?" I ask.

Mandy nods, distracted by examining her project. "Some stores use it as part of inventory systems. Casinos use them to track chips. And those implants in dogs that identify the owner? Those are essentially RFID."

In the commercials, the vet always reads the chip from a few inches away. That hardly seems useful enough to keep track of a human being. "So the chips can only be read up close?"

"Oh, the range depends on a lot of things." Mandy pulls out some stuffing to make room for her circuit. "A powered RFID chip will have a longer range than an unpowered one. Most are unpowered." She gently rearranges her circuit inside the bear. "The amount of power available to the RFID reader matters too, and the shape of the antenna. Some environments have a lot of interference, and if those signals are on the same wavelength, then that will affect the strength of the signal." The information is so automatic to her, her hands don't miss beat as she speaks. "Most RFID chips are close range, but there are some military contractors working on chips that can be read from a hundred feet away."

"Why use RFID at all when there's GPS?"

Mandy is sewing on a zipper to close the teddy bear's wound. "Power, mostly."

The word makes me think of glass prisons and guns, but I don't think that's what she means. "Don't both require batteries?"

"A GPS tracker requires a battery. Most RFID chips don't. The signal from the reader is enough to power the chip. GPS trackers are actually less reliable for close-range tracking. They're finicky if they can't see a satellite."

They didn't use GPS because it would require implanting a battery that would need to be periodically changed, or an external battery pack vulnerable to tampering. Whatever the lab was planning, they wanted to keep track of me permanently.

I assumed I would be used once and then discarded. Now, my upbringing makes more sense. They taught me several languages because they want me to travel. They gave me a tutor so I would know enough of the world to have a casual conversation. They wanted a weapon that could be deployed anywhere. A lifetime of service to a perverted cause. My father would be proud.

I back away and stumble into a shelf, pushing the bracelet under my sleeve so she can't see it. "I'm kind of tired. I think I'll go to bed."

When I'm far enough away not to break Rose's gift, I re-assemble the bracelet. The living room is dark. Tom is gone, probably upstairs. I find the small guest room downstairs, neatly made up for me. I lie, wakeful, in the dark. I want Mandy to think I'm asleep. I really want to sleep. But all I can think of are questions. Why would someone give me the bracelet but not tell me what it does? What if I had managed to remove it? What if the batteries die? How am I supposed to know when to replace them? What else does the bracelet do? Maybe my mysterious benefactor is not as kind as I assumed.

The incisions on my thighs itch. I know I have to get rid of the bracelet. And that means getting rid of the tracker in my leg.

Chapter 8

My naked legs are stretched out on the cold, dry bottom of the tub. The door is locked. A paring knife I stole from the kitchen rests on the edge of the tub. I don't have long. Mandy is assembling breakfast from what she can find in the cupboards.

The approach seemed simple an hour ago. I gathered gauze, bandages, antibiotic cream and painkillers from the medicine closet while they weren't looking. I took superglue from the kitchen to take the place of stitches. I washed my hands thoroughly, even getting under the nails like surgeons do. I sterilized the knife with rubbing alcohol. Evidence of my surgery will be easily erased by running the shower.

On each upper thigh, there is a one-inch-long incision neatly closed with stitches that look like tiny black ants. I hover the knife over my right leg, than my left. One incision holds the tracker; the other holds a capsule. The teddy bear might have told me which one, but Mandy must have hidden Rose's gift. I couldn't find it this morning. If I open the wrong incision, I'll have to open both. Though, to be honest, I'm not sure I can open even one.

The tracker must go.

Left leg or right leg—that's the only decision to make. Flip a coin. I choose left. I place the tip of the knife underneath the first incision and pull. The black thread stretches under the point of the knife. It hurts like a bad pinch. I saw at the thread, grit my teeth. Finally, it gives. I can feel the threads moving inside my skin as I cut and pull out each one. A thin trickle of blood leaks from the wound. I mop it up with gauze before I remember I should save that for later.

Now, to open the incision. I grip the knife tightly to make up for my sweating hands. I push the tip into the wound a quarter-inch. The fragile, recently healed flesh tears easily. It feels like pushing a hot coal underneath my skin, like a thousand paper cuts all at once. The knife clatters into the tub. I need something to bite on. I pull a washcloth down from the sink and roll it into a tight cylinder.

The fabric sucks the moisture from my already dry mouth. I waste some more gauze. Scars are one thing, but open wounds are another; it isn't often that I see my own blood. I force myself to pick up the knife and follow the length of the incision. The pain arches my back, forces my spine against the hard edge of the tub. A curtain of red leaks down both sides of my leg.

I'm panting like I've been running. For a second, before blood fills the wound, I see a yellow layer of fat beneath my skin.

Now, dig.

With one hand, I pull the incision open. It's good I have nowhere to fall. My head hits the tile at my back, and I moan softly. Sparkles dance in my vision. Don't think, I tell myself. Just finish the job. I shove my finger in up to the first knuckle. Each small movement touches a nerve. Something twinges against my finger. A ligament? A vein? Everything feels the same, slippery and soft. There's nothing metallic or even hard. Maybe I've pushed the implant further into my flesh.

There is liquid dripping from my face and my leg now. Tears on my face, blood on my leg. I keep digging. Meditation breaths do nothing to ease the pain. My jaw adds to the chorus, the muscles tired from clamping down so hard. I moan again, despite myself.

There's a slight knock at the door.

"Janine?" It's Mandy's voice. "Breakfast is ready."

I spit the washcloth out, try to find saliva to speak. "Be right there."

The washcloth fell on my leg. I roll it up again, clamp down on it, taste my own blood. I keep digging until it feels like my jaw will break. I can't find anything. It's no use.

The cool tile is welcome against my temples. I keep my eyes closed until the spots in my vision fade and my breathing takes on a less desperate tone. I'll have to deal with the tracker in another way.

I hold the ragged edges of skin together until the bleeding stops. A thin stream of water from the spout soaks the washcloth. When I squeeze it, red water washes my blood down the drain. I rinse longer than I need to, until the washcloth is almost white again. I use superglue to seal the wound, then bandage it with gauze and medical tape.

As I dress, I stare at the hateful bracelet I can't remove. It looks like a shackle. I'm not supposed to take it off without permission. I'm not supposed to know when the batteries run out. I've played this game long enough to know what that means. It's a temporary, conditional gift of protection. Someone besides the lab has plans for me.

Chapter 9

The clock strikes two in the afternoon as we're finishing up another game of Monopoly. It's Rose's favorite game. I think it's because she's so good at it. I don't know about her parents, but I haven't been letting her win.

No one is sick. Not a cough, an open sore, or even a yawn. I brush hands with Rose as I give her my rent. Her skin is cool to the touch. I've made sure to brush hands with everyone at least once to check for fever. There are no signs of that either.

I don't let myself think I'm completely cured. The only thing I can safely assume is that I'm no longer contagious by breath or touch. With all the hours I spent unconscious in the lab's operating wing, they could have done anything to me. They could have made my saliva contagious, or my blood, or—it's no use trying to list the possibilities. I realize I'm trying because this new knowledge has expanded my desires. A life as a celibate hermit was all I had to look forward to before. For a brief second, I see myself flirting with a handsome man and going home with him.

It's a shameful fantasy. I should be grateful that I'll be able to buy groceries every once in a while, not thinking about how to experiment with other people's lives. That's what my father does.

In the background, the DJ is talking about helicopters again. We've been hearing them all day. "Don't let those low-flying helicopters scare you, folks. They're just hauling water to finish putting out that fire."

The roads to the lab can easily handle a fire truck. I think the helicopters are sweeping for my RFID signal. Maybe the chip they implanted in me can be read from a long distance with a powerful antenna, like Mandy said. The bracelet hidden under my sleeve feels like a live snake against my wrist. It's useful for now, but the malevolence of the design itches at me.

The DJ's overly peppy voice continues. "They're also looking for any fires that may have been sparked by embers. Remember, Smokey the Bear wants you to call 911 if you see any forest fires!" I wonder if he's secretly depressed or if he's really always this happy. He's stopped asking for help finding survivors. I don't know if that's a good sign for me or not. I know they haven't given up. It could mean they're on my trail already. Now that I know the Harrises are clear of any symptoms, I need to leave quickly.

The loneliness of the mountains will be simpler at least. I don't have any friends there, so anyone else looking for me is an enemy. I can't deny that I will miss the warmth of this family. Every so often, Mandy reaches out to tousle Rose's hair. When Rose is intently studying her next move, Mandy and Tom look at each other over their daughter's head and smile. I even like Rose's endless questions about everything.

Most of all, I'm glad they will survive their encounter with me.

This morning, I hid my bag in a bush by the corner of the house. Rose is smart enough to figure out what it means if I walk out the door with my only possessions. I don't know if my rehearsed story will fool Tom and Mandy. If I make my escape while Rose is in the room, maybe I can avoid the more awkward questions.

Rose is counting her winnings. Her mouth moves as she softly says each denomination. Mandy rests her hand on Rose's shoulder with an indulgent smile. Tom has an arm draped around them both. I am not a part of this picture. I was never meant to be here.

I stand up, pressing my hands to my thighs. I swallow my grimace from the pressure of my hand against my freshly opened wound. "I think I'll go for a walk."

Tom sees right through me. "We have to go in an hour. The mechanic will arrive soon to replace the flat tires." His tone is sad, not strict. "You'll be back by then, right?"

I shake my head before I can stop myself. Rose doesn't see, still absorbed by her counting. My hopeful imagination paints the picture of what it would be like to go home with them. I'd help Rose with her Spanish. The four of us would eat dinner together, maybe in front of the TV sometimes.

My treacherous, hopeful imagination. I can't expose them to any more risk. The lab won't give up on me easily. The person who helped me escape may or may not be benign. Tom must never know how much I've endangered them.

"You have an important meeting in Claremont, remember?" Mandy says. She's thinking of the fictional PI who I said would come to my defense. She puts her hand on my arm.

I tense. "I'll be back before the mechanic finishes. I promise."

Rose looks confused. She's picked up on the subtext of the conversation, but she's not sure what it means. She hugs my other arm. "I want to go for a walk too."

I might cry for the second time today.

"Have you packed all your toys?" Mandy asks.

Rose buries her head between my arm and my chest. She smells like lavender and innocence. A streak of blue marker runs across the back of her hand.

"That's what I thought," Mandy says. "Go on, sweetie. You'll see Janine later." The way she pins me with her expression, I know she's trying to guilt me into staying.

I remind myself of all the reasons I must go as I pry Rose free. "I won't be gone long." It's a coward's move, forcing Mandy to deal with Rose's disappointment after I leave. I don't know what else to do. I don't have much experience with attachment.

As Rose goes upstairs, my limbs fill with lead. I take a step back in case Mandy is thinking of hugging me again. "You've been very good to me. Thank you."

Mandy frowns. "You sure you won't change your mind? I could go to the PI with you." I can see that she would.

"What if no one believes me? And even if the PI does, I'd still have to convince the police. And then there'd be a trial. I'd have to testify." Even an imagined confrontation with my keepers makes my arms curl around my stomach. I let Mandy think I'm a rape victim, reluctant to confront her attacker. "I just need some time on my own for a little bit. To clear my head."

"Would you say something, Tom?" Mandy snaps. "Tell her to come with us."

Tom studies me carefully. "I think she's had enough of other people making her decisions. She's entitled to her own mistakes."

He's more right than he can possibly know.

"You're useless." She digs through her purse and comes up with a card. On the back she jots down a number and an address. The front says DTouch Engineering—Mandy Harris—Product Designer. "If you change your mind, that's our home phone and address."

I won't. I take the card anyway. As I cross the living room, I hear Rose's light footsteps upstairs. She's turned on some sort of boombox, already distracted. I shut the front door quietly. I refuse to look in the windows as I pass them.

Another helicopter whirs in the distance as I pull my bag out from its hiding place. I force myself to wait long enough to find my orientation. I studied the framed map of the White Mountain National Forest and memorized as much as I could. If I walk due north, I'll cross the road that borders the park. There aren't many trails in that area, minimizing the possibility I'll run into someone else. The mountains are 10 miles distant. Someone without my weak heart could do that in a day. It will probably take me two days.

The helicopter is getting louder. I go for the safety of the shaded forest, where prying eyes won't see me. The protective cover of the forest is a disadvantage for navigation. I won't be able to see the sun's position in the sky. Don't panic, I tell my-self. Think. The slanted beams of light give me a clue. The sun is warmer on my left cheek. I can use that.

My first task is to do what I can to protect the Harrises from retaliation. I'm gambling on two things: that the lab doesn't know I'm aware of the tracker, and that they haven't picked up the signal yet. The helicopters weren't flying last night when I took the batteries out of my bracelet. I walk north for 10 minutes as fast as I can manage, scrambling over branches and trees. An old Swiss Army knife I stole from Mandy's workshop opens the battery compartment on my bracelet. I remove one of the batteries and tuck it into my pocket. I'll need it later.

With the bracelet no longer jamming the signal, the RFID tracker is operational again. My heart flutters even though I'm standing still. I can feel the eyes of lab on me. I dig my heels into the soft soil, to force myself to wait until the helicopter passes overhead. How long would it take from when they find me to when the guards show up? I can't know. I walk facing east now, moving toward the sporadic sounds of cars along Route 49. I want my last known location to be this road. The lab will think I hitchhiked into the city. It's a tempting thought. From the edge of the trees, I watch the oblivious drivers. One man sings along to his radio. A woman talks on her cell phone. A group of teenage boys passes, each with an arm hanging out the window and a hat facing backwards, desperate to look cool.

It's not exactly companionship, but it's more than I'll have for a while. I let myself stay for one more car. A family is inside, with the window open for a black lab eagerly gulping the wind. Lines of saliva have dried against the door. The whirring of helicopter blades tells me it's time to move on.

I put the battery back into my bracelet to block the RFID signal. I head west, back the way I came. Everything looks different going the other direction. I'll just have to walk west for the same amount of time I walked east and hope my pace is similar. The Barbie watch I stole from the junk room says it's 2:30 p.m.

At 2:45, I turn north. I have no idea if I've overshot the cabin or not. The shadows grow longer, the air cooler. Chipmunks and squirrels skitter in the undergrowth and shake the branches. I'm panting more than I should be, even though I'm taking it easy. I slow down to what feels like a crawl, but eventually it becomes clear I have to rest.

I use the time to take inventory. Les Stroud of *Survivorman* always starts by taking inventory. I empty my bag out on a clear patch of ground. I have stolen several things from the Harris family: the knife I used earlier, the Barbie watch around my wrist, a box of granola bars, and a map of New Hampshire. I wasn't able to find a map of the park. I still have the water bottle, the passport, the birth certificate and the roll of cash. Tom said it was $10,000. It seems like a lot, but I know it's less than the annual salary of a waitress.

I gulp some water, then repack my things. 10 more minutes of walking, and I should cross the road bordering the park. 20 minutes pass, and I'm still scrambling around in the brush. I peer through the green leaves, locate the sun to double-check myself. I'm still headed north. I've underestimated how fast I can go without using trails. I'll have to risk using them, or it will take me too long to get to the mountains.

A nice idea, of course, except I memorized the part of the map where the trails weren't. I was avoiding them on purpose. The national forest park entrance would have maps, but the Harris' cabin is closer. They have to have a map somewhere;

they hike here all the time. Now that they're gone, I can do a better search of the house.

I turn until what's left of the sun is on my right cheek, heading south. In just an hour, I find myself at the edge of the clearing for the cabin. Just looking at it calms me. It's the only place I've ever been happy. I see a tow truck in the driveway. The logo says *Trusty Mechanics*.

Something's wrong. I've been gone for two hours now. It doesn't take that long to replace two flat tires. I wait 15 minutes, 30 minutes, and still the tow truck doesn't move. There are no sounds of movement at all.

Maybe they're waiting for me, even though they said they wouldn't. Maybe they invited the mechanic in for coffee. There's my hopeful imagination again. I circle the house, sticking to the woods. The garage door is open. The tires I slashed have been replaced. The two damaged tires are on the ground by the tow truck. I break the cover of the trees to peer inside the windows. First, Mandy's cluttered workshop, also the junk room. Empty. Then, the living room. Empty. The dining room has a large picture window overlooking the yard. I crouch to stay below the ledge, sticking close to the house.

A mirror would be handy right about now, but I don't have anything like that. I peek above the blue-painted ledge, ready to duck at the first sign of movement. I'm confronted by stillness. Three slumped figures in three chairs. Three small, red circles in three pale foreheads. Three cheeks resting on the table, as if they simply fell asleep. In front of each of them, there is a plate with a sandwich. Each plate sits in a pool of blood. Rose's sandwich is only missing one bite.

I stand, press my palms to the glass, already cooling as the heat of the day fades. Fear and grief coil in the pit of my stomach. One shot to the head for cynical Tom, the man who saw through my lies and allowed me my mistakes. One shot to the head for the practical and sentimental Mandy, the engineer who couldn't get rid of grandfather clock that wouldn't keep time. One shot to the head for little Rose, the winner of board games and the asker of questions. Without the reflection of the sun, I can see a fourth body. A man in a gray jumpsuit, near a fallen clipboard. Also shot in the head. There are four circles in the window, showing where the bullets entered. I can reach them with my fingers. The radiating cracks prick at my skin.

Only a coordinated team of snipers could have done this—exactly the kind of team the lab has at its disposal. The lab arranged this little display just for me. They want me to know that my father's virus didn't kill the Harrises. I killed them by knowing them. A sniper's rifle could easily kill me too, if the lab wanted me dead. There's no point in running. The lab knows where I am. They've known for hours, otherwise they wouldn't have known I was headed back here. All my precautions meant nothing. I murdered the Harrises, and my freedom lasted less than two days.

"Sarina."

The voice comes from behind me. It's Dr. Choebach, standing at the edge of the woods. He looks more tired and worried than he ever did at the lab.

"You killed them." Raw grief, like acid, burns my throat and scars my words. "They didn't know anything!"

He shakes his head. "No, sweetheart." His eyes rest on each body for a short moment, then he swallows hard. "They called me after… after it was done."

I take a step back, my weight pressing against the glass. It protests sharply, weakened by the shots.

Dr. Choebach holds up a hand, as if to warn me. "They called me to bring you home."

The lab was never home. It was just a place where I was kept. "I'm not going."

"The snipers left," he says carefully. "I told them it was safe to let the soldiers keep their distance. That you would come with me."

In other words, I'm surrounded. The Harrises were bait on a gruesome trap. I can go with him, or be chased down like a dog. Fine. I turn and run. They'll shoot me or my heart will give out. Either way.

"No!" yells Dr. Choebach.

I keep running. Behind me, I hear the grunts of two men struggling. Then a gunshot. I scan my body for pain, without stopping. I'm not hit.

"Harold!" It's Dr. Werham's voice this time.

A quick glance back confirms my fears and stops me in my tracks. My ragged breaths and a roaring in my ears turns the scene into a silent tragedy. Dr. Choebach is on the ground, gripping a wound on his upper leg. Standing over him is a man I don't recognize. He is short and stolidly built, wearing army fatigues. With his arms up, he looks like an action figure. I follow the stranger's gaze to see Dr. Werham.

She has a gun pointed at his chest. "That's enough, Martin," she says crisply.

There's another gun on the lawn in front of Martin. Dr. Choebach must have lunged at Martin to keep him from shooting me. Now I've hurt Dr. Choebach too.

"Are you happy now?" Dr. Werham yells at me. "Go, you ungrateful little chit, go!" Of course she wants me to run. I'll be killed and then she'll be done with me.

"You—should—go," Dr. Choebach says. Each word costs him dearly, judging by how his face twists with pain.

Could Dr. Werham actually be trying to help me?

"You can—trust her," he manages through clenched teeth.

The radio on Martin's belt squawks to life. "Martin, report in. We heard gunfire."

"Why give her false hope, Jennifer?" Martin says. He turns to me. "We've been tracking you all day. You cooperated nicely. We wanted to capture you in the open. No sense in risking you breaking a leg if you tripped in the forest. You're valuable merchandise."

I thought I had outsmarted them. Silly, stupid me. The cruel joy in the twist of his lips traps me as well as any snare. I feel everything I felt when I was behind the glass walls of my cage. Helpless. Overpowered. Dissected. Used.

"It's true," Martin continues. "The snipers have gone home, but my soldiers are only a few minutes away. They're tightening the perimeter as I speak. There's no way you'll make it."

"Shut up, Martin," Dr. Werham says. She keeps her eyes on him as she talks to me. "Running now is the best chance I can give you. You might be able to slip past them."

She's wasting time keeping Martin alive. The lab won't forgive them for helping me. And she can't help Dr. Choebach while keeping a gun on Martin. I won't run. I can hear every blade of grass bend as I walk toward them.

"Ignore him," Dr. Werham says. "You can make it. If you go *now*."

I pick up the gun in front of Martin. "You need to take care of Dr. Choebach. I'll cover Martin." I'll worry about myself when Dr. Choebach stops bleeding.

Dr. Werham hesitates. Martin's amused. Skin crinkles at the corner of his beady eyes.

I steady the gun and step closer to my target. "I won't let anyone else die for me today."

"How very noble," Martin says.

"Shut up," I tell him. It feels good. Dr. Werham starts on a makeshift tourniquet made form the sleeve of her coat. When I look back at Martin, he is holding something in his hand. It's a small, metallic box, the size of a pack of cigarettes. In the center is a red button, protected by a plastic cap.

Dr. Werham hasn't noticed, focusing on keeping the bandage tight.

"Stop moving," I tell Martin.

His lips twist into a smile.

Dr. Werham looks up and sees the box, but she doesn't seem concerned. "Good luck with that."

Martin's confidence wavers. I decide that if Dr. Werham's not worried, then I'm not either. So I don't shoot him when he flips up the protective cap, and I don't shoot him when he presses the red button.

For the first time in our encounter, he looks like he doesn't have all the answers. "The capsule…"

My finger hovers over the trigger. It seems a thin piece of metal to balance a life on. I wonder if shooting a gun will be like in the movies, if Martin's body will flail or stutter. I increase the pressure slowly. The metal is warm from my hand, not cold like I imagined it would be. Martin doesn't notice. He's so busy examining his precious little box, he doesn't notice I have his heart in the sight.

The gun jerks in my hand as I fire. The sound tears at my ears. My lack of control means I miss his heart and get his shoulder instead. He's still standing, lunging for me with the uninjured arm. I pull the trigger again, this time prepared for the recoil. The second shot does better. On the third shot he crumples. On the fourth, his eyes roll back in his head. One shot for Tom, one for Mandy, and one for little Rose. The fourth shot was just to make sure the first three count.

"Sarina!" It's hard to hear Dr. Werham over the ringing in my ears.

My unsettled conscience tells me it's not quite self-defense. The metallic box had something to do with the capsule in my leg, but it didn't work. Maybe the capsule is RFID-triggered too, and the bracelet blocked it. I let the gun drop, the warm barrel brushes against my jeans. Martin gets paler as his life drains into the soil. I examine myself for any hint of regret, and find none.

"He would have told the lab you helped me," I say. "The lab would have killed both of you. Now you can say I shot him and Dr. Choebach too."

She nods slowly. "You're probably right." There are hand-prints on her pants in her husband's blood. Dr. Choebach's leg is tightly bound.

I scan the tree line. Martin's soldiers must be close. In the picture window, the glassy eyes of the Harris family observe their revenge. I wonder if it's worth trying to run.

"Hand me Martin's radio," Dr. Werham says. "There's one thing to try."

The whites of Martin's eyes watch me pull the radio from his belt.

"Larry, this is Jennifer," she says into the radio.

"Jennifer?" A gruff male voice answers. "Was Sarina shot? Can we take her alive?"

She glances at me. "She shot Martin and Harold, then ran away. Back toward Route 49. She has Martin's pack and his gun."

"She overpowered Martin?"

"She caught us by surprise. I need to get Harold to the hospital."

"What is Martin's condition?"

Dr. Werham clips the radio to her belt without answering. "I'm going to get the car. Lie down on Martin until the helicopter passes over."

"What?" I sputter. "No."

"They have infrared cameras on the helicopter. If you don't lie down on Martin, they'll see a fourth body."

A whir approaches in the distance. I do what she says. My ankles dangle awkwardly past the edge of his combat boots. My back grows sticky in the four spots where I shot him. His nose presses uncomfortably against the back of my neck. When I shift, the last breath of his lungs tickles my scalp. I shift again. The weight of my head turns his to the side. I shriek, nearly forgetting to keep my arms lined up with his.

"It's—okay, sweetheart," Dr. Choebach says. His words are muted by the helicopter that flies over us, high and fast.

I wish I could hear what Larry was saying on the radio. Sooner or later, they'll figure out there's no warm body in the woods near Route 49. In the meantime, I'm stuck on my grisly perch.

A fine sweat covers Dr. Choebach's face; he's in a lot of pain. Every few seconds he winces and takes a sharp breath.

"Here's the car," I say stupidly. He can see the black SUV approaching as well as I can.

"Thank you," he manages. "For staying." It could be my imagination, but the red spots on his bandages are growing.

I'm glad when Dr. Werham kneels next to her husband, rescuing me from having to say anything at all. She still has the radio in her hand. "Martin had a first-aid kit in his pack, right?" she says into it.

"Yeah, what about it?" It's the voice of the man she called Larry.

"Our standard-issue first aid kit has an emergency thermal blanket in it. She could be using it to hide her heat signal."

"Where would she have learned to do that?"

Dr. Werham looks at me. "Well, she's not here. She's your problem now." She turns off the radio. "You can get up now. I bought you a little time. Take Martin's pack, it has some useful supplies."

I scramble off Martin as fast as I can. Getting his pack is more difficult. It's trapped underneath him. "I'll do without."

"Take the damn pack," she snaps, "or you'll make me look like a liar."

I bend one of his arms to free it from the shoulder strap, but the elbow falls against the ground. I have to hold his arm against his side like a chicken wing. Even as a dead man, he's stubborn. It's creepy, touching flesh that isn't alive and isn't cold. Like a mannequin warmed but never brought to life. I use my knife to cut the straps and yank the pack out from underneath him.

When I look up, Dr. Werham is waiting impatiently. "I need your help to get Harold into the car." We each take a shoulder. Together, we lift Dr. Choebach into the backseat. He stretches out his leg with a grimace. The bandages are nearly soaked through.

"Jenny," Dr. Choebach says. He can only manage a few syllables between groans. "I think—bullet—shattered—femur bone."

She frowns. "Spasms?"

I look between his tortured face and her worried one. I didn't know there were good ways and bad ways to get shot in the leg.

"I need you to ride to the hospital with us," she says to me.

I can't. The last place I need to be a place full of cameras and witnesses.

"Please."

"I don't understand," I say, staring in the direction I should run. "What can I do?"

He moans, and my sore heart tears a little more. I want to help. I do. But I don't want to be a prisoner again. I don't think I could stand it.

Dr. Werham's tone turns icy. "Do you remember your physiology lessons, Sarina? What's the strongest muscle in the human body?"

The smell of blood is making me woozy. Martin's blood on my clothes, Dr. Choebach's blood in the car, and mine seeping through the leg of my pants. My superglue stitches didn't hold.

"The muscles of the upper thigh are so strong they can rub the ends of broken femur together." She points towards her husband. "Either I risk letting those spasms cause internal injuries, or I have to delay leaving for the hospital until I can make a tension splint."

The woods are dark and inviting. She won't force me to stay. She's a good person. I wonder if I am.

"The soldiers are searching the woods east of here. They won't follow us. See the tinted windows? No one will see you if you stay in the car. I just need you to stretch his leg out during the drive and hold the edges of the bone apart."

I owe them this. I owe them more than this, and still my mouth won't form a yes. I remember all the times I woke up in my bed, groggy from anesthesia, with fresh wounds no one would explain.

"Please," she says. Desperation is creeping into her voice. "I'll drop you off wherever you want."

I take my bag and Martin's pack, and I climb into the backseat with Dr. Choebach. I hope hiding behind the passenger seat is enough of a shield, only the side windows are tinted. She's already in the driver's seat.

"Take his foot and pull it toward you," she says. "As hard as you can."

And that's how we drive to the hospital, with Dr. Werham white-knuckled at the wheel, Dr. Choebach pressing his back against the door, and me, holding on as hard as I can.

Chapter 10

I don't like the noise of the highway. Jennifer weaves in and out of the four lanes of traffic at dangerous speeds. The blank expressions of all the drivers around us are frightening. And yet, somehow, they get out the way when Jennifer switches on her blinker and merges over three lanes to an exit marked with a white 'H' on a blue background.

"You should hide under the canvas in back," Dr. Werham says. "We'll be at the doors of the emergency room soon."

I didn't notice the cargo area before. A green cloth covers several square lumps. Gear for hunting me, I suppose. When I release my hold on Dr. Choebach's leg, the tortured look returns to his face. But already we are slowing down, and I can see people on the sidewalks. I climb over the seat. Under the cloth, it smells dank and metallic. In what little light there is, I can see the ridged lines of hard plastic cases. Stenciled lettering identifies their contents, but I don't understand most of the words. The rifles that killed the Harris family might be here with me.

"Jennifer," says a voice outside the SUV. "I'm glad you called ahead. We've cleared an operating room for Harold and the surgeon is already in scrubs."

She says something to Harold I only hear as a mumble. A siren wails, coming closer and closer. I pull myself into a ball, wonder what excuse Jennifer will use to explain my presence. But the noise stops and nothing happens. Of course, we're at a hospital. It's just an ambulance carrying another unlucky soul.

I hear the driver's door open and shut, then the SUV pulls away. We drive for a few minutes, then up, up, up, in a spiral. The car stops, then the growl of the engine dies.

"You can come out now," Dr. Werham says.

I'm happy to abandon the dank smell of the cargo area. Outside the windows, I see the endless concrete of a parking garage. Small shudders announce the movement of cars above us and below us. Outside the windshield, a stenciled number reads *345.*

Dr. Werham rubs her forehead. "I never thanked you for agreeing to come with us. And for taking care of Martin." She doesn't look at me while she's talking.

It's just as well. I don't deserve anyone's thanks. "It was the right thing to do."

"Still." A car passes behind us. Each time the tires cross a joint, I hear a tick-thump. She pulls the keys from the ignition and drops them into a purse. "We'll probably be a few hours. I think there's food and water in Martin's pack."

"I'll be okay."

I'm glad when she leaves. I'm not sure how to deal with the kinder, softer Dr. Werham. I still haven't recovered from Martin's little display at the cabin. The guilt will swallow me if I let it. I push my thoughts into a more useful direction, where to go next. Hiding in the mountains is no longer an option. I'd like to go to another planet, but another country will have to do. Transportation is my main problem. I've never driven a car. Even video games that were too close to the real thing were forbidden. That leaves plane, train, or bus.

The airport will require ID. I don't trust the passport I've been given. It came from the same person who gave me the bracelet. They could be tracking me under that name. A train from here will get me to Canada; that doesn't seem far enough away. Mexico might be an option. The language won't be a problem. I'll have to cross half the continent to get there, though.

New Hampshire isn't that far from the coast. There is another possibility: a ship. I think of all the vacation movies I've seen about cruises, and I can't see it working. A single female recluse would attract attention on a ship full of sunburned families. Plus, they're expensive. I need to be conservative with my cash. An article I read in the *Times* pops into my memory. A freighter cruise. That might be possible. Freighter cruises take a small number of passengers. I won't be part of a gaggle of tourists descending on each port. Even better, minimal service is the norm. I'll be left alone. And they're cheaper, a lot cheaper.

I dig in the glove compartment and find a collection of maps for the surrounding states. It's fun to trace the strings of highways. Towns are strung along them like beads with lovely, silly names. Sandwich. Center Sandwich. Some of the names are regal like Campton and Plymouth.

Detailed maps were forbidden at the lab. It made geography a very short unit.

I read the maps like novels for the next hour, getting lost in the parks and lakes and features. My research tells me the closest large port is Boston. That's where I will ask Dr. Werham to drop me off.

With that settled, there's nothing left to distract from the endless waiting. The hours I spent with the Harris family play over and over again in my head, a tape I can't stop that always ends the same: with Rose slumped over, strands of her hair in the crumbs on her plate. The air in the car becomes stale, suffocating.

I'm about to open the door for just one breath of fresh air when I hear familiar voices and the clomp of a cast.

Dr. Werham helps her husband into the front passenger seat. She has to move it as far back as it goes to make room for the full-leg cast. Dr. Choebach gives me a tired smile in the rearview mirror.

"Is it still painful?" I ask.

"Not so bad." He winks. "They gave me some good pills."

Dr. Werham backs the car out. We climb down, down, down a winding circle until we reach the signs pointing to the exit. Perhaps the long wait frayed my nerves, but I don't want to sit exposed in the back seat. Dr. Choebach doesn't need me anymore.

Without asking, I take my post under the musty canvas in the cargo area. I think it's understanding I see on Dr. Werham's face as I make myself disappear. I can't see my Barbie watch in the dark. I play games in my head, matching each noise to an image. First, people on the sidewalks. Someone's brakes, not ours, screech to a stop. Then the road curves and we speed up. The highway again. I think Dr. Werham must be driving slower than she was on our trip to the hospital because cars rev their engines to get ahead of us. I hear the deep, throbbing growl of a motorcycle. Dr. Werham and Dr. Choebach don't speak. I don't know how much time passes before things get quieter. The highway noise is gone, and none of the background noise of the city. I risk a peek out the back window.

We're on deserted, residential streets now. There are no streetlights here, just houses that pose like models, strategically lit to highlight their proportions and expensive landscapes. Lights in the windows of the houses are the only signs of life. It's safe to sit in the back seat now, I think. "Where are we going?"

"Our house," Dr. Choebach says.

Dr. Werham shakes her head. "No, I'm dropping you off and then I'm taking her to a hotel."

"Honey—"

"It's too dangerous for her to be at the house. Larry might come by."

"He won't suspect we're hiding her," Dr. Choebach says. "Our story is she shot me, remember?"

"You heard Larry on the radio. He didn't believe she could overpower Martin."

They're not even asking me what I want to do.

"And you're in no condition to defend yourself," she adds.

If she's trying to add to my guilt for the day, it's working. "Dr. Werham, I'm sorry Dr. Choebach was shot—"

"You might as well call him Harold. And me Jennifer."

Harold and Jennifer. A nice, professional, suburban couple. I wonder how many of their neighbors know what they do. "I never meant for Dr.—Harold to get shot. I ran because…" Jennifer might think my attempt at suicide was weak. I decide

I don't care. I need her to trust me. The thought of spending the night alone with only a flimsy hotel lock between me and a trained military unit isn't pleasant. "I didn't think I could get away. I didn't want to be taken alive."

A spotlight on a burbling fountain casts a marbled glow on Jennifer's face. Her expression softens, then hardens just as quickly as her face moves into darkness.

"I'll sleep in the car," I say. "If they find me here, I'll say I crawled into the cargo area while you were taking care of Harold."

Jennifer shakes her head slightly and frowns at the dark road ahead. "Fine. You can sleep in the car. But if Larry finds you, there's nothing I can do. Even if I wanted to."

I miss Mandy's hugs. "Who's Larry?"

Harold leans his head against the seat. "Larry Broderick," he says tiredly. "The director of the lab."

It's a name I haven't heard before. They took great care to make sure I had as little knowledge of the staff as possible.

On the street where Harold and Jennifer live, all of the houses are variations on the theme of luxury and conformity. The biggest ones have three stories and garages with room for four cars. Automatic sprinkler systems tend to lawns that look like golf courses.

Jennifer gets out to punch a code into a keypad by the garage door. Two of the three spaces are already taken. I feel much better when the garage door closes behind us. She hurries over to the passenger side to help Harold.

Harold bats her away with his crutch. "I'll have to get used to this for a couple of weeks."

I dig in Martin's pack to find my supplies for the night. Aside from the first aid kit and his weapons, there's one energy bar and a half-empty bottle of water. Mandy would think to bring me food and water. I'm not sure Jennifer will.

"I haven't eaten since breakfast." I hate myself for sounding timid and weak, as if I'm asking for her affection. "If it's not too much trouble, after he's settled—"

Her pinched face cuts me off. "You can stay in the house. If Larry comes, you can hide in the crawl space behind the furnace."

Inside, I'm ignored while she fusses over Harold in one of the bedrooms upstairs. Downstairs there is a large kitchen with a sitting area, a formal dining room, a living room, a game room, and yet another room for the TV. She is gone for so long, I have time to explore the upstairs too. There are three other bedrooms in addition to the master bedroom. Each has a massive bed with an ornate, polished wood frame. The bedding arrangements are straight out of a home decorating magazine, sumptuous down comforters with piles of matching pillows resting against carved headboards. What is missing is any sign of life. There are no scratches on the walls. No odds and ends in the dresser drawers. Just closets full of clothes with the price tags still on.

Dried patches of Martin's blood itch at my back. Mandy's shirt is ruined. Her jeans are dirty and torn. Jennifer won't miss one shirt out of her collection. And maybe a pair of pants too. I choose a long-sleeved silk blouse with modern, clean lines. I like how soft it feels. There's a black pair of pants hanging near it that looks promising. The fabric is a sturdy cotton blend, but cut formally enough the blouse will work. I stuff the bloody shirt in my bag. I'll find a place to dump it once Jennifer drops me off.

The rest of the house has the same character as the bedrooms, meticulously decorated and as sterile as a museum. I end up in the cavernous kitchen, hovering near the fridge. An island of gleaming granite holds containers full of brushed metal cooking implements. Everything I've ever seen on a cooking show, and more. The cupboards are nearly bare. I snack on stale chips. I doubt she wants me in the fridge. She might even begrudge me the chips.

"Nice outfit," she says when she finds me. "I suppose you're ready to eat."

She opens the fridge. It's nearly empty. There are two neatly labeled containers, one carton of milk, and one carton of orange juice. "You can have Harold's meal. He won't be up until tomorrow morning." While the microwaves heats up dinner, she opens a bottle of wine from a well-stocked cabinet and pours herself a glass. She doesn't offer me any.

Loud beeps announce that dinner is ready, but she doesn't move from her perch. I retrieve our dinners. A sticker on both containers says 'Prepared for you by *Matilda.*' There's a blank space on the sticker where the name is written.

"We have a chef service that drops off meals for us," she says.

Only the most upper-class families on TV have their own personal chefs. "That must be nice for you."

She's not apologetic. "Yes, they pay us well."

The slam of the microwave door startles me, even though it was my hand that closed it. "Is it worth it?" I can't help how bitter the question sounds.

Her fork is poised over some sort of braised beef. "It was when the project started."

My growling stomach keeps me from throwing my dinner in her face. I'd rather eat alone on her fancy couch. The brown gravy looks like it would stain. Instead, I take the stool next to her. My time here is short, and I have some questions that need to be answered.

She chews thoughtfully, eyeing me. "When the project started things were different." It's almost as if she wants me to like her. "They recruited Harold and me just out of med school. We weren't much older than you are now. We were giddy. It was the most prestigious residency we could have hoped for, and a well-paying one too."

All of my painful hours at the lab added up to someone's paycheck.

"It wasn't so much about money," she says, seeing my look of disgust. "You can't imagine the opportunities that would have lined up for us if things had gone according to plan. We would have been on the team that cured the infamous virus baby. We would have been pioneers in gene therapy. If we could cure you, what else could we cure?" She sips her wine and swallows hard. "Mostly it was about doing good work, but I can't deny the income was nice. You have no idea how student loan debt adds up."

I hope my expression is blank. I don't have any experience with student loan debt. I never will. I can speak five languages and I could ace a college physics course, but I don't have so much as an elementary school transcript to my name.

"With the tools we have now, we could easily cure you, but when you were born—1990?"

"1991."

"1991," she repeats thoughtfully. "When you were born, gene therapy was barely an idea. Your father was years ahead of everyone else. It took us five years just to figure out how he programmed your lungs to make the virus. By then, Congress had lost interest in the project. Funding drifted to other things.

"Harold and I stayed longer than we should have. We nearly quit several times. Most of the original team saw the writing on the wall. But we couldn't make ourselves go."

She wants me to ask, so I do. "Why?"

"You." Her smile is sad. "That first year, we spent most of our nights at the lab in case you woke up and wanted a bottle. You didn't like the night nurse; you cried every time she held you."

My memories are reshaping themselves in uncomfortable ways. All the times Jennifer avoided my eyes, ignored my pleas for help, withheld a gentle touch. I thought her antagonism toward me was jealousy. She was only protecting herself.

"When you were six, the lab was nearly shut down due to lack of resources. They planned to put you in an institution with a biohazard wing. We were so excited when we heard the lab got new funding, that we could continue our work. We were so close to curing you. God, we were naïve." She grips the stem of the wineglass so hard I'm afraid it will break. "That's when Larry showed up. The funding came from secret military budgets. Weapons research. They wanted to make you the ultimate covert bio-weapon. Our protests were overruled." She leans in, her eyes a little wild. "You have to understand that by that point we had sequenced the virus. It could have been weaponized in other ways. We could have cured you, and let you go. But you were just too valuable." The fight leaves her posture. She takes another long swallow. "At first, we stayed to protect you."

My stomach is clenched around the three bites of dinner I've forced down. I'm no longer hungry.

"And then we had no choice. We were the only members of the original team left. What we knew was too valuable, and we had made ourselves a liability by arguing about how they treated you. Larry offered us a choice. We could stay and work for them, where they could keep tabs on us, or..." She drew a finger across her throat. "Larry never came out and said it that clearly, of course. He's a very careful man."

I do the math in my head. I'm 23 years old. The lab became a military project when I was six. That's 17 years of forced labor. Forced to work hurting the child she once cared for.

"So, yes, we have money. Money we have to earn." She waves her hand in a broad gesture at the luxuries surrounding us. "Money we have to spend. A large savings account makes us a flight risk."

"I didn't know," I say. I won't apologize. She could have shown me some kindness over the years. Harold did. Though, she did hold Martin at gunpoint to let me get away. Maybe I should be nicer to her. Free from the pressure of the moment, a memory falls into place. When Martin brought out the box with the red button, Jennifer knew it wouldn't hurt me. She knew the bracelet would block the signal. "It was you. You set me free. You burned down the lab."

She nods. "With pleasure."

The job she hates would have ended with my death. She went to a lot of trouble to get me out. "Why not just leave me there?"

Red shadows swirl in the polished surface of the granite as she twists the stem of her wineglass. "You probably don't remember, but we were good friends once, you and I. You took your first steps into my arms."

The soft tone of her voice is unexpectedly familiar. I hear an echo of a laugh inside my head. The kind, musical laugh used when playing with a child. It's hard to pair that memory with the hard woman sitting next to me; her wrinkles show more scowls than mirth. I think I understand how she feels. Caring for someone makes you vulnerable to her pain. I can't afford to take that risk ever again. To the lab, anyone I'm connected to will become a thumbscrew to be used against me. Behind other curtains, in other windows, on this street, maybe it's different.

I tell myself it doesn't matter. In my life, the burdens of caring for someone will always outweigh the blessings. That's the price I will pay for my father's sins. "I have some questions."

Mandy shrugs. "Ask away."

"Where did the bracelet come from? The one that blocks RFID signals?"

Her eyes skip to the corner of the room. "Online. They sell them for protection from identity theft."

I'll play along. "Did you save the manual? How will I know when the batteries need replacing? Where's the clasp in case I need to take it off?"

She narrows her eyes. "A friend made it for me, okay? I told him what I wanted it to do, and the rest is his design. I don't know how to get it off. I wouldn't try anyway, not for a couple months. Not until the batteries run out. You might damage it."

"How did the lab find me after I escaped? When?"

"The helicopters Larry borrowed are equipped with infrared cameras. They spotted you just before the Harrises picked you up."

"The lab knew I was there the whole time." Saying it out loud just makes it sound worse. The Harrises were dead the second they made the mistake of helping me. Nothing I did mattered. "I didn't hear any helicopters on the first day." My voice is barely a whisper.

"Larry grounded the helicopters when your location seemed stable. He didn't want to spook you."

I hear a dull rattling; it's my fork hitting the edge of the plastic container. I stab the swirl of mashed potatoes and leave the fork there, standing upright. I should have known better. Mentor taught me this lesson over and over again. The deadliest mistake you can make in chess is underestimating your opponent.

She lifts her hand as if to comfort me, then changes her mind. "I'm sorry. About the family. I figured Larry would search quietly, just with soldiers on foot looking for your RFID signal, until we could confirm your body wasn't there. He likes to keep a low profile. On the county books, the building really does belong to a shell corporation called Next Squared Industries. But something spooked him. First thing in the morning, he went to the media with that story about looking for missing employees. A couple hours later, no one had called in, and he was panicking. He told the guard captain to call off the foot search and use helicopters. They found you pretty quickly, but by then the Harrises were already there."

"Why didn't the lab just come get me?"

"Same reason you stayed," she says carefully, as if she's afraid of my reaction. "Larry wanted to see if they would get sick." Jennifer shudders. "I'm supposed to do their autopsies tomorrow. As if I'm a fucking pathologist."

I close my eyes and see their bodies neatly lined up on steel tables, draped with sterile white sheets. It feels like right before I'm sedated for surgery, numb all over. Except this time I'm awake, and I don't want to be.

She touches my shoulder; my arm hits my fork. Lumps of mashed potatoes spray the spotless counter.

"It's good that you were worried about the infection spreading," she says. "It's good that you tried to protect them. It's just, sometimes…" She retracts into herself, hugging her elbows against her chest. "Sometimes nothing you can do is enough."

Escaping Larry's grasp won't bring the Harrises back, but it will spite him. Just the thought of panicking the bastard makes me a little happier. "How contagious am I?"

Jennifer visibly relaxes at my calmer tone. "You're not infectious without the external trigger. We crippled the virus by removing the DNA for a coat protein that's necessary for HF186-2A. Without that protein, white blood cells are able to kill the virus through phagocytosis. Your father made sure the coat protein was unique to his virus so no other virus would allow someone to develop immunity. The trigger reintroduces that little bit of DNA."

"How is the trigger delivered?"

"I don't know."

I'm about to accuse her of lying again, but she speaks first.

"You think they tell us everything?" She tips her wine glass until the last of the liquid drains down her throat. "We're just well-paid foot soldiers."

I try to think like my opponent. My keepers would want an efficient weapon, with an infallible trigger. "My part—the crippled virus—is still manufactured by my lungs?"

She nods.

The easiest way to guarantee infection would be to make the trigger airborne too, something light and easy to disperse. A perfume, or a powder, or… There are too many possibilities. It would help if I knew how they were planning to deploy their weapon. "The lab was going to let me leave. They had a plan to use me. What was it?"

She arches her eyebrows. "I always suspected you knew more than you let on."

"Just tell me."

"Larry sold the project as a weapon against isolated terrorist training camps. Conventional weapons aren't any good against deep caves or in places where it's difficult to target accurately. The target would have to be a day's travel from any other populated location." Her voice is mechanical, like she's reciting someone else's words. "You and the trigger would be exposed to someone headed into the camp. The roads to and from the camp could be monitored to make sure the infection didn't spread. If anyone discovered the camp full of infected people, the military could claim the terrorists had infected themselves with their own biological weapon."

If you don't know much about biology, it's a fine plan. "There's no way they can guarantee that the virus wouldn't jump the species barrier. Ebola jumped from monkeys to humans."

"We told Larry as much several times. I don't think he ever wanted to actually use you. He wanted to run the team that kept tabs on you outside the lab. It's his way of protecting his own little corner of power. For what it's worth, I think the trigger will be destroyed if you can stay hidden."

"That seems too easy."

"The director has a strong self-preservation instinct. He won't risk the virus getting loose. All of the vaccine for HF186-2A was destroyed in the fire, and it will take several months before they can rebuild their stock."

It's the first good news I've heard all day. "What was implanted in my legs during the last surgery?"

"A tracker in your left leg, and a poison capsule in your right leg. Both depend on RFID."

The poison capsule explains Martin's expression before I shot him. "The box Martin had with the red button, that triggers the poison. He didn't know the bracelet would block the signal."

She tips her empty glass toward me. "You always were a smart girl."

"Can you remove the implants?" Just thinking about them makes the incisions hurt more.

Her answer is cut off by the sound of the doorbell and an insistent knock on the front door. "Shit."

"That's—"

"Larry. He's the only person who would come around this late." She grabs my arm, pulling me off the stool, and points to the dining room. "The stairs to the basement are just around the corner. The wooden access panel just behind the furnace leads to our crawl space. Stay there until I come for you."

I find the stairs, but pause on the first step. If I hide in the crawl space, I won't know if it's time to run. Larry's walk sounds more like a stomp. His steps thunder into the kitchen. I hear the floor creak and a cabinet door open. My hesitation has cost me the opportunity to do the right thing. If I can hear those sounds, surely Larry will hear me creep down the stairs.

"You haven't been answering your phone," a male voice says. Without the radio static, it's demanding and sharp. A voice that is not used to being disobeyed.

"We just got back from the hospital. She shot Harold, re-member?"

"So you say." Waiting for Jennifer's reply is torture. I find myself expecting to hear a gunshot. Instead, Larry speaks again. "It was nice of you to help Martin."

"No one could have helped Martin." I hear a glass clink and the faucet run. "Water?"

"No." A glass slams on the counter. I stop my hand from turning the knob on the door just in time. "I want you to tell me what happened. Everything."

"We were following your orders. Harold was waiting just in-side the tree line for her to show up." There are years of fatigue in Jennifer's voice. She sounds nothing like the woman who happily admitted to burning down the lab; she sounds like a soldier. "Martin and I were further back, following her with the thermal imaging cam. When she broke cover, Harold tried to talk her into coming quietly. Instead, she ran. Martin ran after her. He caught up with her first and tackled her."

It's discomfiting to hear an alternate version of the afternoon. It could have easily gone that way.

"They struggled, and somehow Sarina got his gun," Jennifer continues. "She killed him, then threatened us. We tried to get the gun away from her, and Harold got shot in the process. Then she grabbed Martin's pack and ran."

"Martin outweighs her by 50 pounds and has combat training. You're telling me she was able to steal his gun and shoot him four times?"

"I guess she had more to lose," Jennifer snaps. "I'm just telling you what happened."

My mind follows Larry's train of thought just like I followed Mentor's moves in the game. We left Martin's gun in the clearing. I should have taken the gun when I took the pack. A desperate girl on the run wouldn't give up her best weapon.

"We found Martin's gun by his body."

There's a long silence. I wish I could see Jennifer's face. "She must have come back after we left."

"Why would she come back?"

"I don't know, Larry. We didn't talk. I was trying to keep my husband from bleeding to death."

Larry stomps around the kitchen. I wonder if he is circling Jennifer, or just pacing. "The autopsies on the family will have to wait. I have a new assignment for both of you. It starts tonight." I can't tell if he accepted her story or not. He could be baiting a trap, like he did for me.

"The doctor said he needs to stay off his leg."

"That's nice for the doctor. We have work to do."

I hear a thump, like the legs of a chair hitting the ground, or something being kicked. "My husband needs to rest. We're staying here."

"You two were close to Sarina once, you know how she thinks. I need you to help search for her. We have to find her as soon as possible." For the first time, he sounds worried.

"That's not my department."

"There's a been a complication."

"Right, because this was all so simple before," she says.

"Gregory Wocek escaped this morning."

I grab the banister to keep myself from falling down the stairs. The wood protests at my sudden weight. My muscles freeze, hoping the creak from the basement stairs didn't catch Larry's attention.

"More good news I can't do anything about," she says.

"I can't keep the manhunt for Dr. Wocek quiet much longer. We need to get inside Sarina's head so we find her before word gets out that Dr. Wocek escaped."

"Or people will start asking where Sarina is. And what you've been doing to her for the past 18 years."

"You know the deal, Jennifer. If I go down, everyone goes down with me. You operated on her for most of her life. You think people will look past that?"

"I'm not any happier about this situation than you are." She sounds dangerously defensive.

"Convince me."

The floor creaks in the agonizing silence. "You're right, I'm ecstatic," Jennifer says. "My husband was shot, and a bio-terror weapon and her creator have escaped. It's like I won the fucking lottery."

"Careful, Jennifer. For all your complaining, you've always been a loyal soldier. I hope you realize how important that is."

I watch the seconds on the digital screen of my Barbie watch. They count up to 60, roll back to 0, then back to 60 again. I force my rigid stomach muscles to release a breath.

"Fine," she says. The defeat in her voice is painful to hear, even if it is saving her life. "I'll talk to Harold and come up with some places she might hide. He can stay here while I go out looking."

"Don't bother with the forest near the lab. If she's still there, the dogs will find her."

Every muscle in my body snaps taut.

"If not, she must have hitchhiked out. We already swept Ellsworth; she's not there. Think of places she might feel safe enough to spend the night close by."

"Okay," she says dully.

Somehow she keeps her temper in check as he leaves. Larry's footsteps pound to the door, then Jennifer's lighter footsteps come back into the kitchen. I take several steps down, so I can claim I was in the crawlspace, but Jennifer doesn't come any closer. She stomps on the floor so hard the appliances rattle.

I make my way upstairs and gently push the door open. It doesn't matter, I think, that the door squeaks lightly. Jennifer won't hear it. I pad across the dusty, fancy dining room. She's caught in an angry dance on the cream tiles, her eyes closed and her fist contorted. She makes a fist, shoves it into her mouth and screams. Even muted, the desperate pitch chills me. In one explosive motion, she picks up the wine bottle and smashes it against the edge of the counter. Blood-red wine explodes from the jagged bottom and splashes out the narrow neck. Harold appears in the kitchen doorway with his crutch, on the other side of Jennifer.

He circles the granite island to avoid the red puddle sparkling with green glass. When he puts his arm around her, she collapses against his chest. I shouldn't be here. They should be able to suffer in privacy.

For several minutes, he hugs her face to his chest.

"It's okay, sweetheart," he says into her hair. "It's okay."

She shakes her head and steps back. "How much did you hear?"

"Everything."

"Then you know what to tell Larry when he asks you what happened."

"I heard everything between you and Sarina, too." It's the first time I've seen him show any hint of anger. "Now I know where you were two nights ago."

She digs out a mop that looks like it's never been used. "You would've said the plan was too risky. That we should have gone to the attorney general or the press, or—"

"No." The hand not clenched around his crutch is balled into a tight fist. "I would have helped."

I have underestimated him, too.

She finally looks at me, as if deciding whether or not to share something, then back at Harold. "Larry will have to end the project if Sarina can get away safely." Her words stumble with desperation. "It'll just take longer than I thought."

"You couldn't have known Dr. Wocek would escape."

She looks guilty for a second, then nods. "I guess we can call ourselves lucky. Pretending to search for Sarina will give me a good excuse for dropping her off wherever she wants to go."

"Boston," I say.

She seems surprised. "What will you do—never mind, don't tell me."

"Tell Larry we think she'll try for a bus to Canada, where she can use her French," Harold says. "Take the lab's SUV, so Larry can use the GPS to confirm you searched for her. Spiral out from Ellsworth as if you're checking all the bus stops she could have hitchhiked to." Harold picks up my bag and hands it to me. It's more gray than white now, streaked with black charcoal and dirt. "You know I wish you could stay." He hugs me to soften the blow. It's the second hug in my memory. I understand what Jennifer sees in him. Even balancing on one leg and the crutch, he's the most solid thing I've ever felt. I clutch at his cotton shirt. It smells of pine needles and antiseptic. It's wet. From me. I don't fight the tears this time. I cry for all the lives I ruined without meaning to and with exhaustion for the task ahead.

My father will try to find me. He's never given up on his dream. I will have him and the lab stalking me.

There's another hand on my back, not warm like Harold's, but just as gentle. "Sarina, sweetheart," Jennifer says, like she's said it a hundred times. "We have to go."

Chapter 11

I try to hide behind Jennifer's seat as she drives. I don't want to be visible through the windshield. The closer we get to Ellsworth, the more my shoulders hunch with tension. I suppose it would make more sense to hide under the canvas again, but it also means I won't be able to see what's going on. The graffiti on the wall of an abandoned gas station in Ellsworth reminds me of my unwanted cargo. Cut wires dangle from the security cameras. A red light holds us at the intersection. "Can you stop at that gas station across the way? And dump Martin's pack for me?" And the bloody shirt inside it.

"You'll want the supplies."

I shake my head. "It smells like him. Everything in it smells like him." To be more precise, the pack smells like his blood.

Jennifer raises her eyebrows. "If you insist." She taps her finger on the steering wheel as we wait for the light. "I'll let you off there and you can put the pack in that dumpster behind the family restaurant."

The cameras mounted on the brick wall look very new and functional. "And get caught on camera?"

She nods. "Exactly." The light turns green. She rolls through the intersection slowly, but speaks quickly. "Tomorrow I'll say I thought I spotted you here, but I wasn't sure. When Larry sees the surveillance footage, he'll think you're on foot, alone. I'll wait for you at the intersection at the end of the block, where that park is. There are no cameras there." She pulls over and unlocks the doors. "Well?"

The street is deserted. There's no one to see me. It's just one block. One block outside the protection of the car.

"Trust me. It means they'll concentrate their search far away from Boston. And they're not looking for you here. Larry's men already cleared the area."

Her logic works. The dark night mocks me anyway. My fingers brush the door handle but refuse to open it.

She sighs. "Fine. I'll dump the pack at the gas station. But the less evidence of you they find, the wider the search area will get."

"No, I'll do it." I can do this. Or, at least, that's what I tell myself as I push open the door of the SUV. One step across the sidewalk. 10 strides across the gas station parking lot. The rigid unevenness of the cracked asphalt makes me unsteady. My feet have only known the perfectly level surfaces at the lab or the soft mounds of the forest floor. Five strides left. Then across the alley.

I find my chin tilting to look at the cameras, then point it back down. I can't look like I'm trying to be seen. An engine passes me; my attention snaps back to the road. It's Jennifer, heading to the park. Every palpitation of my heart muscle ripples through my chest. The speeding rhythm could be my weak genes or my nerves.

Walk. Behind the restaurant, across a parking lot to where Jennifer waits. I spin every few steps, trying to avoid any blind spots, but it just makes the walk take longer. My hands are sweating when I get back in the car. I'm glad to be hiding behind Jennifer's seat, where she can't see how rattled I am.

She ends her fake search of town at the bus station. We're stopped by the second of the two traffic lights in town on our way out. A dark SUV, exactly like ours, approaches from the dark highway. Jennifer swears under her breath. "Larry said they were sticking to the woods."

Panic tumbles my words together. "They saw me get in this car earlier. And now they're—"

"Quiet," Jennifer says. "They would have picked us up sooner if they knew where you were." But she doesn't sound sure. "Get on the floor. Let me handle it."

I curl myself into a tight ball on the carpet. Small pebbles poke through the seat of my pants; my shins are pushed against the metal frame of the driver's seat. I peek around the edge, even though I know I shouldn't. The other SUV ignores the red light. I curl up tighter, press my knees into my forehead.

Jennifer dealt with Larry, didn't she? Everything's going to be fine.

I hear the growling engine of the SUV stop next to us. Jennifer rolls her window down. Night sounds creep into the car. It reminds me of the night I escaped, when every sound seemed to be evidence of a creature stalking to me. A dog's barking cuts the air into staccato beats.

"Shut that dog up," a vaguely familiar male voice says. "What's got him so excited?"

My scent. It's one of the dogs Larry mentioned at the house. Jennifer's sharp intake of breath echoes my thoughts.

"Oh, I thought you were another field unit," he says. In the background, the dog's whines blend with the voices of other men discussing coordinates on a map.

"We have Martin's car," Jennifer says. "I had to use it to take Harold to the hospital."

"A shame about Martin, huh?"

I don't think it's a shame at all. The other driver doesn't ask about Harold.

"Yeah," Jennifer agrees. "Larry wanted us to search places she might have hitchhiked too. Seen any sign of her?" Her question is drowned out by another round of barking.

"I said shut that dog up," the male voice says.

Another male voice, more distant, speaks. "Sir, the dog smells something."

For a second, I feel canine teeth closing around my wrist. I will Jennifer to say something. Anything.

"Smart dog," she says.

Anything but that.

"The dog must be picking up Sarina's scent from this afternoon," she continues. "Harold and I tried to get the gun from her."

In the other SUV, fingers drum against a door. It could mean boredom or suspicion. "We're moving the dogs to a new quadrant. The IR cameras picked up something."

"Good luck."

There's no reply, just the sound of his window rolling up. The other SUV continues on its way. Another 30 seconds passes before the light changes and we move again. I count the minutes on my watch. I'll move in 10 minutes, I tell myself. When that passes, I give myself another five.

"You can get up now," she says.

Despite the pain in my shins, I hesitate.

She sighs. "It's fine, Sarina. We're past their search area now."

Pins and needles attack my legs as I climb back on the seat. I rub at my feet, then wince as the feeling comes back. "Who was that driving the other car?" I ask.

"Captain of the guard unit."

I used to have a crush on him. When I thought the lab was a friendly place, he was my handsome, dashing protector. After I realized what was really going on, I noticed how he spent most of his time bragging about his deadlift personal best at the gym. A road sign lists how far it is to each town on the rural, two-lane road: 11 miles, 13, 21.

"One of us might as well sleep," Jennifer says. "I'll be making a lot of stops so I can pretend I asked about you."

I think she wants to avoid talking to me. I'm okay with that. I'll need to be alert when she drops me off, and I am tired. The plastic upholstery grabs at my clammy skin when I try to lie down. As the encounter with the guard unit fades into the miles behind us, I notice how cold it is. Jennifer has barely turned the heat on. I decide not to complain. She has protected me, after all. And I won't have any more companionship for a while. The research on social isolation doesn't bode well for me. Lack of meaningful connections increases the risk of death in elderly patients. Studies on childhood development show that human contact is nearly as important as nutrition. For some reason, my ever-wise panel of psychologists never bothered with that aspect of my life. I suppose it makes sense if you realize what I really am. The military doesn't tuck their missiles into bed at night; why am I any different?

My rest is fitful. The hum of the rural highways and the dark night lulls me to sleep, only to be woken when the car stops. The door opens, lighting up the interior. It's bright even with my eyes closed. Jennifer gets out. The door slams shut. Five minutes later, she's back. Hours pass as we repeat the charade.

The shallow sleep brings a parade of uncomfortable dreams. I watch the Harrises die, but this time I shoot them. Martin presses the button, and I hear him laughing while I die. The Harrises are alive again. I roll the dice and move my acorn two spaces ahead. Rose smiles and holds out her hand for the rent. It seems real. It feels real. The living room jerks. Part of me knows it's the car stopping, part of me refuses to believe it. I fight consciousness, clawing to hold on to the mirage.

It's like grasping at a reflection in water; the simple act of reaching destroys the image. I wait for the door to open, for Jennifer to get out. Nothing happens. I open my eyes to slits and find a gray dawn. We've been driving all night.

"We're here," Jennifer says. "Boston." She stretches her arms and opens my door.

I expect to see the city limits. But no, the air smells different here. Salty, like miso soup. The humid air is heavy in my lungs.

"I figured you didn't want the airport," she said. "We're close to the main port."

"Thank you," I mumble. "And thank you… for everything else." I lift the bag with the unspent roll of cash and my emergency supplies.

"You're the closest thing we have to a daughter." There's an edge in her tone that belies the words. "We decided not to have kids. It'd be one more thing the lab could hold over us."

Her unhappiness forces me out of the car. The door hasn't even shut before she drives away.

The port is nothing like I imagined it. It's utilitarian, not romantic. I'm surrounded by large, one-story buildings with parking lots occupied by rundown cars. The warehouse workers shuffling to and from their shifts take no notice of me. I wander until I see a map of the waterfront displayed for tourists. Plexiglass pockets for brochures line the bottom. The slogans are ridiculous and engrossing at the same time. Have a "magical good time" at the mock dungeons in Salem and see a recreation of a witch trial. Get "crabby" at Uncle Eddy's crab shack, where all kids get free crab hats.

I find the star that says, "You are here!" and head toward the docks. The main port announces itself before I can see it. Large engines rumble under the deep-throated horns of the boats. The voices of weathered men cuss at each other. I pass a diner with a buzzing neon Open sign that proudly offers 24-hour service. It's deserted, except for a table of rowdy men. Someone tells a story that ends in boisterous laughter that carries through the thin glass. The men lean over each other, competing for the right to tell the next one. One of them, an olive-skinned man with a broad nose and sparkling dark eyes, catches me looking and winks.

I hurry on.

The hive of activity at the docks leaves no safe path to walk. A forklift crosses in front of me, carrying a shrink-wrapped pallet of dolls. Rows of faces, distorted by the stretched plastic, smile at me. Even the doll on the bottom row that's been speared by the forklift operator is smiling. I find the directory listing and see it has only one freight cruise operator, called Harbor Freight Cruises. I navigate the maze of shipping containers until I find their ticket office.

It won't open for another hour. My stomach grumbles, reminding me of how little I ate last night before Larry showed up. I didn't think to take the rest of my dinner with me. The diner I passed is the only place I've seen that serves food near the docks.

The entrance to the diner is inviting, if grungy. A waitress leans over the table of rowdy men, bending over like Nurse Rita always did for Harold. She fills their white ceramic cups with steaming coffee. Some of the men add splashes of liquid from a silver flask. The good-looking man who winked at me catches my eye again. My stomach tightens, but not like when I heard the dog barking at my scent. A curious warmth rises into my chest. Good-looking? I force my eyes to the empty tables. I can't afford to think that way. I need to be invisible.

The waitress looks me up and down, frowning. She's plump, in an attractive sort of way. The lines between her angled eyebrows betray her age. I must be dirty. I was sweaty even before the confrontation with Martin, and the last time I showered was at the Harris' cabin. After a night's sleep in the car, I could use some mouthwash. A little toiletry kit in my care package would have helped. But as I notice her eyes darting between me and her other customers, I realize my lack of hygiene is not what disturbs her. She's noticed how the table of men has responded to my entrance, and she doesn't appreciate the competition.

"Sit anywhere you want," she says with that thick Boston accent I've only heard in movies. Then she turns on her heels and disappears into the kitchen.

I love her accent and her rudeness. And the way the metal counter gleams under the heat lamp, even though it's dented and scratched. Plates of waffles and pancakes and eggs wait to be delivered. The whole place smells sweet and salty, like syrup and bacon. Anything high in calories was a treat at the lab. Saliva wets my mouth as my stomach, insistent now, announces its hunger. I choose a booth where the good-looking man is out of sight.

The men's overlapping conversations distract me from the menu. They speak a mix of languages. I don't recognize all of them. Spanish is the lingua franca. They must not know I understand them. They are teasing one of the men at the table about me.

"Tienes una hora," says one. "Pídele una cita." *You have an hour. Ask the woman out on a date.*

"Estás celosa porque no tienes una cara bonita, como yo." *You're just jealous you don't have a pretty face like me.* I like his smooth, jovial voice.

Their stories turn to life at sea, about shipments that spilled or sunk or spoiled halfway across the Atlantic. A sharp sound jerks my head up. It's the surly waitress, tapping a pen on a thick pad of paper.

"Ready?" she asks.

I close my menu. "The special." That's what I always ordered in my daydreams of life outside the lab. She brings me a plate heaping with pancakes, another plate with scrambled eggs, and a third, smaller plate with bacon. A yellow square of butter turns shiny as it melts on the stack of golden circles. I drown them in syrup, then cut a triangle out. They're better than I imagined. Thick and sweet and buttery and light and fluffy. I feel like Eve taking a bite of the forbidden fruit. The empty growls of my stomach lessen. I take another bite of pancake, then shove a whole strip of bacon in my mouth. The salty meat makes my taste buds tingle.

I look up from my plate to find a napkin for the grease on my fingers and the syrup on my chin; instead, I see my admirer. The group at his table has rearranged.

My mouth is so full, my cheeks are stuffed like a chipmunk's. Very attractive, I'm sure. He has shiny, black curls and a wide face. A shadow of a beard hugs his chin. His smile is brazen. He looks to be about my age. Okay, he's not just good-looking. He's handsome.

I nearly knock over my water as I reach for the napkin holder. Ignoring the flush on my cheeks, I stare down at the table. It's not difficult to focus on my food. My unintentional fast has sharpened my appetite. I finish everything.

Through the windows, I see the busy docks are getting busier. Cranes load shipping containers onto the docks of ships so large that they make the men look like ants, scurrying around on the deck. Semi-trucks hauling only frames arrive, then leave laden with cargo. The rumbling of their engines shakes the diner as they pass. The containers have labels in dozens of languages. I love the poetry of it, like blocks for a giant baby.

I check my watch. It's time to move on. The ticket office will open soon. The diner is empty except for me and the handsome man, who is flirting with the waitress at the cash register. I find myself taking note of how she tilts her head, how she smiles slyly, with one side of her lips lifted higher than the other. Her fingers twist around the extra set of salt and pepper shakers on the counter, and she giggles at everything he says. The rising sun glints off the metal spike that holds the morning's receipts. I wait, hoping he'll leave. He doesn't. I can't risk missing the first boat of the day. I can control myself for a few minutes. There will be other attractions, after I'm in a safer place.

I take the piece of paper with my order to the counter, just like I saw the other men do. I try to keep my eyes on the waitress. When that fails, I try to keep my expression neutral. That doesn't work either. His warm brown eyes melt my caution. There's a sparkle in them I can't help but answer with my own.

The waitress glares at me. "Eight ninety-five," she says.

I take out my roll of money and peel off a hundred-dollar bill. Her eyes widen. She almost puts it in the pile with the other twenties, then shakes the bill in my face. "You trying to pass funny money? You think I stand here all day on my aching feet for fun?"

"I—uh—" The money is real. I think the money is real. I guess I wouldn't know. I've never handled cash before.

"Dolores," says the man. He has the elongated 's' and first syllable emphasis of a native Spanish speaker. "Calm down, let's take a look." He holds the bill up to the light. The strong, angular sunrays illuminate a thin line of writing. "See the plastic strip? The one that says USA 100? The bill is real."

She huffs and shoves the bill into the cash drawer. "I'll have to clean out the register just to make change."

"I'm sorry," I manage. "I don't have anything smaller." I would tell her to keep the change, but I'll need every penny.

He winks at me. "Don't mind her. They don't get many high rollers around here."

She slaps a stack of bills on the counter and puts a nickel on top. My knuckles scrape against rough fabric as I put the handful of cash into my bag. I can still feel her glare on my back as I walk to the door. The man—my rescuer—is holding the door for me.

Why won't he just go away?

He falls into step beside me. "I'm Paul. I'm a motorman on one of the freighters here."

I shake my head and walk faster.

Without breaking stride, he matches my pace. His smile hasn't wavered either. "Don't I even get a thank you?"

I stop and count the pockmarks in the asphalt between my shoes. "Thank you." A light touch on my shoulder sends me jumping back.

He holds his arms up, looking apologetic. "I didn't mean to startle you. I was just going to ask if you were okay."

All the reasons I should brush him off fade in my head as I look at him, taking in every detail of his friendly, concerned face. The full, dry lips. The cheekbones and dimples. The bushy eyebrows that arc towards the crinkles at his eyes. It's my turn to say something, but nothing acceptable occurs to me. *Hi, I'm a biological weapon on the run from my creator and a government lab.*

I really like you, so don't take this personally, but I can't get involved right now.

My examination emboldens him. "Let's start over," he says. "I'm Paul." He holds out a callused hand.

"Not Pablo?"

He looks surprised.

I must have offended him. "I'm sorry—it's just, it's your accent. I mean, I shouldn't assume. I'm sorry." It's probably better for both of us if he walks away angry.

He laughs. "That's the third time you've apologized in the last five minutes. No one has that much to be sorry about."

If only he knew.

"It's Pablo, you're right. But I find Paul is easier when we dock here. Otherwise, people notice my accent and assume I forgot to get off the bus at the tomato farms in North Carolina."

I have no idea what he's talking about. I'm trying to think of some news article that might explain his comment when he speaks again.

"You don't get out much, do you?"

The lies came easily to me at the Harris house. I should lie to him for all the same reasons, but my throat rebels against it. "This is my first time away from home. It's a little overwhelming."

"Where's home?"

I've said too much. I have to end this conversation. I think back to the stilted scripts I followed with my language tutors. "It was nice to meet you, but I have to go now. Thank you for the help." I start walking again, tunneling my vision toward the ticket office. I only make it three steps before I run into Pablo's arm. When I blink, the arm is wearing a military uniform. I'm about to throw him off, when an insistent beeping interrupts my flashback. I nearly walked into the path of a reversing forklift.

Pablo offers the operator an affable smile. "Sorry."

The man doesn't look any less annoyed. He disappears, like a large yellow insect buzzing away, down an aisle between towering stacks of containers.

"Thank you, again."

He grins. "Tell me your name, and we'll call it even."

"S—Janine. And I really do have to go. I have to get to the ticket office."

He points to the small, locked shed with the weathered sign that says *Harbor Freight Cruises.* "That office right there?"

I nod, hoping he won't follow me.

"There's no need to hurry." He's smiling like he knows something I don't. "It won't open until I get there."

He said he was on the crew. Is he joking? Trying to trick me into something?

"Our office manager is running late. He asked me to fill in. The ship I'm on is the only one leaving port today anyway."

Great. I'll just have to lock myself in my room. He opens the office door and flips a switch. Dust swirls over cluttered stacks of paper and boxes as a fluorescent tube blinks its way to life. The desk is a warped board with a filing cabinet holding up each end. Behind it, a series of laminated pictures advertise my cruise choices. The whole office isn't more than 15 feet square. The disorganization makes it seem smaller. Being alone with Pablo in such a small space makes it hard to concentrate.

He gestures at the photos of smiling retirees in front of European landmarks. "Well, Janine, where would you like to go?"

"You said there was only one cruise leaving today?"

He studies me. "I kind of thought that'd be your answer. The Mediterranean cruise leaves in two hours. Our first stop is Algeciras, Spain."

"The Bay of Gibraltar." I'm a regular encyclopedia.

"It's one of our most popular stops. You'll have a whole day there. Long enough to visit the big rock and sample a couple good restaurants. From there, we go up the Spanish coast, then to Italy, then back across the Atlantic to New York, then Boston." He slides a price list across the desk. It lists the cost based on which stop I choose.

When I lean in to read it, we're less than two feet apart. He smells like grease and cologne and the salt in the air.

"So?" he asks. "Which stop would you like?"

I push my daydreams away. Someone on the run would order a one-way ticket. It'll look better if I pretend I'm coming back. "Round-trip."

He's skeptical. "That's the most expensive. Are you sure? It's non-refundable."

"Round-trip," I insist.

He shrugs. "Okay, then."

I give him a fifth of all the money I have in the world. He gives me a ten-dollar bill in return. At some point, I'll have to find a way to make a living. Maybe I can make costumes for a circus or something.

"Last name?" he asks. At my hesitation, he glances out the door and speaks softly. "I'll skip the ID check. It's just for the ticket."

"Harris."

An aging printer spits out my ticket. He extends it to me, but doesn't let go. "I've been sailing with this crew for a couple of years now. They're good people, mostly. But I'd be careful flashing that money around, just in case."

Right. I'm going to have to get better at this whole subterfuge thing.

Chapter 12

My fellow passengers are two retired couples, one from Texas and one from Maine. Each forms a matching pair with the same sort of smile, the same accent, the same taste in clothing. They are the happy ending everyone wishes for and I will never have. The man from Texas wears jeans and a belt buckle the size of my hand. His shirt is meant to look like a rancher's, but I saw it in the Macy's catalog last week when I was waiting for Dr. Choebach. The woman's belt buckle sparkles with pink and purple sequins. The couple from Maine is dressed entirely out of a Land's End catalog.

The couples have made best friends of each other already. I went to the balcony to get away from the chatter, and all four of them followed me out for the view. We're not allowed on deck while the ship is leaving port, but our rooms aren't ready yet. I'd go back into the main lounge, but my path to the door is blocked.

"Whereabouts are you from?" the Texan woman asks.

I try to remember what my passport says, then decide it doesn't matter. "New Hampshire."

The Maine woman descends on me. "Oh, you're a local then. Don't you just love the fall? We're flying back just so we can be here for peak foliage season." When my expression doesn't show enough interest, she turns to the other woman. "You really should see Maine in the fall sometime. The colors are beautiful. You never saw such a beautiful thing."

Her w's sound more like r's. She turns to me again. "Don't you agree? It's so nice in the fall."

"Beautiful," I agree.

The Texas woman nods enthusiastically. "Well, now, maybe we'll just have to have a vacation swap. You can come down for wildflowers in the spring, and we'll come for the leaves in the fall."

"That's a lovely bracelet." The Maine woman reaches for my wrist. "Where did you—"

I snatch my arm back. I'm saved from offering an explanation by a groan from the Texas man. He puts one hand on his stomach and the other over his mouth.

"Poor baby," his wife says. "He always get seasick on the first day of our cruises."

He hurries into the lounge, rushing for the door labeled *Men.* I use the space he cleared to make my escape. The thin door doesn't cover the sounds of his troubles. Still, I'd rather have that than suffer small talk.

I distract myself by wandering the room. It's a large room, about the size of my quarters at the lab. As I boarded, Pablo told me that everyone eats here, crew and passengers alike. All of the square tables are bolted to the floor. There's a shelf with books and board games. No Monopoly board, thankfully. Still, I can't help but think of Rose. The books are mostly well- thumbed, paperback thrillers. I take one of the books to the only cushioned spot in the room, a blue armchair with lumpy upholstery.

The first chapter proves the book is as much about romance as adventure. Like with the waitress at the diner, I find myself taking notes. I wonder if I could be that fun, flirty girl with Pablo.

"Hello again," he says, as if my thoughts had summoned him. He's standing in the doorway that leads from the main deck, holding three sets of keys. "I volunteered to play steward."

"I bet you did," I hear myself say. It's the last line of dialogue I read for the heroine in the novel. Time for a new book.

He smiles, then frowns as he hears the retching from the bathroom. "There's always one. I think I'll let him finish. Let me show you to your room."

My eyes linger too long on his face. "Sure."

I follow him down the metal steps, past two other doors. The economy passenger quarters are stacked like layers of cake below the lounge. He opens the bottom door and flips on a light. It's tiny compared to my room at the lab. The bed takes up most of the space, but at least the windows have drapes I can shut. I can hide here all day if I want.

"If you think this is small, you should see the crew quarters," he says, misreading my silence.

"No, it's perfect."

He sets the key on the nightstand carefully, then studies me. "That's a first."

I should end this conversation. "What's a first?"

"Never heard anybody say that about this room."

A *Do Not Disturb* sign sits next to the lamp. The plastic is smooth on my fingertips. "If I hang this on the door, no one else will come into the room?"

He nods slowly. "No one."

"Could I have my meals brought to my room?"

"If that's what you want."

What I want is to throw my arms around Pablo and feel my first kiss. Hibernating in this room until we dock is a close second. What I don't want is to answer any more friendly, nosy questions.

"They'll go to bed early," he says.

I look at him, confused.

"I noticed you were avoiding the other passengers. You don't need to stay in your room the whole time. Trust me, I know their type. They'll be in bed by nine every night."

I really should end this conversation. "They seem like nice people. It's just…" Again, my lies fail me.

He waves my excuses away. "Promise me one thing, at least."

The harbor looks like a watercolor on the horizon in my window. I can't believe I made it here, away from Larry and his dogs. I keep my expression blank to hide my smile.

"Come outside and see the stars after they go to bed. You won't see anything like it on land."

"I will," I say, even though I shouldn't.

That cocky smile comes back to his face. "Bon voyage. I'll see you around."

Not if I can help it. I wait for him to leave before closing the door, and I sit down on the bed and open the book. I continue reading as the heroine, a deep-water scuba diver, and the hero, the ship's first mate, discover the first clue in their maritime treasure hunt.

Chapter 13

I spend all day in my room, with the drapes closed but the windows open. The way the breeze stirs the curtains reminds me of how kelp moves underwater in nature shows. I try to imagine what's beneath the slow sway of the boat. Thousands of feet of blue water, and a bed of sand. Or maybe deep canyons hiding bizarre creatures. Or a pod of whales migrating to their winter homes to calve.

My thoughts of escape only went as far as the mountains. Even that seemed like a fantasy most of the time. It was a fantasy I kept alive to stay sane, but part of me never expected it to happen. Now that I'm out in the real world, smelling the real sea, my forgotten fantasies are resurfacing. I could learn how to scuba dive and come face-to-face with the creatures I saw on television. I could go hiking in a rainforest.

The semi-circles of light cast by the undulating curtains fade as I finish the last chapter of my book. Footsteps come to my door and someone knocks twice, politely, before picking up the lunch tray I left and leaving another. The sunset tempts me to open the curtains while I eat dinner. The clouds take on the hues of cotton candy, then fuchsia. Not too long after, I hear my fellow passengers on the stairs saying goodnight.

Before nine, just like Pablo said they would. I wait, to make sure, then ease the door open. Crewmembers pass by on the deck and take no notice of me. When I take the stairs up to the lounge, I see a card game in progress. The silver flask I saw at breakfast is out on the table. I head back to my room and grab a pillow so I can sit on the corrugated metal of the stair landing. Pablo was right about the stars, too. A canopy of yellow stars twinkles in a deep black sky, a painting in two shades.

A walking silhouette, a man on deck, startles me. He has a large flashlight in his hand as he scans the water. The light illuminates waves that are gunmetal gray. He moves on, stopping every few steps to search the water.

I get lost in the blizzard of stars. The shapes of constellations always eluded me in my astronomy textbook, but these stars look nothing like those simplistic diagrams anyway. The Milky Way is a sparkling road, with the stars around it nearly as dense. I make my own shapes, connecting the dots as I please. There's a section of the Milky Way that could be the cap of an acorn, and below it the body. I can make the shape of the trees that sheltered me and leaves with veins and points and stems. I can make the faces of the dead.

Some Native American tribes believed the spirits of the dead rose to the stars. I'd like to believe it. I'd like to believe in a god. But my existence seems to be proof of his non-existence. I lean my head against the metal wall and focus on the stars again. It's strange how comforting they are. They're a reminder of our fragility, the pettiness of our existence. A gust of wind cools the trail of liquid on my cheeks.

It's only been two days. I tell myself even the pain of grief can't last forever, then feel guilty for it. The pain should last forever. It was my fault.

The night watchman passes again. I check my watch, out of habit. I used to track the guard's schedules at the lab. It took the watchman 40 minutes to walk the ship. Not that it matters, he's not after me. I don't need to escape from here.

He passes once more before I go to my room. I take a long shower, the longest shower I've ever taken. There's no one watching a timer. I brush my teeth using my finger and the complimentary toothpaste and then head to bed. Sleep captures me quickly. In my dreams the lab is animated, a bogeyman that stalks and pounces and swallows me whole.

Chapter 14

The second night on the ship, I wait long enough for the crew to finish playing card games before venturing up to the lounge. The lounge is blessedly empty. I pick out a new book, a military thriller which I hope doesn't contain any romance. There's a clipboard hanging on the outside of the shelf, a list of names with tasks and shifts. Before I realize it, my finger has scrolled down to the Pablo's name. He worked a 10-hour shift that ended at midnight. Hopefully, he's in his quarters.

On the balcony, I find a pair of lounge chairs folded and propped against the wall. When I release the legs, the loud snap makes the night watchman look up. I freeze, like I've been caught doing something wrong. Then I remember where I am and that his job is not to watch me.

The stars are better on the balcony. I fall in love with the sparkling dome all over again. The forests of New Hampshire were beautiful, but I think I prefer life at sea.

"You kept your promise," Pablo's voice says from behind me.

I quickly pull on the long-sleeved shirt I brought for warmth. I don't want him to see the scars on my arms. "I thought you'd be asleep." The comment didn't seem as rude in my head.

Pablo leans on the railing in front of me, an uncertain smile on his face. His t-shirt outlines his body in all the right places. "I can leave?"

Yes, you should. "You don't have to."

He unfolds the other chair with more grace than I did. As he relaxes, he crosses his long, muscular legs at the ankles. "I was right about the stars, no?"

"They're lovely." I can't look at him. I can already feel the corners of my mouth turning up. I feel the same nervous anticipation in my stomach, the same warmth, as I felt in the diner at our first meeting. A trail of yellow streaks across the sky, then disappears in a blink. I sit up quickly. "What was that? Did you see that?"

He looks at me strangely. "A falling star. You've never seen one?"

My bracelet clinks against the armrest as I lean back, reminding me of how much I can't tell him.

"You're a puzzle."

I cross my arms over my stomach. I think I can see Orion, with his arrow threatening. Though, at this point, it makes me think more of Cupid. "How's that?"

"You know where the Bay of Gibraltar is, but you don't know how to tip a waitress."

A tip. I should have remembered. "That's why she was glaring at me as I walked out."

"Oh, there were other reasons," he says. He sounds amused, like I made a joke.

I find myself looking at him again, even when I promised myself I would keep my eyes on the stars.

"So, Janine, what brought you to Harbor Freight Cruises? You've probably figured out that you're not our typical passenger."

I was bothered by questions like this from my fellow passengers. With him, what bothers me is how little I can tell him. "It was a cheap way to cruise to Europe."

He senses the evasion in my answer. "Okay, enough about you. We can talk about me. Ask me anything."

I don't even know where to start. There are no awkward moments in romance novels.

"Let's see. I was born in Sevilla." His voice rolls over this birthplace with a deep, pleasing rumble. "My parents still live there. It's where I fell in love with boats. There's a port, not as big as Algeciras, but it's still impressive." His eyes are focused on me the whole time he's speaking. I can't decide if I like it or not. "When I was a kid, I used to sit at the port and watch all the ships come in. My parents wanted me to go pre-med. Instead, I dropped out of college and became a sailor."

The flirt in me answers. "It must be a romantic life."

He laughs. "Hardly. I share a room with five other men. I get one bunk and one shelf. Our normal runs take six weeks, give or take. Sometimes I'm gone for months. It's hard being away from our families that long."

It occurs to me he might have a girlfriend, or even a wife. My attempt to observe subtly his left hand fails.

He holds up the hand and wiggles his fingers to show there's no wedding ring. "I have an older sister with kids. And my parents and my friends. I miss them when I'm here."

"But you seem so happy."

"I am. I wake up tasting the sea every morning. My mother tells me I should have been born with gills. Now it's your turn. Tell me something about yourself."

"Just your typical spoiled American college girl." The lie hurts, but it's unavoidable.

"I don't believe that for a minute."

He's reaching for my hand. I can feel the ghosts of the Harrises watching me. I won't bait another trap for Larry. I scramble off the chair, feel the railing against my back. "I need to go. I'm tired." I have to climb over his chair to get to the door.

"Janine—" He starts to get out of his chair, still reaching for me. Then he thinks better of it and sinks back, with an expression that is equal parts hurt and confusion.

The door to the stairs is only a few strides away. My hand is on the doorknob when I hear the chair scrape. In the reflection of the windows, I see Pablo framed in the balcony door.

"Janine, I'm sorry. Come back."

I escape down the stairs to my room. I huddle on the bed with my knees drawn to my chest. Eventually, I hear Pablo's footsteps down the stairs. They pause at my door. The small, rectangular windows with their thick glass dim the brilliance of the sky. The room makes me feel more claustrophobic than protected.

When I finally sleep, I dream of what would have happened if I held his hand.

Chapter 15

The knock on my door comes the next day, between breakfast and lunch. It's not the steward delivering my meal. I set
down my book and pad cautiously to the door. The ship isn't entirely cut off from the world. Maybe the lab has finally released
my mugshot. The fish-eye lens in the peephole shows Pablo.
The distortion makes his head as big as his body. His dark, wavy
hair bends in a circle around an earnest face.

He knocks again.

I could pretend to be asleep. It's not like he'd know. He starts
to mouth a word, but is cut off by a pressure washer starting up
on the deck behind him.

He holds up one finger, as if he senses I'm watching, then
searches his pockets for something. A pen appears in his right
hand. Then there's a scratching sound on the door, like he's
using it as a writing surface. The drawing he holds up is distorted by the lens, but I think it's some sort of fish with a spout
on its head.

Curiosity wins out. I open the door.

He takes a careful step back. "I can make it up to you."

I made him feel like he did something wrong last night. How
stupid of me not to realize it. "There's nothing to—"

He smiles mischievously. "We have to hurry, or your present will be gone."

"My present?"

"Come on." He takes two steps down the stairs to the deck, then turns to see if I'll follow. "Trust me, you won't regret it."

I can't disappoint him. I follow his eager steps to the stern of the boat. A few sailors are there with binoculars. In the distance, land shimmers on the horizon. A spray of water interrupts the quiet rhythm of the waves, then a smooth gray back cuts the surface.

I grab the rail eagerly. "A whale?"

"A whole pod of them," Pablo says. He holds out a pair of binoculars, still careful to keep his distance. The other sailors ignore us, except for sidelong smiles.

The world gets blurrier when I hold them up to my eyes. I move the two halves back and forth, but it doesn't help. I hear an ooh from the other spectators and know I've missed something.

"The focus knob is on top," Pablo says. He hovers, wanting to help but reluctant to get any closer.

I find the knob and twist it until the waves come into focus. The binoculars flatten the image as they magnify it. Two spouts of water burst from the surface, then two tail fins slide out of the water and go back down just as quickly. The whales leave glassy, smooth circles in their wake, slow to be reclaimed by the sea. These are the majestic giants I've only seen in nature shows, with their unblinking, strangely human-like eyes.

I overhear the sailors say we're off the coast of Cape Saint Mary's, which shimmers on the horizon. Pablo leans on the rail two feet away. I can feel every inch of the space between us, a sharp contrast to the hazy images I remember from my dreams.

A black and white belly rises out of the sea with acrobatic grace, sunlight glinting off the smooth skin. The flippers are spread like arms outstretched. The splash as the whale lands is distant, but audible. White foam spreads out in circles. Then a smaller form, with similar large patches on its belly, follows. "It's a mother and her calf." The sight is as wondrous as my first sunset.

Pablo nods. "Last year's calf, most likely. They're migrating south for the winter."

We stand at the railing long after the other sailors leave and the whales have passed. I keep the binoculars, scanning the water for any other signs of life. Eventually, the land on the horizon is reduced from a shimmer to nothing, and there is only sea, as far as my eyes can reach. Regretfully, I pass him back his binoculars.

"Am I forgiven?" His smile is confident, the brazen Pablo I remember from the docks.

My own smile fades. How can I explain that my hesitation has nothing to do with him? Even I know *It's not you, it's me* is a shitty line. The waves lap at the side of the boat. It's an awful long way down. Behind us, the ship leaves its own mark, a line of bubbles and an elongated triangle whose edges weaken as it expands. I look steadfastly at the water as I search for the right words. "There's nothing to forgive. And thank you. This was lovely."

Then I walk away. This time I leave him confused, instead of confused and hurt, which I suppose is an improvement.

Chapter 16

After a week at sea, I have established a routine of sorts. Between meals, if the lounge is empty, I check the work schedule so I know when Pablo will be on deck. I don't spend much time outside during the day. The lounge is empty only for short periods of time, and the deck is always busy. The vessel is a floating city with an astonishing array of moving parts. The fickle mechanics take turns being broken, whether it be a pump or a motor or a generator or one of the many machines that beeps on the bridge. Evidence of the crew's hard work is on my clothes. Every walk I take adds a streak of grease.

I come out to the balcony at night, after the passengers have gone to bed and the crew's card games have ended. Then it's just the night watchman and me. I no longer tense every time he passes. There's an easy rhythm to life at sea. I wish we weren't docking in two days.

The voyage has been educational as well. When I am in my room, I leave the windows open so I can hear everyone's conversations. Now I understand what 'swear like a sailor' means. I've learned all sorts of new words. And not just in Spanish. I listen especially for things that will help me survive when I leave, things that the sailors take for granted knowing. How to tell if you pay at the counter or at the table in a restaurant. How you tip waiters in the United States, but not in Europe. Apparently, I owe Dolores $1.78, even though she was rude. The sailors exchange tips on how to sneak small items through customs. Their stories tell me what guys expect on a first, second, third date.

They don't know I understand them. They tease Pablo about me often. It's been surprisingly easy to avoid him, even though we are stranded on a steel island together. It's important to avoid him. I still find myself thinking of his deep, brown eyes. The crew works punishing 10-hour shifts. So for most of the men, if they're not on shift and there's no card game, they're sleeping.

I don't know what's waiting for me when we make port. There are only so many ways to leave the country. Jennifer's trick with the backpack will only buy me time. The captain of the guard could be waiting for me the second I step off the boat. My father could be waiting for me. I bet the waitress Dolores would be happy to point either of them in my direction. In the best of all possible worlds, getting off the boat means choosing a direction to run. And then another. And another. Survival shows always point out that staying in one place makes you easier to find.

The night watchman passes for a second time. That means I've been on the balcony for nearly an hour and a half. I've learned his job is to watch for pirates, which the crew curses as a silly exercise mandated by the insurance company. There aren't many pirates in these waters, and the shifts cut into their drinking and card-playing time. The other passengers joke nervously about it, discuss articles they've read about pirates in Somali waters. These are not the pirates of Disney movies. These are the ones who ransom ships for money. I'd be nervous about it too, if I didn't have bigger things on my mind.

The stars are so enchanting that the night watchman passes two more times. When he comes around again, I promise myself, I will satisfy my heavy eyes and go to bed. But then the next thing I hear is the friendly swearing of men below the balcony. The sun is warm on my face. I rub my eyes and look behind me. Breakfast has already been set out in the dining area. The couple from Texas smiles politely at me, no doubt wondering why I spent the night outside.

I swing my legs off the chair, eager to hide in my room where breakfast will soon be delivered.

A round of catcalls below startles me. I look down to see a man struggling with large, circular handle on one of the hatches. A taunting crowd surrounds him. Finally, sweating and red in the face, the man gives up. Pablo is the next person in line to try. He waves at me and, before I can stop myself, I wave back.

It's hard to follow the jumble of voices on deck. Something about needing to check the temperature on the refrigeration units below deck. Pablo eggs on the sailors, motioning for applause. The men boo good-naturedly instead.

He looks up at me and shrugs, never losing his smile. Then he grips the painted blue circle with two large hands and grunts as he struggles with it. I can't help but notice how pronounced the muscles in his arms are. Like the man before him, his skin grows slick with sweat. His shirt sticks to his back. With my eyes, I follow the indent of his spine between his broad shoulders down a slim waist and a well rounded... God help me.

The men don't let up.

"!Ni siquiera para tu novia!" one says. *Not even for your girlfriend!*

"!Muevete!" says another. "Le voy a enseñar lo que es un hombre." *I will show her a man.*

Pablo takes it goodheartedly. He holds up his hands. "Sé cuál es el problema," he says. *I know the problem.* He doesn't look at me, but I know I'm the audience. Slowly, and with great aplomb, he pulls off his shirt. I'm officially done for. I know what a body sculpted by the gym looks like, thanks to movies. His body is sculpted by hard work. A dusting of dark hair covers his chest and lean stomach. His back is smooth except for a mole on his shoulder. There's a ring of flesh that hangs over his waistband just a little bit.

He's back to wrestling with the handle, and I can't help but stare. The catcalls and cheers raise in volume.

"¡Debilucho!" *Weak.*

"¡Mi madre es más fuerte que tú!" *My mother is stronger than you!*

"¡Mi hermana es más fuerte que tú!" *My sister is stronger than you!*

"¡Mi hermana pequeña es más fuerte que tú!" *My little sister is stronger than you!*

"¡Yo también puedo quitarme la camisa!" says a grizzled man. *I can take my shirt off too!* His arms are muscled too, but unlike Pablo, he has a potbelly that hangs over his belt. "Las chicas me adoran." *Girls like me.*

"Mejor que le adoren a él, que a ti," I call down. *Better him than you.*

There's a shocked silence—then laughter. Pablo is just as surprised as the rest. He turns back to the handle and gives it one last twist. There's a groaning sound as the mechanism gives. He bows to me and disappears into the hatch.

Chapter 17

It's my last night on ship. I'm determined not to waste it. I decide to ignore the men playing cards in the lounge, and I go out to my favorite chair on the balcony. I've managed to avoid Pablo since the incident at breakfast yesterday. According to the schedule, Pablo's shift in the engine room started at 6 a.m. this morning. I imagine he's already in bed.

Glass clinks behind me. I look behind me and see the card players filling a motley collection of shot glasses. Never mind them. I'm here for the stars. Tomorrow night I don't know where I'll be, but I doubt it will be somewhere where I can see the sky.

The card player's voices slur, and their laughter gets louder. I concentrate on the breeze that always seems to be on the ship. It's cold in a t-shirt, but I don't mind. I like the goose bumps on my arms.

There's a swoosh, and the player's voices from the lounge break into my thoughts. The sliding glass door behind me has opened. It's Pablo. Judging from his wet hair, he's just showered. He is, sadly, wearing a shirt.

He takes the lounger next to me without asking. It's right next to mine, nearly touching. "Buenas noches," he says.

I like his voice better when he speaks Spanish. It comes more naturally to his tongue.

"I thought I'd never see you out here before midnight," he says.

So he's been keeping track of my habits. "Es la última noche. Por las estrellas." *It's the last night. For the stars.* Certain words in English don't sound right. One clunky syllable isn't adequate for an object as complicated and beautiful and massive as the burning orbs holding court tonight. The Spanish word has more of a lilt and a sparkle to it.

Pablo clears his throat. "I didn't realize you spoke Spanish before yesterday. You… um… probably overheard some of what the crew has said about you."

I smile and look away. This flirting thing might not be so hard after all.

"They like to talk, that's all. Don't believe everything they say." He scratches at the metal frame of the chair. "Better yet, don't believe any of it."

It's the last night. After tomorrow, we'll never see each other again. One conversation between us won't hurt anything. "So you don't wake up in the middle of the night calling my name?"

He's blushing. It's adorable. "Nobody said that, right?"

I laugh. I like how the feeling loosens my shoulders. I can't remember the last time I laughed during a conversation with someone. "No, nobody said that. They spend most of the time making up stories about their own conquests." It took me a few days to notice how the story from the same man would change with each telling. Always in ways that made the teller inch closer to James Bond and further from the everyman.

"You must have spent some time abroad. You speak Spanish like a native. Where did you study?"

I smile to make it a joke. "A government lab."

He looks hurt. The clomp of the watchman's footsteps fills in where our conversation should be.

I didn't want him to be here, and now I'm afraid I'll drive him away. "I'm sorry. I keep saying the wrong things." My bracelet clinks against the armrest. I turn the brushed metal circle in my hand. The moonlight tugs on the waxy lines of my surgical scars on my forearms. I don't have a shirt to cover them up this time. And I don't want to. The isolation my secrets have forced on me feels like a punishment I don't deserve. "I didn't grow up like most other kids. I was given a good education, but not much of a life. I was provided with things, not people. I was sheltered…"

His eyes count my scars, then move to my face. "But not safe."

"I don't like to talk about it. It's behind me now." Not quite the truth, but close enough. "Can you understand that?"

His lips form around a question he doesn't ask. He taps a finger on his leg, thinking. That smile comes back to his face. "Makes it hard for a guy to start a conversation."

I cling to the first topic that pops into my head, the lovely desert that came with dinner. "Ice cream. What's your favorite flavor? Mine is raspberry."

"Oh, that's easy. Pistachio. What's your favorite music?"

I collected every jazz CD I could. I liked that the musicians got to make up the tune as they went along. "Jazz. You?"

"Anything by AHI."

The name isn't familiar to me.

"Yeah, no one else knows him either. Rap music. But with soul." He laughs at my reaction. "You were expecting me to say salsa?"

I expected something with a guitar. He's watching me, waiting for an answer. I realize I'm too used to having conversations with myself. "Country rock, I guess. Something more with a singer/songwriter vibe."

His teeth flash in a smile. "Sorry to disappoint."

"Favorite book?"

"Most recently? *El coleccionista de relojes extraordinarios*, a graphic novel."

We're finally having a conversation I don't need to run away from. "Tell me about it."

"It's science fiction and fantasy sort of stuff. The hero has to save the soul of his stepmother by finding a magic clock." He glances behind him. "I know, it's a little silly. Don't tell the guys. They'd never let me hear the end of it. The Kindle was a great invention. Now they don't have to know what I'm reading."

Silly imaginings were the only thing that kept me sane in the lab. "I think it sounds lovely. Fantasies are important." I want to take back the last sentence as soon as it slips out. I keep talking before Pablo can ask what I meant. "My favorite book is *Matilda*, by Roald Dahl. I read it when I was... I don't remember how young. But I keep going back to it."

"That's the one where the little girl manages to escape her horrible family?"

Even in a casual conversation, I share too much. I should think of a new topic, but all I can think of is how he must see me. A desperate, scared, pathetic girl who can't even pass for normal for five minutes. "I used to play tricks on them, like she did." Like spilling the pins on the floor so the guards had to count them. Or making bullshit art the psychologists thought they could use to interpret me. "The little victories helped."

His hand touches mine and my entire body feels it. There's no pity in his expression when I look up. His features are set; his eyes are hard. "Let me help—"

"No." Whatever his offer is, I can't accept it. I can only have him for tonight. It's either kiss him or start crying. I choose the kiss. His lips are chapped, but warm. The kiss ends abruptly as he pulls away, leaving me cold as the breeze moves between us. I've done something wrong. Of course I have. I should have ended this conversation before it started. The bracelet falls halfway to my elbow, tight around my flesh, a souvenir of all the reasons I should just walk away.

Even though the bracelet blocks the RFID tracker. Even though I've seen no trace of the lab or any sickness on the ship. None of that saved the Harrises.

He points at the sliding glass door behind us. The normally raucous card game is muted. "We have an audience here. I don't mean to be forward, but I share my quarters with five other men."

I won't walk away for the same reason I didn't let myself burn to death in the lab. I am just an animal. Wounded animals need connection nearly as much as they need air.

We walk pass the gauntlet of eyes to my room, holding hands. I'm giddy and terrified and everything in between. I keep the lights off to hide my scars. The darkness concentrates every sensation: the callused pads of his fingers on my skin, his stubble rough against my cheek, his chest hair against my collarbone. His movements are graceful and practiced; mine are fumbling and unsure. I ignore the questions in his eyes. Sex isn't like any of the romance novels I was allowed to read. It's awkward and messy and oh so much better.

Chapter 18

The small window over my desk only shows glimpses of the busy port of Algeciras. There's little hint of what lies before me. I review my belongings on the small desk while Pablo snores softly on my bed. There's not much to pack. One clean outfit, my passport, the granola bars I have left, and my diminished roll of cash. Remembering his advice about not showing the roll of cash around, I put two smaller bills from the change at the restaurant in my pocket. I gather the rest into a neat pile. There's something mixed in with them, thicker than money and smooth to the touch. It's the back of a wallet-size photo. Strange, I didn't have any photos when I left the Harris' cabin. A note is scrawled on the white surface in black pen.

Jenny's had a hard time of it. Don't think too badly of her.

When I turn the photo over, my hand shakes. There are three smiling faces, a younger Harold and Jennifer tickling a toddler. Me. It's hard to tell exactly how old I am. The lab didn't figure out a vaccine until I was one, so it would have to be after that. Jennifer's hair is missing any streaks of gray. Harold's forehead isn't so prominent. We look for all the world like a happy family. I was loved once.

The photo is a vote of confidence on Harold's part. If I'm caught with it, Larry will know they helped me.

"Are those your parents?" Pablo asks.

I didn't even hear him get out of bed. I press my cheek against his warm stomach, grateful for the hair that tickles my skin, then curse myself for it. I'm too old for a teddy bear. He rubs my back in slow circles while he waits for an answer.

I do not deserve so much kindness from this world. I stand up and snap a rubber band around the small pile of cash. "They're not my parents. It's a long story."

Like last night, I can tell he wants to ask but doesn't. "How would you like your personal tour guide to Algeciras for the day? I know the best tagine place for lunch, and I can take you to this club near the docks where we can see some salsa music and dancing." He winks at me. He's making a joke about our conversation last night.

I'm about to ask him to show me his favorite rap club instead. He's got that adorable, vulnerable look on his face again. I get the feeling he's been practicing the line in his head for a while. I don't seem to be any good at lying to him though. I choose the simplest explanation possible. "It sounds lovely, but I need a day alone."

He frowns as I put the cash in my bag. "Are you planning on taking all that cash on shore with you?"

I have to think of a good excuse, or he'll figure out I'm not coming back. "I'm not sure it'll be safe on the boat."

"They might question you at customs. And you'll have to fill out paperwork to carry that much through."

"Customs?"

Now he looks worried. "I suppose you wouldn't know, would you? You don't have to go through customs when you board."

The cash and my language skills are the only advantages I have. Without the money, I'll be reduced to begging with a perfect accent.

"Are you sure you can't leave some of it behind? I can help you find a good hiding place."

I'll have to be selective with the truth again. "It's all the money I have. I can't risk it."

"Those declarations forms are kept by customs for a while. It could leave a trail."

My face must have betrayed my fear.

"It would be easier to help if you could tell me who's threatening you."

I shake my head. Pablo touches my cheek and kisses me lightly on the forehead. "Stay here a minute. I have an idea."

As he dresses, I feel the intimacy of last night slipping away. He rushes out the door and returns, panting, a few minutes later carrying a small metal thermos.

"From the kitchen," he says. "They'll never notice if you bring it back tonight."

I turn it over in my hands, not sure what I'm supposed to do with it.

He divides my pile of cash in two, then rolls each stack into a tight cylinder. The two cylinders just fit stacked inside the thermos. "The metal in the thermos will make the cash harder to see in case they x-ray your bag. You might get away with it, if they're not looking too closely."

The thermos feels heavy in my hands as I weigh the logic. "But if they catch me, they'll know I was trying to sneak it through."

"There's another option, you know." This time he kisses me on the lips. The passion from last night stirs. "There's nothing saying we have to go on shore at all."

Regretfully, I end the kiss and push him away. There's no way around the lie. "I don't want to miss seeing Algeciras. I might not be here ever again."

My voice sounds hollow and forced. The worry creasing his forehead shows he notices. "I'll see you at dinner tonight?"

I nod, hoping my gestures are less transparent than my words.

"I'll be waiting." He runs a hand from my shoulder down to my waist. I hold myself still to avoid the temptation of leaning into him. "The ship doesn't wait for anyone," he says. "Be sure to come back on time, or you'll have to catch up with us at the next port."

I nod again. He gives me one last kiss, then leaves. He doesn't close the door behind him. A crystal blue sky beckons. For a second I consider his proposal. We have several stops before we head back. I could get off at the next one, or the one after that, or... no. It won't get any easier to leave him. Better to cut ties now.

My breath catches when I walk out on deck. The peninsula curves like a semicolon from the shore, where a majestic peak rises from the otherwise flat land. The sun casts one side of the mountain in deep shadow. At its base, buildings cluster like eager children. On the dock, I see Pablo with a group of his friends. I let them get well ahead of me before leaving the ship.

The delay puts me in customs at the same time as a large group of passengers from a real cruise ship. The long line snakes in front of a row of customs officials in plexiglass booths. Their uniforms bring back unwelcome memories of the base. Between visitors, two of them exchange eye-rolls. Their annoyed expressions tell me the extra traffic is to my advantage. I watch the exchanges between the guards and visitors carefully.

Each visitor steps up to a window and pushes their passport through a slot cut into the glass. All the visitors get asked two or three questions. I can tell from the officer's faces they aren't paying attention to the answers. They are looking for non-verbal clues that might indicate someone is lying. One of the officers notices me watching. I pretend to stare at the person in line in front of me as I prepare myself.

Lying to authority will be easier than lying to Pablo. I lied to people in uniforms all the time at the lab. I lied to the psychologists in their I-don't-want-to-say-I'm-better-than-you-but-I-am suits. I lied to the medical staff in their white coats. I lied to the guards in their clomping boots and their camouflage pants and shirts. By the time I get close to the front of the line, I'm more angry than I am nervous. I take a few deep breaths. I learned early on that I can't let anger show. People don't trust anger. They'll believe anything you say if you let them think they're smarter than you are.

"Next," an officer says in English.

I walk up to the free booth with a friendly smile, the metal thermos bouncing against my spine and my passport in hand. The officer has a moustache that doesn't suit him and hard, beady eyes. I fix my smile in place and hand him the passport, like I saw everyone else do.

"What is the purpose of your visit?"

I'm a fugitive on the run. "My cruise ship is docked here for the day."

"Where do you live?"

Nowhere. "New Hampshire."

A stamp hovers over a blank page in my passport, like he hasn't made up his mind. "Only here for a few hours then?"

"I wouldn't want to miss my ship." I feel my smile slipping.

"Your bag looks like it's been through a lot."

That's four questions, one more than anyone else I saw. I had all that time on the boat to wash my bag, and I didn't think of it. I think of the gleaming decks I saw as I walked past the vacation cruise ships and how they contrast with the cluttered, working decks of the freight ships. "I'm on a freighter cruise. I borrowed this from on board for the day. I found it on deck."

He studies my face, then looks at the line. The stamp slams down on my passport. "Have a nice visit to Algeciras, Ms. Butler."

I follow the flow of the crowd, trying to stay in the center, as it moves toward the glass doors that mark the exit. I keep expecting someone to grab my elbow, pull me aside. No one does. There's a desk beyond customs with a large tan machine and more uniformed officers. A woman is arguing with them in rapid-fire Spanish, almost too fast for me to translate.

"These seeds are from the conservatory, of course they're safe. They're a gift for my mother."

"I'm sorry, ma'am," the female officer says. "They don't have the proper agricultural stamp to cross the border. We need to x-ray all of your luggage." Another officer behind her loads a bulging roller bag into the tan machine. I hurry on.

A day alone, what a ridiculous thought. From the moment I step out of the harbor station, I'm swept up by the crowds. The people move like currents in a river; I simply float along. Most of the signs are in Spanish, some are in the sweeping, graceful arcs of Arabic. The air is fragrant with mint from steaming cups of tea, and cumin from meat slowly roasting in the windows of shops. I find myself in an old square with a fountain in the center. White bricks radiate out from the fountain. A guide leads a tour group into the square and stops them by the fountain.

"It's such a nice day, folks," the guide says. "I'll give you some time to take pictures here." He's speaking in English, with a barely detectable accent. Half of his tour group has bags advertising Carnival cruises. A parade of families and couples poses in front of the fountain while the guide checks his watch. He herds them into a group before everyone is finished.

"Everything you need to know about the history of Spain is in this square," he says. "It was originally known as Plaza Alta, the same name we use today. But from 1725 until today, it's changed names more times than Prince. At one point it was known as the Plaza del Almirante, or Plaza of the Admiral, and then it became the Plaza del Rey, or Plaza of the King. In 1821, King Ferdinand VII had a bad day and it became the Plaza de la Constitución, the Plaza of the Constitution."

The energetic, hypnotic cadence of his voice sounds like a TV pitchman. It reminds me of the blank hours I had to fill while I was imprisoned.

"Two years later, the French decided to help a brother out, and the square once again became Plaza Alta. When Isabel II took the throne in 1830, the name was changed to Plaza de la Reina. The name kept changing for the next hundred years or so until 1975, when it once again became Plaza Alta." He gives the crowd a well-practiced wink. "The locals never called it anything else."

If renaming is the right of conquerors and liberators, I should take a new name. It frightens me I can't think of any. A psychologist would call it evidence of institutionalized personality traits, the internalization of external restrictions. I escape to the cool interior of a tiny church. The massive wooden doors and stone walls block the noises of the outside world. Underneath the rubber soles of my sneakers, I can feel the unevenness of the tiled floor, worn down by the footsteps of the faithful and the sinners alike. Near the altar on a wooden platform, tea lights flicker and sway in the air, perfuming the air with roses. The polished wood is formed into steps and drilled with holes made for the silver circles of fragrant wax. Some of the circles are empty. A woman in black picks an unburned tea light from a box on the floor, and sets it in an empty circle on the platform. She slips two bills into a donation box before lighting the candle and crossing herself.

A tribute to those who have passed. I wonder if the Harrises ever went to church. I decide it doesn't matter. It's not like I've been in a church before. I don't need to believe in God to honor the dead.

There's no sign that says how much to donate per candle. I put 10 dollars in the donation box and light five candles. One for each member of the Harris family, one for the unfortunate mechanic, and one for Harold and Jennifer's safety. The woman and I sit there in silence for several minutes, each pretending the other isn't there. I hope her faith will carry my prayers.

I have to concentrate on my next move. I must find food and then a way out of this town. The sun seems too bright when I step into the square. The tour group is gone. For lunch, I choose the next tea shop I find, a small place with only four tables inside, plus a battered wooden shelf haphazardly piled with books. I see a few guidebooks that might be useful. When I step closer, I see a friendly sign telling me I can take a book or leave a book.

I take a guidebook on Spain and a free table. A door swings open in the back, filling the small room with the sizzling sounds from a kitchen. A weathered man enters, wearing an apron streaked with oil and spices. On one hand, he expertly balances a tray with a metal teapot and a tall glass cup. He carries a cloud of the most mouth-watering aromas with him. There seems to be no one else around; I suspect he's the owner and the cook as well.

With a flourish, he places the cup in front of me and holds the teapot above my head. I shrink back, afraid of the steaming liquid, but he only smiles. A pale green column of water slowly fills the cup. He doesn't spill a drop. The tea foams as he pours. My stomach growls. Finally he puts two mint leaves in the cup, sets the teapot down, and hands me a small menu from his apron pocket.

There are only three choices: beef, chicken, or lamb tagine. I order the beef. He disappears into the kitchen.

I sip, then gulp the tea as it cools. The flavor of the mint is soft and lovely, like walking through a garden. Instead of reading the guidebook like I should, I watch the jostling crowds of people on the sidewalk. I pour a second glass. I'm not that far from the boat, I think. I could eat dinner with Pablo tonight.

No. Just because the lab hasn't found me yet doesn't mean I'm safe. I open the guidebook to find how best to move on. After a few minutes, it's clear I've chosen the wrong country for my escape route. The mountains crisscrossing Spain complicate rail travel. The only line leaving Algeciras goes to Ronda. When they trace me to this port, it will be obvious where I've gone. I'll have to leave Ronda as soon as I get there.

My food arrives as I pour my third glass of tea. The beef, prune, and sweet potato stew is honeyed and hearty. In between bites, I study the rail map for the cities I can reach from Ronda by train. I choose Màlaga. I like how the name rolls over itself, and it's by the coast. After so many days under the upturned bowl of the sky, I can't imagine being hemmed in by the hard earth.

The owner's friendly demeanor drops when I pull out my money.

"Euros o tarjeta de crédito," he says.

Of course, I should have exchanged my money for the local currency. His delicious meal sours in my stomach. "Lo siento. Solo tengo dólares."

He swears at me in a language I don't understand, his volume raising as his hands flap at his sides. I throw the wrong currency on the table and back away while the other customers stare, my face red with humiliation. I've only eaten at two restaurants in my life, and I won't be welcomed back at either one.

Chapter 19

The train station has a window where I exchange some of my dollars for euros. My remaining American dollars look drab next to the shorter, wider euros. I buy a train ticket to Ronda, which costs an alarming number of the vivid bills. If I weren't in the middle of a busy station, I would count what's left of my cash. While I was first wandering the city, the constant crowds seemed new and exciting; but now, with a ticket in hand for a train I don't want to take, the combined din of hundreds of conversations is overwhelming. For a traitorous second, I miss my quiet room at the lab.

The train is little better. Nearly every seat is taken. I elbow my way to a window seat in the back, where I can see most of the car. My eyes linger most on the young, male passengers with solid builds and short hair, the type of men who guarded me at the lab. I can't help but wonder if Larry has tracked me to this place and is waiting to spring his trap, like Martin did.

Despite myself, I relax after we leave the crowded tracks at the station for the countryside. My nerves can't compete with the scenery. It's too beautiful.

We pass through forests of trees with gnarled branches and wrinkled bark, and knots in places that give them faces. Next we cross a patchwork quilt of steep golden fields of grain, alternating with soft green fields of sugarcane. The slanted, fecund hills give way to mountains, sweeping gray hunks of rock that are sparsely forested.

The late afternoon sun illuminates whitewashed buildings clinging to the side of green hills. The train is slowing down. We must be near Ronda. I was wrong about feeling land-locked. I feel like if I could stand at the top of one of those mountains, I could soar between those peaks.

I remind myself I must move on. Ronda is a predictable destination from Algeciras. I must catch the train from here to Màlaga. The train empties its cargo of people onto a long platform. Unlike the crowded sidewalks, the passengers have no common direction. Some are pushing to get to a different platform. Some are reuniting with loved ones, their heartfelt hugs preventing other passengers from getting by. Some are struggling with large roller bags that tip at every opportunity. In the confusion, I nearly miss my train.

My second train ride is already more promising than the first. There are only a few other passengers. I have my choice of seats. Just as the doors are closing, one last passenger arrives and nods at me in greeting. He is an older man with a salt-and-pepper beard and dark, green eyes. Even though he could easily sit alone, he takes the seat across from me.

I angle myself toward the window and try to ignore him.

"Pretty country, isn't it?" he asks in English. If English is not his first language, he hides it well. The words are innocuous. His smile isn't. It's not flirtatious, but he seems to want something from me.

Surely the lab wouldn't send one solitary, old man after me. I look around at the other passengers with suspicion. But it's too ridiculous. There's a grandmother with arms as thin as chicken bones knitting. Her needles click in time with the train's wheels. And a little girl, painfully like Rose, sharing lunch with her mother from a paper bag.

I jump and shrink away from the man when he reaches into his leather satchel. He laughs, and not kindly. In his hand he holds a metallic box, hinged at the middle.

"I'm sorry if I startled you," he says. "It's just such a long ride. Would you share a game of chess with me?"

I move seats. Thankfully, the man doesn't follow. When he opens the metallic box, a 3D chess board folds out. The game must be more popular than I thought. He plays against himself for the entire two-hour train ride. He's very good.

When we arrive in Màlaga, I am hungry again. The feeling is still new to me. All of my meals in the lab and on the boat arrived on schedule without any work from me. I find myself wandering the sidewalks of a strange town again, looking for a good place to eat. Wisps of clouds in a gray sky capture the sunset, each cloud a different shade between rosy pink and fire red. Buildings, modern and ancient, glow softly against a horizon of tall green trees. The necessity of constant movement isn't all bad, I think. There are so many beautiful places in the world. I want to see them all.

The smell of saffron slows my steps as I pass the next restaurant. I stare through floor-to-ceiling windows at well-dressed couples enjoying elaborate paellas. The large pans of yellow rice are precisely decorated with curled shrimp and circles of sausage.

Open mussels ring the edge like a crown. It's tempting, but the meal is clearly meant for sharing. The bearded face of the chess master shows briefly in the reflection. I snap my head around, but I see only a scatter of people walking across the street.

I hurry on to quieter streets, where anyone following me won't be able to hide. There's a narrow shop—a shack, really—with a wall of chickens roasting on spits. The one table that sits outside the shack rocks back and forth on uneven cobblestones as a noisy group of friends shares a meal. They argue over the drumsticks good-naturedly and pass around plates of roasted vegetables and seasoned rice.

A man in a white apron behind the counter sweats from the heat of the chickens cooking behind him. I wait for him to notice me while the laughter of the group behind me echoes in my ears. Someone is telling a story about an octopus that came up with one his traps and how it escaped out a drainage hole on the deck. Behind his understated humor, there is a reverence in his tone. The conversation then turns to fútbol, and impassioned arguments spring over strategies.

I will not concentrate on the loneliness of my new life. I am free. I am grateful.

The cook finally looks over to me. "¿Qué quieres?" the man asks. His abruptness seems more matter-of-fact than rude.

"Dos piezas de pollo, por favor." *Two pieces of chicken, please.*

"¿Qué?"

I repeat my order louder, but he just cups his hand over his ear and shakes his head.

"Ha dicho dos piezas, sordo," calls a friendly male voice from the table. *She said two pieces, deaf man.* It's the same man who told the story of the octopus.

The man in the apron points to his ear. "La guerra." *The war.* I assume he means World War II, but he doesn't seem old enough. I want to ask, but it's obvious he won't hear me.

He hands me two pieces of the chicken wrapped in thin white paper. The smell alone makes my stomach growl. They are almost too hot to touch, but I'm so hungry I can't wait. The taste doesn't disappoint. The skin is crispy, and the flesh is moist. Grease drips down my chin after the first few bites. I look around for napkins. The only dispenser is in the center of the rickety table dominated by the four friends.

One of the men in the group notices me looking. "Ven a comer con nosotros," he says. *Come eat with us.* It's the same friendly voice. "He's lying about the war," he says in English. "Fireworks accident last year." His skin has the same olive tone as Pablo's, but his hair is longer and straighter. He doesn't have the same bravado. His strength seems to come from a quieter place.

"Hablo español," I tell him.

They introduce themselves in between mouthfuls. The man who invited me over to the table is Manuel. The other man is named Alejandro. His smile flirts without shame. The girls have names that sing: Valeria and Julieta. They both have dark hair down to their waist. When Alejandro flirts with them, they grin and flick their hair like a horse's mane. They are beautiful. I realize I was hoping to have Manuel's attentions all to myself, then chastise myself for it. I can't do anything besides eat a meal with him. I shouldn't have done anything with Pablo.

Luckily, I don't have many opportunities to talk. They have so much to say, they're always talking over each other. After a few minutes, I determine that the women are Manuel's sisters. Alejandro is a friend of the family. Every other minute, he mentions a different club for the night's entertainment. I should leave. My food is done. I must learn to be alone. I thought I knew what that meant after all those years living in a fishbowl, but I guess I don't. Maybe it's because, aside from Dr. Choebach, there was no one there I wanted to talk to.

The streets get darker. The sidewalks get busier. Every man with salt-and-pepper hair and a round belly reminds me of the man from the train. I stay rooted to my seat. Manuel is quiet as his sisters debate over which club is their favorite.

"Come with us for once," Alejandro says to Manuel. "You'll have fun, I promise."

"Too loud for me," Manuel says.

Alejandro turns to me, his eyes full of mischief. "You should come, then."

I shake my head reflexively. "I should go to my hotel." It's hard to keep track of the faces on the busy sidewalks. "Thank you for sharing your table."

Manuel follows my eyes as I scan the crowd. "Can I walk you to your hotel? It's easy to get lost in this part of town."

"That would be nice," I hear myself say. It's a small matter that I don't have a hotel. A short walk, I tell myself, until I find a place. Then we will part. When I can lock a door in between the world and me.

Alejandro gathers the paper plates and used forks. The whole time he has a sly smile aimed toward Manuel and me. I already regret accepting Manuel's invitation. I have no idea which direction to go, and now I will have to look like I do.

I choose a quieter street, away from the crowds. Manuel shoves his hands in his pocket as he follows me.

"Alejandro loves dancing," he says. "They'll be out until 4 a.m. at least."

"Your sisters, too?" I'd rather keep the conversation on him.

He drops behind me to let someone pass, then catches up with one long stride. "Much to my mother's dismay. With Alejandro, they're safe at least."

The jokester we ate dinner with isn't a likely bodyguard.

Manuel laughs at my expression. "Appearances can be deceiving."

The comment makes me doubt my own judgment. I was wrong about Jennifer being an enemy. I was wrong about Mentor being a friend. I could be wrong about the trust I'm putting in Manuel, or about my mistrust of the man on the train. "How long have you lived here?" I ask.

"I grew up here. On Alejandro's father's boat, actually."

We come to the end of the block. I flip a coin in my head and turn left. "What kind of boat?" As if I even know one kind of boat from another.

"A fishing trawler. He catches mackerel."

I spot a modest hostel the same shade as the dark blue sky. A tall, narrow neon sign announces the hostel's name and that there are no vacancies. I walk on, like I never meant to stop, but I'm not sure my act convinces Manuel. He's content to talk about himself as we walk though, which is a relief.

We come across a large hotel with a set of glass double doors that leads into a blandly, if tastefully, decorated lobby. A cloud of cigarette smoke lingers where I stop. At my feet, the end of a crinkled, still-lit cigarette butt glows red.

Manuel stops next to me, lingering.

"This is my hotel," I say, to fill the silence.

His hands push deeper in his pockets. "Guess you didn't need my help finding your way."

"Thanks anyway." A handshake seems inappropriate. A kiss is definitely inappropriate. A man in a white jersey cuts between us to get to the door, pushing us further apart.

Manuel gives me a short nod and a smile I can't read. "You're welcome. Enjoy the rest of your trip."

I turn to hide the sting of his casual goodbye. Not that I was going to do anything, right? Out of the corner of my eye, I see him take out his phone. He's probably calling up another girl. Someone who knows how the script better than I do. The door shuts behind me with surprising force, as if I slammed it.

The man behind the desk stands up. He wears a vest that matches the carpet over a long-sleeve white shirt.

"Quería una habitación sencilla," I say. *I'd like a single room.*

He sits back down. "No quedan habitaciones, lo siento." *No vacancies. Sorry.*

I stare at the doorway. From the lit lobby, the night seems blacker than it did before. "Are you sure?" I ask him.

The phone rings, and the clerk picks it up without looking at me. He promises someone more towels then disappears into a door behind him. A guest sitting in the lobby, reading a magazine, watches me. I take one slow step toward the door, then another. I'll just keep walking until I find something. Or someone finds me.

I feel something squish beneath my foot as I step onto the sidewalk. More remains of cigarettes.

Manuel is still outside, leaning against the wall his phone stuck to his ear. "They went out with Alejandro, Mama." He spots me and says his goodbyes. "What happened?" he asks as he pockets his phone.

"They lost my reservation. I guess I'll have to find another place." I hope I sound more confident than I feel. A man with a hat pulled down low over his face jostles me as he walks by. I stumble back, trying to rearrange my face to hide the fear.

If he notices, Manuel doesn't show it. "You won't find any rooms. Your clothes are wrong."

It's true I'm not dressed like the locals. But I've seen plenty of tourists around. "There's a dress code?"

He smiles. "Màlaga played Real Madrid today. Fans have had all the hotels booked for months."

"Oh." If I have to spend the night out in the open, maybe I can find a place where I can hear the sea.

"You're welcome to stay with me, though I'll have to kick you out early."

I'm not that naïve. From the corner of my eye, I see a shadow slipping into alley in front of us. The shadow has the same build as the man on the train.

"No expectations, I promise," Manuel says. "Consider it a random act of kindness."

I'm not sure if I believe Manuel, but the shadow has the hair on my neck standing on end. "If it's no trouble."

"I own my own lobster boat," he says. "I'll be headed out to check the traps early. But you're welcome to spend the night on board."

I follow him through a maze of streets he navigates without thinking. The smell of the sea, a new friend, gets stronger with every step. Finally, I can see the black water. Small, lapping waves catch the light from a weak moon. Masts of varying heights sway against the dark horizon. The brick courtyard we cross to get to the docks is nearly deserted, except for one man stumbling in our direction. A glass bottle clinks against his teeth as he sways and swallows. He is wearing what I have learned are Real Madrid colors. We swerve to avoid him, but he falls against us so we both have to hold him up.

"¡Hala Madrid!" He smells like the card games on the cruise ship, like beer and hard alcohol. But the smell comes more from his shirt than his wide-open mouth. His drunkenness seems like an act to me, but Manuel doesn't seem worried. And Manuel would know better than I.

"Sí, hala Madrid," Manuel says. He pushes the man away, gently but firmly. The drunk continues on his way.

I realize I'm holding onto Manuel's arm.

"You should see a soccer riot." He moves his arm so we're holding hands. Our intertwined fingers swing between us as we walk. The wooden dock bobs underneath our steps. I look behind us; there's no sign of the man from the train. He leads me to small boat that's cluttered with equipment. The wheelhouse is the size of a large bathroom. He hops on the boat, then extends an arm to help me. "I'm supposed to be a Sevilla fan since I live in the south, but I'm a Real Madrid fan. Like our drunk friend. Normally I'm in the minority at the stadium."

He sweeps one arm over a narrow bench padded with red cushions. "My bed." He lifts the bench and pulls out another set of cushions that fill the space on the floor not covered by equipment. It's slightly longer than the bench, but not any wider. "Your bed."

Blankets and pillows appear from a closet inside the wheelhouse. He hands me a set, then drops his own on the bench. "You said you were traveling. What's your next stop?" It's the first question he's asked about my plans. It's a nice change from Pablo's insistent, well-meaning inquiries.

"I haven't decided yet."

His eyes light up. "Care for some recommendations?" This starts a conversation about his adventures around Europe, and then about soccer and cooking and the whales he sees when he is out on the ocean. For someone with such callused hands, he knows a lot about art. He loves the Picasso museum.

The superficial conversation comes easily to me. Art was one of the few topics my tutor was allowed to cover in detail. It was considered safe. I tell him that Picasso lived in France during the occupation and was exiled from Spain in 1939 by General Franco. Picasso was a Communist, but the Soviets banned all of his art because they didn't like his portrait of Stalin.

I find myself losing track of when we speak Spanish or English. We talk about everything but ourselves. It's a relief. Soon, pink tinges the sky, and it's time for him to leave and for me to move on. I watch him ready the boat with graceful, practiced movements—tidying up ropes, rinsing out large plastic bins, checking the engine, making sure the spare gasoline container is full. I don't want to go. It must be desperation, I think, for me to be attracted to two men in such a short time. But this feels different. I never imagined anything beyond one night with Pablo. I want to go to a fútbol game with Manuel. I want to see the porpoises that he says follow the boat sometimes. I want to curl up with him and watch the stars. Every corny love song I scoffed at makes sense now.

"How long do you think you'll be in town?" he asks. "I'll be back in two days from checking my traps."

There are worse ways to spend 48 hours. A lobster boat in the middle of the Mediterranean is as good a place to hide as any. "Can I come with you? I have a little money I can give you for food. I don't know anything about fishing, but I can help if you show me a few things."

He smiles. "Consider yourself hired. No money needed."

I want to hug him, but instead I stow my bag in the wheelhouse.

"Just a couple things before we take off," he says. "The inflatable life raft is in the bench there. If the engine is on and I fall off, close the throttle like this. I'll swim to you. If you fall off, don't swim towards the boat. Just stay clear of the motor, and I'll circle back to you. Also, there's sort of a uniform." He lifts up the bench and pulls out two sweatshirts and what looks like two large rubber boots that grew together. "You'll want the waders, they'll keep you mostly dry. Should be just about your size. My sister wears them when she comes out with me."

Somehow the waders don't make Manuel look any less handsome, but I'm sure I look like a bloated balloon. That's okay with me. Maybe it will keep me from doing one more thing I shouldn't.

I watch the sunrise as we motor out into the sea and then fall asleep on the plastic cushions, rocked by the ocean swells. I wonder if this is what it feels like to be happy.

Chapter 20

I have signed up for hard work. In comparison to the freighter, the lobster boat is a child's toy, rising and falling with every swell. The traps are marked with buoys that must be caught by a long stick with a hook at the end. Manuel does it effortlessly, no matter how much the boat is rocking. I feel like I'm trying to thread a needle with yarn while riding a seesaw.

Once the buoy is hauled in, the rope is attached to a winch that hauls the trap up from the depths. The traps are full of snapping, red beasts with beady black eyes. Some are only six inches. Some are a foot or longer.

I take a step back as Manuel muscles a full trap onto the deck. Their claws click ominously.

"Don't be afraid of them," he says. "I've never seen a catch this good this time of year. You're my good luck charm."

It's nice to make someone happy for a change. My arm brushes his as I tentatively come closer, still careful to keep Manuel between the beasts and me.

"Now they have to go into the live well." He lifts up a panel on the deck to reveal a deep fiberglass compartment. Water sloshes around inside. It smells like the sea, concentrated. "Take one lobster at a time." He reaches into the bramble of snapping claws and comes up unharmed. "Then put rubber bands on their claws so they can't hurt each other." He uses metal tool to snap a rubber band around each of the lobster's claws, despite its squirming. The whole procedure takes him less than five seconds. He does a few more, then motions for me to take his place.

The trap is a writhing mass of red shells and claws.

"It's not as scary as it looks," he promises. "The trick is to grab the lobster on the back, where their claws can't reach."

"How strong are their claws?"

"Best not to think about that." He steps behind me, resting one hand on my shoulder and extending the other as a guide. The distraction of his touch overcomes my fear. With his sure hand leading mine, I snatch a lobster from the trap and drop it on the tray next to the bands. Free from the confines of the trap, it flaps its tail vigorously and exercises its claws. One claw is larger than the other, making it look even more like a monster.

Again, he guides my hand, sweeping from the back of the lobster to the front. "You see, once you have the claw, he can't do anything to you." The metal tool is a reverse set of pliers that pulls the strong rubber band apart until it's easy to fit over the claw.

After a few tries, I'm able to do one on my own, though I'm not nearly as fast as he is. We work side-by-side emptying the traps. His proximity is somehow comforting and distracting at the same time. He shows me what must be thrown back. Anything that's not a lobster, of course. I pick out a few shrimp, a fish with glassy eyes, and even a small octopus. Female lobsters must be thrown back, too.

He finds a male and female and holds them up next to each other, so I can compare. The females have a hairy, claw-like appendage on their undersides that the males are missing. It's easy to tell the difference when the females have eggs; they have clumps of tiny, dark circles sticking to their body. They remind me of slimy seeds.

We can't keep all the male lobsters. Each tray has measurements on it. Lobsters that don't fit within the lines must be thrown back. Once I have the process down, we don't talk much. We find a rhythm in our movements, synchronizing so we can stay out of each other's way. Grab a lobster, snap the bands on, toss it in the hold. Grab, snap, toss. Grab, snap, toss.

Then, the traps are baited again, with a putrid, sloppy mixture of chopped up fish parts, and returned to the ocean.

In between traps, I am alone on the deck while Manuel steers. It is nearly dusk when he pulls the boat into a small cove.

"We will spend the night here," he says.

Tiny cuts and bruises pepper my arms. I'm pleasantly exhausted from the day's labor. Manuel opens a small pantry, and prepares a dinner of canned beans and instant rice using a camp stove on deck. We eat on the bench, even though the constant wind adds a chill to the air. Our food tastes better than any gourmet meal I've ever had.

For dessert, he brings out a sweet wine that tickles my tongue. All day we have worked together easily, but now he seems shy and awkward, keeping more distance between us than he did last night.

It could be the fish smell. The lobster bait is pungent. Even with the gloves and waders gone, I'm sure we both smell like an expired seafood buffet. I'm not exactly dressed to kill either. In the harbor at Màlaga we were protected, but now I'm wearing two sweatshirts and a windbreaker just to stay warm.

"More wine?" he asks.

I nod, just so he'll come closer. When the next wave pushes him against me, I stay there. Hesitantly, he puts his arm around my shoulders. It will stop here, I tell myself. Being touched is enough. We watch the sunset—I think I will never grow tired of these—as the waves rock the boat, brushing his chest against my cheek.

Being touched is not enough.

I bring one hand to his cheek, rough with stubble, and pull his lips down to mine. The kiss lasts until the sun has disappeared from the horizon. I can hear the lobsters scratching at the sides of their prison below deck. He uses both sets of pads to make a bed on the floor of the wheelhouse. The chill wind is cut off when he closes the door. It's odd how quickly the cold fades as our fingers touch. I take off one sweatshirt. He takes off his wool sweater. We proceed in turns until we are both naked. His torso is two shades lighter than his arms and his face. His arms and stomach are toned from hauling up traps. He lets me guide his hands. His eyes don't ask any questions. There's no need to be quiet here. We're utterly, wonderfully alone. And, as I listen to the seagulls pass overhead, I see that I was wrong about earlier. *This* is what it feels like to be happy.

Chapter 21

Breakfast is oatmeal and hardboiled eggs, cooked on the camp stove before sunrise. We eat at the small table in the wheelhouse to stay warm. The seat is really meant for one. I don't mind, and he doesn't seem to either. Manuel keeps his arm draped around my shoulders.

After we have eaten, Manuel lays out the map. Yesterday, we did a semi-circle starting at Màlaga and ending in our little cove, about 20 miles east of the harbor.

"We'll retrace our route today to pick up the traps we missed," Manuel says.

"I slowed you down." The pleasant blush of last night's encounter fades.

He hugs me close. "You did fine. Besides, if our catch is as good today as it was yesterday, we may fill up the hold before we finish checking the traps."

"Do we have to head back early?" There's nothing good waiting for me on shore.

He mistakes my nerves for something else. "We don't *have* to do anything. That's the nice part about being your own boss."

I feel his kiss all the way down to my toes. For a moment, I forget I will have to leave him. He is warm and strong and kind and gentle and... not for me. I must not get greedy with my happiness. I count the freckles on his arm with my finger. There's a dark spot, a mole I didn't notice before.

No, not a mole. A sore.

"Hey, that tickles." He captures my hand, and I notice his skin isn't just warm. It's feverish.

On my next swallow of oatmeal, I taste blood. "Are you feeling all right?" The Harrises didn't get sick. How could Manuel? What if Pablo is sick?

"I feel a little achy." He rubs his arm, dislodging the scab on his sore. A perfectly round drop of blood forms in its place. When he moves, the drop collapses into a thin ragged, red line. He takes a napkin and wipes the blood off. "Boat bite, I guess. I do feel a little warm. Maybe I have a fever. I hope I don't get you sick."

Guilt curdles in my belly. My hearty breakfast threatens mutiny. I've seen sores like the one on his arm before. In the news articles describing the early stages of HF186-2A. His cell phone vibrates on the table, rumbling. I swallow my scream of frustration. The picture on his cell shows one of his sisters.

"They know to call early," he says, mistaking my anxiety for confusion. "While I'm close to land." He answers with his free arm, one arm still around my shoulders. "Dinner tonight with Mom and Dad sounds great." He looks sideways at me. "Maybe I'll even bring a guest."

He should be cursing my name. He should hate me with every fiber of his being. I curl into myself to hide my expression.

Jennifer said there had to be a trigger, that I wasn't infectious. She had no reason to lie. But, like she said, they don't tell her everything. Maybe closer contact is contagious. Maybe the man on the train really was from the lab. Maybe he had the trigger with him. What if Jennifer was wrong about them not using the trigger?

"Are you and Julieta feeling okay?" he asks. "I feel a cold coming on. Something might be going around."

Do the math, I tell myself. That's the only way to think this through. All contagious diseases have an infection rate called the reproduction number, R_0. Measles has a reproduction number of 12, meaning every one case of measles will result, on average, in 12 other cases. HF186-2A has reproduction number of 20.

I list the people I had close contact with since leaving Boston. Pablo, Manuel, Alejandro, Valeria, and Julieta. If I infected Pablo two days ago, there will be thousands of cases already. An outbreak of hemorrhagic fever would be the top story on the news. I turn on the small radio on the table at low volume. The top story is a surprise win by Real Madrid. The weather calls for sun and spotty clouds.

No outbreak.

There's still the possibility that Manuel's friends were infected. They would be in about the same stage of infection.

Manuel puts his phone down, stretches, then drops his arm back on my shoulders. "I hope you don't have dinner plans. My parents want to meet you."

The sharp knife twisting in my gut distracts me at first from the obvious. "Was your sister feeling okay?" I think I sound casual. I hope I sound casual. But what would Manuel suspect? He thinks he just has a cold.

"She said everyone's fine and to not be late. My mom is making her specialty, almejas a la marinera. If we don't get there in time to fight for our portion, it'll be gone."

I nod against his chest, still not daring to look at him. Somehow Manuel was exposed to the trigger, but no one else.

Good news for the rest of the world. Bad news for Manuel and me. I can't let him return to shore. I can't let his body return to shore. I can't let the boat return to shore. The virus is airborne. Everything he has breathed on is infected.

I watch him go about the business of prepping for our departure. From a few feet away, he doesn't seem sick at all. He is graceful and charming and sexy and easy to be around. It would have been hard to say goodbye. The word love comes into my head, but I push it away. My task is grisly enough.

"We better get going," he says. He kisses me on the forehead and stands up. I escape to the fresh air on deck. The waves look the same as yesterday. The sky looks the same as yesterday. I try to convince myself I'm imagining things. But when I see Manuel in the wheelhouse, reviewing maps, he's scratching at his neck. A line of blood appears and runs down to the collar of his sweater.

I could just tell him. Maybe that's the right thing to do. If I tell him why, he'll understand that we can't go back to shore. I could be his nurse, comfort him until the end. There's not much you can do for HF186-2A patients but hold their hands and keep them from swallowing their tongues.

No, I can't afford to be silly. Just because he wants me to meet his parents doesn't mean he'll believe the story of my life. And even if he believes me now, he might not be so cooperative when the hallucinations start. He's too strong for me to keep him here against his will. I study the geography of him, from his broad shoulders to his strong legs, not yet hidden by waders. It's easy to strip away the layers of clothes and see him as I saw him last night. Warm flesh against my flesh, strong fingers running down my back.

I force myself to strip away more layers, to imagine how he must look beneath the skin. Muscles, ligaments, organs, joints, arteries, and perfectly round eyeballs that do not blink. Underneath the skin, like me, he is simply biology and mechanics. A picture in an anatomy textbook. The image of his sleeping face competes with my analysis and threatens to subvert my will. A cold voice reminds me this isn't just about him. This is about everyone who will die if he makes it to shore.

I search the deck for a weapon. There's rope, of course, but I don't think I can overpower him. The hook for the buoys is solid enough I might be able to knock him out, but in the confines of the deck I might just as easily knock him overboard. There are knives in the galley. I saw them while we were making dinner yesterday. A cut to an artery will disable him quickly. Something stings my hand. I look down to see white knuckles gripping the railing. A nick in the metal digs into my palm.

Halting, shallow breaths tense my muscles. It's the same grief I felt at the Harris' cabin. It will be worse this time. My presence killed that family. This time it will be my hands doing the killing. Manuel is now rolling up his maps. He stows them next to the instrument panel and turns a key to start the motor. As he leaves the wheelhouse, he flashes me a smile. I can't return it, but it doesn't matter. His attention is on the growling winch pulling up the anchor.

This is my opportunity to get a knife from the galley.

Crossing the small distance from the rail to the door feels like moving through water. I'm hoping, begging, that the universe will find a way to stop me. A lightning strike, the boat capsizing, the lab people showing up in a helicopter. Let them kill him if it has to be done. They could have cured me, and they didn't. I never asked for this.

But the sky is clear, the waves are slight, and there are no noises on the horizon. We are alone, except for a scattering of other fishing boats. I slip a steak knife up my sleeve just as he comes back into the wheelhouse. He wraps an arm around my waist, kisses me like he did last night.

"Don't be nervous," he says. "My parents will love you."

If only he were a bastard. He deserves better than this. He deserves better than me. I can't do anything more than nod. He pushes a handle forward and the boat kicks forward. I hug him from behind, keep my head on his shoulder.

Manuel will die regardless of what I do. The only question is how many other people will get sick. I repeat this in my head as the boat eats up the miles to the next trap. It's the kind of day where we should be enjoying each other's company. The dirty windows in the wheelhouse don't keep the rising sun from warming my left cheek. I close my eyes, hear his breath as it moves in and out of his lungs. He twists, briefly, to kiss me on the forehead. I shut my eyes tighter. One tear escapes anyway, tracing a cold path down my cheek.

When I open my eyes, I see the sore on his neck is bleeding again. It stains an inch of his collar crimson before his blood manages to clot. It will only get worse for him. I force my breaths to be even so he doesn't ask why I'm crying. I watch the GPS screen to track how far we are from shore as the cove gets smaller behind us. Five miles behind us, then 10. There are still boats visible around us. We're not far enough away. 15 miles, then 20. The shore is only a wink on the horizon. We're alone on the water. His life pulses in his neck. I kiss the spot on his throat I should stab.

His fever is getting worse; his neck is flushed red.

We have traveled far enough. I should do it now. Every foot farther is one more foot I'll have to row. The edge of my hidden knife scrapes against the vulnerable skin of my shaking wrist. I can feel every beat in the palm of my hands as I slip the weapon into my sweating fingers. I waste another minute, two minutes on regret. I watch the delicate, olive skin over his carotid artery move in a steady rhythm. My heart beats twice for every pulse of his. Why can't he hear it? Why doesn't he see the wicked gleam of metal next to his thigh?

The droning of the motor hides my gulp of breath. "I'm sorry," I whisper, just like Harold did during my surgeries.

The sound makes him turn to me as I bring the knife down. It lands true, scraping against his collarbone as it sinks deep into soft flesh. Blood spurts out in sync with his heart, painting the windows of the wheelhouse in garish, dripping stripes lit by the sun. I stumble against the small table where we shared breakfast.

He tries to lunge at me and crumples to the floor. His life escapes through the fingers he holds against his wound. As he weakens, his hand loosens and the trickles turn to streams.

Without him steering, the boat goes wherever the waves demand, veering erratically. A swell catches the bow and throws me to my knees. He uses one hand to pull himself over to me. Coated in red, the hand resembles a lobster's claw. I recognize his instinct to survive. Anger and confusion swim in his eyes. With one last pull, his head lands heavily in my lap, and his eyes close. His soft, brown eyes, flecked with gold.

His hand falls from his neck. Weak spurts of blood push through the ragged edges of the hole I cut.

I'm crying so hard I can't breathe. "I'm sorry," I say again. But he doesn't hear me. He's already dead. He rolls off my lap with the next swell. A crimson pool quickly spreads to the whole floor of the wheelhouse, rocked as we are by the waves. The metallic smell is so strong I can taste it. The liquid slips between the toes of my bare feet. I am bathed in it. I will be bathed in it forever.

But my job is not done. The boat is still a biohazard zone.

I tell myself to stand. The floor is so slippery that I have to hold on to the walls to make my way to the throttle. I shut the engine off, just like he taught me to do in case he fell off. My handprint leaves the throttle dripping with Manuel's blood. The circles splash against a glass dial showing the oil level. My breakfast comes up on the maps neatly stashed by the steering wheel.

When I'm done, the silence is jarring. It's only the waves and me. I swish water in my mouth and spit into the sink.

I force myself to take the life raft out from the bench Manuel showed me. The directions are printed on the side in three languages. One pull on the red cord and the life raft inflates itself, bobbing on the water like a yellow duck. In most situations, I suppose, a life raft should be easy to see. I scan the space around us—around me—and see no one. I'll have to move quickly, just in case. The boat is still contagious to any would-be rescuers. I find the oars for the life raft and toss them in. There are other things I need. I tear my eyes away from Manuel's contorted body. I have to think.

I need my bag. It's the only money and ID I have. I haven't opened it since we came on board, so everything inside should be safe. The outside will need to be disinfected. The raft needs to be disinfected. I have to be disinfected. There's soap and bleach in the wheelhouse. I put both in the life raft with my bag.

Now, the spare gas canister. I pour gas on every surface of the boat I can reach. Perhaps it's my imagination, but the lobsters scratching in the hold start to sound desperate. The fumes nearly make me faint. I fumble and drop the first match, unlit, with shaking fingers. The second falls, too. The third match finally lights. It lands on the bench where we shared our first kiss.

The small, eager flame blossoms as it feeds on the rainbow liquid. By the time I climb in the life raft, the flames are as long as my arm. At least Manuel won't feel anything. The shifting orange curtain of the fire and the waves of heat rising off the deck distort his body, like he's melting away. Black, acrid smoke rises from the white fiberglass. The fire is so hot, I'm afraid it will melt the raft. I strip quickly, throwing each item onto the boat.

Naked, I do my best to row as far away from the heat of the fire. The chill of the ocean raises goose bumps all over my body. I get the absurd feeling I'm abandoning Manuel. As if that's the worse of my sins.

Grieve later. Finish the job now. I scan the horizon again. The coast is still clear. I wash one arm with soap and water to disinfect it, then take out a pair of socks from my bag. I soak them in bleach, then wipe down everything in the life raft, including the outside of the cotton bag and the raft itself. The smell of bleach reminds me of the lab. I throw the socks into the gray, unforgiving waves.

By now, I'm shivering, but I can't bring out the second outfit just yet. I scoop cold handfuls of seawater and use my hands to scrub every part of my body for 20 seconds. The water is colder than the air. My teeth chatter and my fingers turn blue. I dress with stiff fingers.

I hug myself and look back at the fire devouring Manuel and his boat. Already it is lopsided, sinking. Eerie, keening screams rise from the hold as the flames reach where the lobsters are kept. I read somewhere that lobsters can't scream, but now I'm not so sure. It's just the air escaping their shells as they're burned alive, I tell myself. Like that's a more pleasant thought. The smell of burning flesh and plastic forces me to row away.

Which direction is the shore? I remember the sun on my left cheek as we headed out of the cove, away from shore. The sun hasn't reached the peak of the sky yet. That means keeping the sun on my right cheek will take me back to shore. I row for 10 minutes and nothing seems any closer. In the distance, all that's left of the boat is burned plank floating on oily water. The sea swallowed my secrets. There's nothing for miles. I'm alone and I have no idea how much farther I need to go. I'll have to get used to this feeling. It'll be the rest of my life.

I row in spurts, stopping whenever my arms demand it. The bleach bottle rolls around at my feet. The bleach bottle. It's not something a survivor would think to take. I fill it to the top with seawater, cap it and drop it over the side. The bar of soap follows.

The sun changes from a warm, comforting friend to a vicious taskmaster. I stretch the sleeves of Mandy's shirt over my hands to keep them from burning. I can feel my face prickling from the exposure. Leaning forward a little helps. By late afternoon, my aching arms and fluttering heart are rewarded by the sight of bobbing masts in the distance. When dusk arrives, I am close enough to see the lights of the harbor. I aim for the steady stream of boats returning to harbor. This far away, they look like toys.

My arms demand another break. I lean back against the cold rubber of the raft, stretching my sore muscles under the first star of the night. The distant sound of a growling motor snaps my head up. There's a white boat with a sharp prow headed toward me at full speed, leaving a large wake. As it gets closer, I can read *Guardia Civil* in blue letters on the side. A spotlight aimed at the raft from the boat nearly blinds me. I don't bother to wave them down. They knew where to look for me.

I hadn't considered what I would tell the authorities. A fire, obviously; there will be some evidence of that where the boat sunk. What makes a boat start on fire? A leaking gas can. The gas can was leaking and—no, we would have smelled it. He had to use the gas can to refill the tank, but we were in choppy water so it spilled, and—who would be stupid enough to light a match then? Do electronics on boats ever short out?

Any elaborate story I might have told is lost when I see the two anxious figures on my rescue boat. Two girls with hair like a horse's mane. Manuel's sisters. Of course, they were expecting Manuel for dinner. They're yelling rapid-fire questions at me in Spanish, before I can even hear them over the motor.

The questions don't stop when a woman in a blue uniform helps me off the rope ladder and onto the deck of the boat. They're speaking so fast I can barely understand them. I try to put together a sentence in Spanish, but I hear Manuel instead, speaking every word in his soft, lovely voice. I bury my head in my hands and find my cheeks are wet.

Something crackly and silver is dropped over my shoulders. A survival blanket.

"Fuego," is all I can manage.

"Manuel?" his sisters ask together.

I shake my head. "Muerto."

Their faces contort into masks of grief. They fall on me, sobbing, trapping me in a tangle of arms and long hair. Every wail stabs at my heart. I start crying like I did on the boat, sobs that feel like muscle spasms. I killed the man I loved. I can use that word now. Naming my feelings can't save Manuel.

When our tears stop, I am bone-weary. The woman who helped me onto the boat tries to ask me what happened, but most of my Spanish has deserted me. I couldn't confess to her even if I wanted to. The sisters don't suspect a thing. Why would they? Manuel was going to bring me home to meet his parents.

They offer me a bed at their house, but I refuse. They insist. I keep refusing until, confused, they leave me alone.

I find a bench and sit in the dark. I'm not cold. I'm not warm. I feel nothing. I can't run anymore. Someone from the lab found me and used the trigger. Maybe as a cruel reminder, maybe as a test. It doesn't matter. I wait for them to show themselves and take me home.

Chapter 22

I watch the restless docks go quiet. The fishermen are either gone or sleeping on their boats. They start their days early. More stars appear in the darkening sky. I can't find any joy in them. I smell blood beneath the salty air, but I know it's my imagination. An impatient wind stirs the trees, their leaves and the streetlights leaving shifting dark blotches on my palms.

I loved Manuel. I killed Manuel.

My head falls into my hands, and I dig my fingers into my scalp. Larry must take pleasure in my suffering, in making me wait. Finally, I lift my eyes at the sound of footsteps. The bearded man from the train appears out an alley bordering the courtyard. He doesn't brandish any weapons. The only thing he carries is a small leather briefcase. He sits down next to me without saying anything.

I wait for his reinforcements to arrive, for my body to be claimed as property again.

"You still don't recognize me," he says.

There was no one at the lab with a beard. Or green eyes like mine. Those eyes—of course. I should have seen it. 23 years in prison has aged him. The first and only picture I've seen of him was taken the day he was arrested. "Father."

He pats my leg. I squirm away.

"I suppose it has been a long time," he says. "The last time I saw you, you barely weighed—"

"You only cared about how far your virus had spread."

My enmity doesn't faze him. "You were an adorable child. I chose your mother for her beauty. I knew a cute baby would get more attention. Are you going to thank me?"

He's never given me anything worth having.

"You have your mother's figure and her cheekbones. Did you think it was your language skills that attracted your fishermen?"

I dig my nails into the soft wood of the bench. "You don't get to talk about Manuel."

"You really cared for him." He's genuinely surprised. "I thought I raised you better."

Raised me? I was raised by surgical equipment and television.

He pulls the metal box he had on the train out of his briefcase. When he opens it up, the pieces are arranged exactly where my last game with Mentor paused. "I was hoping you would figure it out on the train. You were watching me play."

My father is Mentor. The one person I thought who was always honest with me. But if he's Mentor, does that mean he was working with the lab? Was the lab aware of our conversations the entire time? "Why did the lab send you?"

His laugh mocks me. "The lab doesn't know either of us have left the country. They're still chasing their tails in New Hampshire."

"Then how did you—"

He taps my bracelet with a long, graceful finger. "GPS tracker and RFID blocker. Quite brilliantly designed. I couldn't have done much better myself. I have such friends now."

The biographers were right. He loves to hear himself talk.

"I expected prison would be the end of my plans, but you should see the letters I get from admirers. It was actually much easier to continue my work than I expected. Your bracelet was designed by an engineer in Calcutta, built by a hobbyist in Virginia, and delivered to Jennifer by a truck driver named Steve."

"Jennifer would never work with you."

"She's sentimental when it comes to you. I convinced her and Harold I had a change of heart about what I'd done. How do you think I setup those chess games with you?"

Jennifer and Harold have been working with my bastard of a father. I close my eyes and remind myself to breathe. But if the lab doesn't know where I am, how did Manuel get sick? And what did my father mean about his plans?

"The first time your doctors came to see me, it was about curing you. Later, their questions changed. I realized they were going to weaponize you instead. That's when I saw my opportunity."

He leans back and smiles as he continues. "One of my most promising acolytes was an impressionable young man in California. He wrote me while he was in high school, asking if I could teach him how to make a virus. The prison censors would never let me do it, so I told him to keep his record clean and join the Army. Eventually, I knew I'd have need of him.

"When the gene therapy trials began at the lab, I told him to volunteer. They didn't ask too many questions about how my acolyte knew about the project. They were having trouble getting volunteers. The early animal trials didn't go well, you see. If they'd just put me in the lab, Sam would have been operational years earlier."

If there's someone else like me, why didn't Jennifer know? "You helped them make another carrier for the virus."

His eyes light up. "Oh, that would be a wonder, wouldn't it? Sarina would spread so much faster then."

I look away in disgust.

"You don't know how special you are." He looks at me as if he's admiring a painting. "Jennifer didn't tell you how you were made?"

"We had other things to talk about." It's not surprising my father thought his brilliance was important enough to be the main topic of conversation.

"You're a chimera. It was the only way."

It would be nice if I could blame all my mistakes on whatever beast he crossed me with.

"The DNA that programs your lungs to make the virus had too many instructions. It interfered with other vital functions. No matter what I tried, the best I could ever achieve was a stillborn baby. He never even took a breath. Useless."

What torture it must have been for my mother. No wonder she cracked. She suffered through endless rounds of IVF and miscarriages, and then a stillborn child that my father never even grieved.

"I figured out a way to combine two zygotes without triggering an immune response that rejects the foreign tissue. You have the lungs of your stillborn brother."

I taste the acids of my stomach. I want to claw my chest open and tear out the offending organs.

"That's the technique I kept from Larry all these years," he continues. "I thought eventually they'd let me out so I could create more Sarinas. Instead, they decided to use gene therapy to insert a small number of genes into someone else."

The coat proteins Jennifer was talking about. "The trigger isn't a what. It's a who."

My father grins. "I knew you'd figure it out. My acolyte, Sam, is the other half of you. Together, you're contagious."

He waves his arm, and someone else emerges from the shadows. The drunken Real Madrid fan who accosted Manuel and I before we got on the boat. His white-blond hair is shaved close, accentuating his long face and milky blue eyes.

"I know technically we're not related," Sam says. "But I'd like to call you sister. Is that okay? How did our test work? When did you first notice symptoms?"

I see Manuel's face after I slit his throat—confused, angry, and twisted in pain—and I launch myself at my 'brother'. I almost get my nails into his eyes before my father's strong arm pulls me back at the waist. Sam dabs at the scratch I left on his cheek with a napkin.

Without loosening his grip, my father picks up a phone that's fallen on the ground. I see a red dot blinking on the screen—my GPS signal. "We're your family now," he says firmly. "Sam, kindly grab the kill button from my briefcase please."

Sam pulls out a metallic box like the one Martin had. My father's grip doesn't let me move.

"Keep it between the bracelet and her leg," my father orders.

Sam does. The bracelet won't do much to help me now. My father releases me, with Sam hovering close. Sam gives up the box easily when my father reaches for it. With a gentle finger, my father flips up the protective cover. He holds his palm over the red circle. "Come with us."

My eyes narrow, and my lips form a snarl. "You would destroy your masterpiece."

"I'm a patient man. Your lack of cooperation would only delay the inevitable."

"I guess I don't have much of a choice then."

His hand doesn't move. "Every time you won a chess game, it was because I let you. Do remember that."

"Fine. I'll cooperate." It's not because I want to save myself. I'm going to kill them both. And I won't be sorry.

Chapter 23

My father takes us to a camper van parked on a nearby street. He was never far away. Inside, it's about the size of the wheelhouse on the boat. The kitchen is a three-foot section of counter with a tiny stove. The only thing on the counter is a drying rack with a set of dishes for two. My father is, apparently, a neat person.

He handcuffs me to a bar he's installed at the doll-sized table next to the kitchen. Sam follows us in and stands just outside my reach. He has a bracelet like mine; I wonder if he has a poison pill in his leg too. If he does, he was awfully calm earlier when he was holding the kill button. My father opens up a small cabinet filled with green bricks. He must have a small fortune sitting there.

The look of shock on my face makes him smile. "Some of my friends are richer than others." He weighs one brick in his hands. The plastic snaps as it tears, and he pulls out a handful of bills. They crinkle in Sam's hand as he accepts them.

"To get home," my father says. "And for the bribe."

My father places his hands on Sam's shoulders. Sam bows as if it's a blessing.

A beneficent nod from my father completes the bizarre ceremony. "Thank you for coming."

After Sam leaves, my father digs around in the small refrigerator. "We'll have dinner now." It's nearly midnight, according to the microwave clock. He pulls out a small package of chicken, some vegetables, and a bag of salad.

From the cabinets, he pulls out plastic jars of spices. "I'm sorry I don't have fresh herbs for you. It's hard to keep them on hand when I'm on the road so much."

That's what he feels the need to apologize for. I try to find a comfortable spot to sit with my arm awkwardly hanging above my shoulder. He chops an onion with precise strokes of a knife, then drops the slices into a skillet glistening with oil. Herbs are sprinkled in the pan next, measured by scent rather than instruments. I smell tarragon, thyme, and parsley. My mouth waters, and I hate myself for it.

"You must have questions," he says. "I want us to be able to work together. Ask me anything."

I could start with why he's such a bastard, but I should take advantage of this to find my quarry's weaknesses. "Where is Sam going?"

"Sam was ordered to report to the auxiliary lab." He washes several carrots in the sink, then puts two on a cutting board. The knife slaps against the wood with every cut.

"Don't they know he left the country if they're tracking him like me?"

My father smiles a chess master's smile. The thwacks of his knife punctuate the silence. "His surgery is scheduled two days from now. It was supposed to happen a week ago, but your escape interrupted their plans."

Waiting for Sam to get back will save me the trouble of finding him, if it won't be too long. "When will Sam return?"

Circles of orange fall through a cloud of steam as my father scrapes them into a pan of boiling water. "I haven't decided yet."

"You play chess with him, too." Sending orders via a chess game could take weeks. Weeks I'll have to spend stuck in a van with an asshole.

"Jealous?" he asked, mistaking the bitterness in my tone. He pats his pocket. "We use coded texts. The lab thinks I'm his girl-friend. Sam isn't smart enough for chess. I chose him for his loyalty."

He smashes a clove of garlic with the knife turned flat. The pungent, fresh, aroma stings my nostrils.

"The things we will do, Sarina." When he says my name, the first syllable hisses. "You were created for a purpose."

"What if I don't want to help you?" The question comes out before I think better of it.

My apparent disloyalty doesn't rattle my father. He gently places two chicken breasts on top of the cooking vegetables and sets a teapot to boil. "You will."

I want to slap the smug expression off his face. "You think because I'm your daughter, I'm a monster like you."

He chuckles. I didn't know I could hate him more. "You left the lab when you thought you were contagious."

I thought I was partially cured. I hoped I was partially cured. The animal that drove me to leave the lab stirs inside me, coy and sly.

Watching my father plate a meal is like watching a surgeon at work. His long graceful fingers waste no motion. Each piece of chicken is precisely centered on a bed of mushrooms and caramelized onions. A third of the plate is filled with carrots, still steaming. The last third is covered with dark spinach leaves and drizzled with a simple dressing of olive oil and balsamic vinegar.

He sets both plates on the small table, then he goes back for the teapot and two cups. He sets the hot water outside my reach. My chicken has been cut for me. I wonder how much damage I could do with a fork. The tea smells hauntingly familiar. It's mint tea, the fragrance of the streets of the Algeciras. I'm reminded of how much I enjoyed my meal there, then how much I missed Pablo, which feels like betraying Manuel all over again.

"I bought some from the shopkeeper after you left," my father says. "In honor of your clever escape."

"If you wanted to be sure I escaped, you should have given me more help."

"Jennifer thought so too. But I had to make sure Larry didn't suspect anything."

I poke at the food on my plate. I'm famished and it smells delicious, but I don't want to give my father the satisfaction.

"I never doubted you would make it."

A flush of pride warms me before I can push the feeling away.

"You are my daughter, after all."

I stab a carrot and swallow it without chewing. I'll need my strength to get out of here.

He sighs and dabs a napkin at the corner of his mouth. "I suppose it's understandable you think I'm a monster. They never told you the real purpose of Sarina, did they?"

"I don't care."

"Larry has all my files locked away in a vault, I'm sure. Of all the questions he asked me, he never asked me why."

I take a second bite and chew quickly to avoid savoring the taste. My father really is a good cook.

"Didn't you ever wonder why the Sarina virus causes seizures and hallucinations?"

To create fear and suffering, I assumed. It seems to be his specialty.

"It rewires the brain, creates new connections." He leans in, a fanatic gleam in his eyes. "It makes people smarter. The worthy ones survive."

I choke on a piece of onion. "You started an outbreak to raise the IQ of the population by a couple points?" It explains why my father told his followers the virus was a test of purity. He believes it himself.

"Not a couple points, Sarina. The survivors are geniuses. Imagine a world where you and I aren't expected to follow rules designed to protect idiots from themselves. A world where I would never need to suffer the company of fools."

My incredulous look only encourages him.

"I'm going to tell you something even Sam doesn't know about me. Before I was Gregory Wocek, I worked at a private genomics company. I was researching the role genetics plays in intelligence. I developed a test that could predict intelligence in utero."

Practical eugenics. I shiver, despite the warm van.

"My superiors didn't appreciate my brilliance either. They fired me, destroyed my research, and ruined my reputation. I couldn't get hired anywhere. I was forced into menial labor until I could get a new identity.

"I had to find a new way to fulfill Nietzsche's vision. So I created Zarathustra's overman in a virus. If it had been allowed to run its course..." He takes a breath, an almost religious fervor in his eyes. "It would have been a beautiful world. It still can be."

"And the 300 people that died, what they wanted doesn't matter?"

He blinks and swallows the last of his dinner. "That's the whole point. I'm not bound by the values of normal men—I have a legacy to protect. You are my legacy. You are the purpose of my life." He leans over and holds the tip of my chin between his fingers. The smell of tarragon drifts to my nose. "You are the purpose of humanity."

My father is a madman. He's used his genius to rationalize genocide.

"You're not convinced," he says. "It doesn't matter."

"I don't have to help you."

He laughs. "You have it backwards. You need my help. They'll never stop looking for you. Do you know how many years of research are in your tissues? How many powerful people will fall if your story is ever told?"

"Jennifer said—"

"Jennifer set you free because she wanted to be rid of you. She would have left the lab years ago if they had let her. Don't you remember any of your lessons? There aren't any good people in the world. Not you, not me. Not Jennifer, or Harold, or that cute little family that hid you. There's no one worth saving. There's no reason not to use your gift. Your only duty is to look out for yourself."

It's not true. I think of Mandy, laboring in love to build a present for her daughter, and Tom, who forgave me even after all the lies I told him. I think of Pablo, who warned me about flashing the money around so I could protect myself. And Jennifer, who caught me after my first toddling steps, and Harold, who gave me the picture that proved I was loved. My father's own logic has defeated him. I wouldn't have escaped with my 'gift' without their help.

My father grazes my cheek with the back of his hand, almost tenderly. "You don't understand yet, but you will. The only way you can be free is by starting the epidemic. All evidence of the lab will be destroyed so they can deny your existence. Once the infection spreads far enough, there will be no point in recapturing you. You'll just be patient zero. The rare, lucky girl who could carry HF186-2A without dying from it."

I see his weakness now. His lack of empathy means he only understand the actions of others rationally, not viscerally. Typhoid Mary was a real person. She wasn't the only person who carried typhus without getting sick, but she was the only person confined to an island for the rest of her life. There's something stronger than utility in the human spirit—there's love. And when that is torn away, there's revenge.

"You'll see, my dear." His tone is fond, but I don't mistake it as a fondness for me. He clears the table and neatly wipes down the kitchen until everything is spotless again. "Now, I have a few errands to run, so I'll be gone for a while. I'm afraid it looks like I'll need to keep those handcuffs on you. Would you like to use the bathroom before I leave?"

The only image in my head is my hands around his throat. I don't think I can convince him I was converted by his little speech right now. "Yes, I'd like to use the bathroom."

He retrieves a gun from a drawer before he unhooks the handcuffs. He points to a tall, narrow door near the foot of the bed. "Be quick, please. I have a lot of preparations to make."

After I'm done, I let the water run to cover my search of the bathroom. All I can find a paperclip. I was hoping for something with more stabbing potential. Paperclips can be used to pick locks though, right? I have to try.

I tuck the metal oval into my pocket before I come out. He handcuffs me to the bar again, and then he disappears into the early morning light.

Two hours and one mangled paperclip later, it's clear I won't be able to pick the lock on the handcuffs.

I channel my frustration into trying to yank the bar off the wall. All I have to show for my efforts are red marks on my wrist. The bar rattles in its braces as I try to find a comfortable spot to rest. I examine the bar closer. The attachment to the wall is secure, but the bar itself is hollow. If I can bend it enough, it will fall out of the braces entirely. I grab the rod in the middle with my free hand and lean back. The edge of the table digs into my spine. I hear something snap inside the braces, like plastic breaking.

The damaged rod holds on stubbornly. There's no hiding the fact I tried to escape now. I have to be gone when my father returns. I lean back again and use my feet to push against the wall. Pain flares in my back where the table has slipped between two vertebrae. I keep pushing.

With a creak and a groan, the rod gives. I'm thrown to the floor, hitting my head and my elbow on the way down. But I'm no longer his prisoner.

I'm his executioner. After searching all the cabinets and storage places, the only weapon I can find is a knife. He must have taken his gun with him. I hide behind the door.

Then I wait. Minutes pass like hours. My mind spins on our meeting at the docks, remembering how much my father outweighs me. He was strong enough to pull me away from Sam without breathing hard. If the first stab doesn't disable him, my chances of winning are low. The fight will be messy. Maybe even noisy. Someone might hear us and call the police. The van might be contagious—Sam and I were in here together, even if he was keeping his distance. I should have spent my time cleaning instead of crouched against the wall, knife in hand.

There will be a better time and place to kill my father. I don't doubt he will find me again.

I scrub myself with soap and water and every exposed surface in the van with bleach. Sam is far away by now. I don't need to worry about being contagious.

I find a duffel bag and fill it with anything that could be useful to me. There's a small stack of clothes in my size, and a coat. Granola bars from the kitchen. Several bricks of cash. I check the clock on the microwave and find I've been packing for 10 minutes already. Too long. But the key for the handcuffs dangling from my wrist is nowhere to be found, and I can't walk around on the street with them.

The last cabinet to search is the one under the sink. It has spare cleaning supplies and one toolbox. I dig it out, but there are no tools inside. Just a heavy black rectangle with a short antenna, like the radios the *Guardia Civil* carried. The screen shows two red dots blinking on a map: Sam's bracelet and mine.

It's a spare GPS device. I'll figure out how to read the coordinates later. Behind the toolbox is a gray case labeled 'Dremel.' A quick glance inside shows it's a power tool of some sort. Another five minutes have passed. I throw the box into my bag along with the GPS. I can always ditch it later.

I throw on the coat I found, making sure the sleeves will hide the handcuffs. As I step out into the afternoon, I notice how warm it is and how much I stick out. It doesn't help that carrying the heavy duffel bag is making me sweat. I won't be able to lose my father unless I can block the GPS signal somehow. I buy a ticket on the metro for the next train with a stop at an underground station. It's also the line to the airport, unfortunately. A predictable destination.

The sign at the platform tells me my train will be arriving in five minutes. I stare at the station entrance, waiting for my father and his gun to come running through the turnstiles. But he doesn't, and the train arrives with a screech of brakes. I choose to board the car that's empty. I dig the gray case out of the duffel bag and read the directions in the manual. There's an attachment for everything from cutting to sanding, if I can find a power outlet. If.

The train stops at the underground station. I see two bathrooms. I might as well try. Wet toilet paper and dirty footprints decorate the floor of the women's room. I step gingerly over the worst of it to look for an outlet. I find one near the floor, under the hand dryer. The manual tells me which attachment cuts metal. I crouch near the outlet, careful to hold the cord away from the floor, then gingerly push on the slider switch. The high-pitched motor echoes loudly against the tiled walls and floor. I almost cut my hand, flailing, as I try to turn it off. I can't use this tool in a quiet station.

I take a deep breath and count to 300. As I was hoping, the roar of the next train becomes audible. The cutting blade hovers near the handcuff ringing my wrist. Not yet, not until it's louder… Now. Hot sparks of metal sting my skin. The tool cuts through so quickly that I nearly cut into my wrist, too. In the quiet after the train speeds away, the handcuffs fall with a clang to the disgusting floor. My knees protest from crouching for so long.

Count to 300 again, I tell myself. This time for the bracelet. Someone knocks on the door. I ignore them. One minute later there's a more insistent knock. "Metro police," a voice says in Spanish. "Everything okay in there?"

I tell him I'm fixing my makeup.

I can't risk using the tool again. There has to be another way to get this bracelet off. My father is not the brute force type. I close my eyes and run my hand along every single surface, every single edge. There's a small hole, no larger than a pin. Too small for the mangled paperclip to work. My eyes land on the plastic biohazard container on the wall, with directions to dispose of needles. I pry the container open where the red tabs meet the clear plastic top. The top snaps loudly as it releases. There's another knock on the door.

I ask for one more minute.

The point of the needle on top fits into the small hole on the bracelet. It pops open. I let out a long breath. The policeman knocks on the door. I'm about to throw the bracelet away when it occurs to me it could still be useful. Since I didn't destroy it, it can lead my father away from me. The handcuffs are just extra weight. The garbage can in the restroom is nearly empty, so I lift the top off the toilet and lower the handcuffs into the tank. I'm careful to set the porcelain top down on the tank silently.

There's no hiding the damage to the sharps container.

The next train toward the airport has finally arrived. I leave the bathroom and walk past the waiting policeman. I choose a car with people this time. Odds are someone on this train is flying out of the airport today. If I can slip the bracelet into their luggage, my father will follow the signal away from me. As the door closes, I hear the policeman report on his radio that I'm just another druggie. That's fine. As long as he doesn't think I'm a fugitive.

On the train, I sit next to the woman who is speaking a language I don't recognize. It's that and her open, bulging purse that attracts me. I can see her plane tickets on top. She's flying to Iceland today. Perfect. She is deep in conversation with her companion, so she doesn't notice when I slip the bracelet into her purse and get off at the next stop.

Chapter 24

I shed the heavy coat as I leave the station, glad I no longer have handcuffs to hide. Something else feels different. There's no bracelet bouncing against my wrist. For the first time since I left the lab, I feel free. I'd start skipping, if it weren't for the heavy duffel bag on my shoulder. My steps slow as I recognize the neighborhood. It's the neighborhood where I met Manuel. I walk past the chicken shack with the rickety table and the surly vendor, who's pointing at his ear while a customer yells his order.

Manuel lived here. Somewhere, not too far away, his sisters and mother and father are grieving for him. They will never see his body. What's left of him will be food for scavengers along the ocean floor. I hold the image close as my punishment. My father's laugh mocks me. *You left the lab when you thought you were contagious.* My hands start to shake. I shove them into my pockets and go into the next hotel I see. The emotions of the day are catching up with me. I need to be alone.

The lobby is decorated with abstract murals of city life and furniture too modern to be comfortable. I swallow the hard lump in my throat and go up to the desk clerk. He raises his eyebrows when I pay in cash.

"I had to use my ATM card to get cash," I say. "My credit card was stolen." I read something about carrying an ATM card for backup in the guidebook. I can't tell if he believes me or not.

Mostly, he looks bored. He holds out a hand with yellow nails. "Passport, please." His breath smells like cigarettes.

The only passport I have is the one Jennifer—and by extension, my father—gave me. My father said he had friends all over. Does that include someone in Interpol who will be watching for the name Janine Butler? I pretend to dig in my bag. "I'm sorry, I can't find it. Can I bring it down later?"

"I can't give you a room without a passport. Unless you've already registered with the police here?"

Registered? I have no idea what he's talking about. I'll have to read more of that guidebook tonight. "Oh, here it is," I say, handing him the passport. I can't spend the night out in the open and risk my father seeing me. He may not have followed the bracelet to Iceland. If I weren't so tired, I would leave Màlaga tonight.

"The old style, huh?" he says.

Is the passport not good? Pablo is the only other one who's seen it.

"No RFID chip yet. When you renew, you'll get one." The clerk makes a copy of the passport and hands it back to me with a room key. "Upstairs and to the right."

After the cramped quarters of the boat, and my father's van, the room seems palatial. There's a queen bed and a small couch, and a bathroom that doesn't require contortions to enter. I open the curtains so I can see the procession of people on the sidewalks below. They are people headed home from work, families on their way out to an early dinner. In a few hours, they will be replaced by a younger, louder crowd. Men like Alejandro, Manuel's friend, who wander out to the clubs for the night.

It's a life I will never be a part of, all because of one madman and his sick visions of utopia. I wonder if he's right about the lab never giving up. If Jennifer was lying to herself, so she could justify setting me free. I feel his knuckles brushing my cheek.

I need a shower to wash away his touch.

The needles of hot water massage my sore shoulders. It occurs to me that I am washing away Manuel's touch too. Our brief interlude of happiness is a fragile memory compared to what followed. The steam of the shower is transformed into the cold spray of seawater. The water at my feet reminds me of the splashing of waves on the deck. I feel his arms around me as he demonstrated how to band a lobster's claws. As hard as I try, the tape won't stop there. My mind fast-forwards to us in the wheelhouse together, me with a knife hidden in my hand and him steering the boat. I squeeze my eyes shut. I see his brown eyes, stung by my betrayal. I'm covered in his blood again.

I put a hand against the wall as I slide down to my knees. It's safe to cry here. There's no one to hear me. I stay under the hot needles of water until the tears stop. The walls are wet with moisture when I finally turn the shower off. The mirror is fogged over. I leave it that way. I don't want to see if I'm the monster my father says I am. I left the lab. People died because of it. The fact I feel guilty doesn't make it okay. Do I have something to offer the world that's worth letting the virus in my lungs live?

A voice inside me answers yes, but it's not the reassuring voice of Harold. It's the sibilant voice of my father. The sociopath who wants to start an epidemic just because he can.

There is one way I can justify my existence. I can make sure the Sarina project is destroyed. I will kill Larry. I will kill Sam. I will kill my father. I will tell the world what they've done. And since there's no possible way I can survive all of that, the rest will take care of itself.

Chapter 25

My growling stomach wakes me. I realize I missed dinner last night and slept until nearly lunch. The prices on the room service menu are outrageous, but I have some cash to spare now. And I'd rather not show my face around town. A man in a crisp hotel uniform, light green with black trim, arrives 20 minutes after I order. I'm so hungry I nearly grab a muffin off the plate. When I pay him, I even remember to tip like the guidebook said.

"Check-out time is in one hour, ma'am," he says diplomatically, noting that I'm still in pajamas.

"Thank you."

The GPS unit I stole from the van shows my marker in Iceland and Sam's in New Hampshire. The auxiliary lab must be near the original. I take a sip of orange juice. It's much better than the orange juice I was given at the lab. The breakfast menu calls it freshly squeezed.

I have to leave the hotel soon, and I'm not sure where to go. My father may have followed the bracelet to Iceland. He may have also tracked my passport to this hotel.

The task I've set myself overwhelms me. What does it take to destroy a lab and kill three people? I can't even think of the supplies I need. Should I buy a gun? I don't know the first thing about how to find one. Or how to get it across an international border.

The bright blue sky outside the window mocks my black mood. I remind myself of the first step of survival: Take inventory. I empty the duffel bag onto the bed. The case for the Dremel tool slips off the mound of clothes and breaks open. The manual spills out, along with a manila envelope. I examine the case closer. It's not broken at all. My father built a false front into the case. I tilt the envelope over the comforter, afraid of what I'll find. Research from his latest experiments? Records of the original Sarina epidemic? Miniatures of my face sprinkle the fabric like puzzle pieces. Sam's face, too. My father has variations of his face, with and without beard, dark hair and gray hair. There are blank passports from several countries, some even with my face already printed in them. There's also a small toolkit, including glue, stamps and inkpads. I pick up the U.S. passport and see my picture is there, with the rest of the fields left blank. The old style, the clerk said yesterday. The ones without the RFID chip. I can go back to the United States as anyone I want to be, if I can figure out how to use my father's kit.

I call the front desk and tell them I'm staying one more night.

There are no directions, but I use the Janine Butler passport as my guide. The letters are in sheets that catch the light as I turn them. A plastic sheet over paper backing. The letters stay on the plastic when I peel the corner up. I choose the Nigerian passport for practice. My first task is to cut out a letter from the sheet using the razor blade provided. I have to work directly under the lamp to cut between the small letters. Next, I separate the plastic from the paper backing. When I finally have one cut, I'm not sure what to do with it. Surely, the image isn't applied with water. I try anyway and end up with a wet passport streaked with ink.

Scratching doesn't work either. There are only two tools in the kit, a roller and a razor blade. I cut out another letter and place it carefully on the page, then use the roller to apply even, firm pressure. I have to use my fingernail to move the small square of plastic out of the way. The letter W looks exactly as if were printed on the page. The big problem, I discover, is that it's hard to line up multiple letters so that it looks printed from a machine. I ruin several blanks from other countries before I have the confidence to try the blank U.S. passport. Once my biographical details are filled in, I scan Janine's passport for other details I need to replicate.

There's a stamp that says 'USA' above the picture on my passport. I find a matching stamp in the kit. I try all five inkpads to find the right blue and practice. If I press too hard, the lines bleed into each other. Too soft, and the image isn't clear enough. It's impossible to line the stamp up exactly the same way twice. I'll have to get it right on the first try.

I use up two pages of hotel stationary before I raise the stamp over my own photo in the U.S. passport. I let out my breath slowly and press down. I'm afraid to look after I lift the stamp. The result is a pleasant surprise. It's almost a perfect copy. The last feature to add is the holograph that covers the whole page of biographical info. I find a sticker the size of a passport page with the same holographic pattern. There's only one—no practicing this time.

I lay the passport out on the nightstand in preparation. The stiff paper refuses to stay open on its own, but I'll need both hands to place the holograph correctly. I can hold down the signature page with a tourist magazine, but I can't put anything on top of the page with my picture.

I'm so close. I examine and reject each of the tools at my disposal, then do it again. Something in the disorganized pile on the bed can help me, if I just think hard enough.

The glue. I find another sheet of hotel stationary and slip it under the page with my picture. Then I add two very small dabs of glue between the passport page and the stationary. I press down until the glue sets. When I lift my hand, the stiff passport pages lift the stationary up a fraction of an inch. All I need is a little more weight. I use some socks from the collection of clothing to weigh down the stationary, which in turn holds the passport page open for me to place the holograph.

My appreciation of that small triumph fades quickly as I turn to the holograph. I have one chance to get this right. I peel the holograph from its backing a millimeter at a time. Micro-currents of air in the room make the thin sheet of plastic sway, threaten to stick it to itself. I have to arrange my fingers in awkward claws to hold the sticker flat over the passport. Meditation breaths steady my hands as I lower it down. I can feel my pulse in my thumbs, where I grip the sheet. I put the edge of the holograph just below the creases where the pages meet, like where the holograph starts in Janine's passport.

Then, breath by breath, I press the sticker down. I see one small bubble, but I know better than to try to reverse the process. The iridescent ink catches the light from the lamp, dances as the sticker curves, then flattens against the page. I try to use my fingers to smooth out the bubble, and it doesn't help. Anxiety flutters my heart. I've spent hours on this one passport, and I don't have the materials to make another.

I attack the small flaw with the roller. After a few strokes, it's nearly invisible. I study my handiwork under the lamp. It's early evening now, and the sun is setting. The passport isn't perfect, but it might be close enough. If I get caught, the mere mention of my real name will be enough to put me in quarantine and keep the rest of the world safe.

The room service menu beckons again. I order a burger before remembering that evidence of my recent criminal activities is all over the room. I finish cleaning up just in time for the knock on the door.

As I eat, my stare alternates between the city sidewalks and my new passport. My mind worries over the next challenge. Transportation. The lab doesn't know I've left the country yet, but they are likely watching airports on the Eastern seaboard. I could catch a flight into the Midwest, Chicago maybe, and then head east. Without a car, it will be tricky to stay under the radar.

Or... I could finish my cruise. I fish the crumpled freighter cruise schedule out of the pile of clothes on the bed. My ship leaves Malta tomorrow. I could fly there. I tell myself it's a good plan because there's no way my father can get to me once we're out of port. And Jennifer said the trigger might be destroyed if I can stay hidden long enough. The 10 days it takes to cross the Atlantic might kill Sam for me. The truth is, I want to see some familiar faces. One face in particular.

I won't have Pablo in my heart, but I want him in my bed.

Chapter 26

The customs desk at Malta is one woman with the intimidating stare of a matron underneath thick, black eyebrows. They move like caterpillars when she says how much cash I declared. I hid what I could in the metal thermos, then carried as much as was legally allowed. I know from the guidebook I'm allowed to take 3,000 over the border, but her questions make it seem otherwise.

"It's my life savings," I explain. "I just graduated and I'm taking the year off. I'm here to catch up with my cruise."

"No cruise ships are coming in today."

I keep the smile pasted on my face. "It's a freighter cruise."

She nods, then turns to her examination of my passport. I am Sara Warren of New York, New York. That is, if my passport holds up to scrutiny. This is a good dry run. The real test will happen when I go through customs in Boston, with the agents who see thousands of U.S. passports every day. She frowns at me, but I think it's just to see if I'll squirm. Finally, she stamps the passport with a huff and returns it to me.

They are loading the last of the crates when I find my ship in the maze of the docks. I see Pablo there, pushing a cart loaded with food supplies into a wide door at dock-level. He does a double take and abandons the cart, coming over to fold me into a bear hug.

"You're all right," he says.

I can only nod. It feels like I've swallowed glass.

Pablo is about to say something else when the pot-bellied man who had threatened to take his shirt off before thumps me on the back, and I nearly fall over.

"Now Pablo can work again," he says.

Pablo was worried about me? We only spent one night together. The question on my face when I look at him makes Pablo's smile waver.

The sleeve of my coat falls back as he holds my arm up to the sailors lounging against the rail. "Look what I found!" His eyes pause on the red rings around my wrist, marks of my escape from my father's van.

I shake my head before he asks. He doesn't, though I have a feeling he will later.

"Can you finish loading the rations?" he asks the pot-bellied man.

Before his friend even nods, Pablo has taken my duffel bag and is leading the way. He takes me to the room I had before. My presence has been erased. The bed is neatly made. Everything is straightened, tucked away, and rigidly in order.

"The captain didn't think you were coming back," Pablo says.

I nod again, still unable to form any words.

"I told him you had family to visit so he wouldn't file a missing persons report." He slouches in the doorway, as if he's not sure if he's welcome. "Was that the right thing to do?"

The right thing to do would be to forget about me. "Yes," I manage. "It was the right thing."

"And you're okay?"

"I'm okay." The vulnerability in his eyes frightens me. But I'm scared of being alone more. "That's kind of heavy, isn't it?"

He looks confused, then adjusts the duffel bag on his shoulder. "Yeah, you've collected a few things."

"Can you put it by the window for me?"

His smile returns as he steps inside. I open the curtains to a gunmetal gray sky. Blue wouldn't suit my mood anyway. He hovers behind me. I can feel the warmth of him, even though we aren't touching. "Do you still have those binoculars?" I ask.

He nods.

"I'd like to take them to the balcony. See what I can spot as we head out. After your shore duties are finished, you could sit with me." I don't dare look at him. Rejection is nothing less than I deserve. "You know, if you wanted."

His hand rests lightly on my shoulder. I hold myself still to keep from leaning against him. "It's a date," he says. "I'll only be a little while."

I go up to the lounge area by myself. The selection of books on the shelf has changed slightly. Presents from my fellow passengers, I guess. The new romance novels smell like the Texas woman's perfume. I wonder if there are any passengers westbound. I haven't seen any. The quiet is nice. If I lean on the railing and crane my head, I can see one of the tugboats pulling us out of port. The physics of it seem impossible. Behind me is a massive pile of shipping containers. It adds up to over 50,000 tons of furniture, electronics, food, and toys. Yet the little tugboat, a dwarf in comparison, can pull the giant. All it takes is a little bit of pressure in the right place.

Like a bracelet slipped into a purse headed in the wrong direction. Imagining my father in Iceland makes me smile for the first time in two days. I think he was lying when he said I only won the games he let me. It doesn't really matter. He may be smarter than I am, but I'm more desperate.

Pablo finds me there, leaning on the railing. "Penny for your thoughts?"

"I'm thinking about the Immortal Game."

He leans on the rail next to me, just close enough that our elbows touch. "You mean the Highlander movies?"

"No, it's a chess thing. A famous game played in London in 1851."

His expression is indecipherable. I know it's unfair, but I can't help but compare him to Manuel. Conversation flowed so easily with my fisherman.

"The game happened during a break in the tournament between two of the greatest players of the time, Anderssen and Kieseritzky."

Pablo's waiting for me to get to the point.

"Anderssen won by giving up both of his rooks, his bishop, and his queen." The tugboat disconnects from our ship. I hear the heavy rope slap against the side as it's reeled in.

Pablo frowns. "You mean he won because he was willing to sacrifice more."

The smell of melted butter drifts out to the balcony. The cook has arrived with a plate of fish swimming in a butter sauce, dotted with green capers. "Exactly."

"You going to tell me what happened in Algeciras?"

My head shakes slightly before I can stop myself. I watch the gray waves fall over each other, an endless, ever-shifting pattern that stretches out to the horizon. "I spent too long at lunch and missed the boat."

"Fine. Don't tell me."

His anger stings. I don't dare look at his face. "You shouldn't get involved."

"You don't have to—" He stands back and loops his thumbs through his leather belt. "Never mind. Let's go have some dinner."

That's it? This is my first lover's spat, but I'm pretty sure it's not supposed to end that easily. "You don't want to see me anymore," I say. "I get it. I'll stay out of your way." I move to brush past him. If I'm quick enough, I can grab a plate of food before others arrive.

"No." He surrounds with me his arms, and I automatically curl into his chest, my hands in fists under my chin. My treacherous heart is still comparing him to Manuel. Manuel was content to let me keep my secrets. Pablo's lips brush my ear. "I have 10 days to change your mind. And you'd be surprised how convincing I can be."

As it turns out, I am the only passenger westbound. Dinner is less formal than before. Even though the men know I can understand them, they don't bother to keep their conversation clean. I do enjoy practicing my language skills. I speak French with the Algerian, Russian with the man from St. Petersburg, Mandarin with the Taiwanese man, and Italian with the Sicilian.

"Where'd you learn to speak so many languages?" demands the Algerian goodheartedly.

Pablo waits expectantly. My delayed answer draws an uncomfortable silence. "I was an army brat," I say. I squeeze Pablo's hand under the table, an apology for lying to him.

The pot-bellied man is happy with my answer, at least. "Then you must know how to play poker," he says.

I shake my head. "I don't know that game."

This excites him. He pulls out a pack of cards with naked women on them and deals in everyone who isn't leaving for a shift. I stare at the unrealistic, ponderous breasts on all the women. The pot-bellied man's face reddens, then he quickly scoops up all the cards and digs out another deck from behind the shelf. These cards have pictures of naked men on them. "We keep these around for Aleksey." That's the name of the Russian.

Those cards make me blush. "Let's just use the other ones," I mumble.

They pair me with Pablo, since I don't know anything. It's hard to concentrate on the rules leaning so close to him.

"This is a pair," he whispers in my ear. "Not a great hand, but I know Aleksey's tell. He's licking his lips. That means he's nervous. And our dealer, my fine, round friend, has a full house. He's never happy about anything less."

Our hand loses to a flush in the Algerian's hand. Brightly colored chips clack and slide as they change places. Pablo doesn't seem upset.

On the next deal, he has me hold the cards. He points to the middle card. "Jokers are wild, so we have five of a kind. Excellent hand. But I should keep talking, so they won't know the hand is good and they'll bet more." His hand tightens on my waist. "You can trust me with anything. I want you to know that. Anything."

"Enough consulting," says the Sicilian. "What's your bet?"

I nervously push two of the white chips into the center of the table, then look up at Pablo. "Good bet?"

He nods with a wink in his eye. "Good bet."

The men mistake my nervousness for uncertainty about our cards and we win the pot. The next few hands go back and forth. When our pile of chips is gone, it is dark. I yawn. With all the entertainment, fatigue snuck up on me.

I excuse myself. Pablo does, too.

We share a kiss at my door. My heart speeds up in the wrong way. Too close, too soon. Even though it's what I thought I wanted. Still, I don't want him to leave. His presence is comforting, if I can ignore his questions.

I break away and put my forehead against his chest. A tiny spot of grease stains the cotton fibers of his shirt. "I want to invite you in," I say without looking up. "But not... not for that, you know?"

He rubs my neck with a callused hand. "Not everything is about sex."

True to his word, he only curls around me when we lie down. He doesn't speak, except to whisper, "Good night." I lie awake for a long time, ashamed of the tears that leak onto the pillow. Finally, lulled by his warmth and familiarity of his arm thrown over mine, my anxieties give way to a restless sleep.

Chapter 27

By the third day at sea, I've read all books I didn't read on the voyage to Spain. Including a poker manual missing half its pages. To keep my mind occupied, I tour the deck of the ship. It's not like strolling through the park. I have to concentrate on staying out of the crew's way, and not tripping over all the equipment that clutters the deck.

Aleksey waves and smiles at me. I'm slow to wave back. As much as I try to blend in, I can see in their expressions how awkward my attempts are.

"Janine!" It's Pablo's voice and his hurried footsteps.

My heart stutters, in a good way. He spent last night in my room. And the night before that. On both nights, he did nothing more than whisper good night and hold me until I fell asleep. "More whales?" I ask jokingly.

"Follow me and you'll see." His eyes are as eager as a little boy's.

We walk up the stairs, past the lounge to a room above it. I didn't know there was anything above the lounge. He fishes a key out of his pocket, then throws the door open. It must be the fanciest suite on the boat. It's three times the size of my quarters downstairs and it has a TV with a DVD player. The windows are wider too. And in the center of the room, a bright shaft of light comes through the ceiling—a skylight.

My bag is sitting on the bed. I don't know much about what Pablo makes, but I saw the price sheet when I chose my room, and this must be more than he can afford. "It's lovely, but I can't ask you to pay—"

He grins wider. "Nobody's paying anything extra. I talked to the captain and mentioned that it doesn't cost the company anything more if you take this room. We don't pick up any more passengers until we reach Boston. Also, you've had a hard time of it because your aunt died in Spain. If he asks."

I throw myself on the bed. "I can stare up at the stars all night. I love it." Then softer, "Thank you."

He cups a hand around his ear in mock surprise. "What was that I heard? A thank you?"

I throw a pillow at him. It comes back at me before I can bring my arm up. A second later, Pablo lands on the bed. "Careful, you're smiling," he says. "You might hurt yourself." The skylight is blocked by his broad shoulders as he rolls on top of me. His face pauses inches from mine, serious and playful all at the same time.

My hands brush his cheeks of their own accord. "I'm not going to tell you what happened."

He shrugs a little too casually. "Did I ask?"

I decide not to let him. The force of his lips surprises me. He's more confident than the last time we were together. When the kiss ends, I hear myself gasp twice.

"Good?" he asks, fingers poised on my chin.

"Good," I answer.

"I have to work an overnight shift," he says. "I told the boys I'd spend the afternoon resting."

The corners of my mouth turn up. "Resting, huh?"

He releases the first button of my shirt. "A bunch of gossips, every single one of them." A second button undone. The cool air raises goose bumps on my chest. "They say you wake up in the middle of night calling my name."

A laugh bubbles up from an unfamiliar place. "You're right. A bunch of gossips." I get lost in his kisses and the blue sky I can see over his shoulder. My hands explore all of his angles and curves. We leave the windows open. We're up so high, no one can see. In the full sunlight, he can see all of my scars, and I don't care. The hum and clank of the ship's work falls away in a languid heat that stretches out for the rest of the afternoon.

Chapter 28

We have been at sea for six days now. We will dock in four. Even the distractions of pleasant nights with Pablo can't settle my nerves. I don't want breakfast. The thought of pasting on a smile for the whole crew makes me nauseous. I'll just tell Pablo I slept in.

I put another movie in the DVD player. I've made the collection of action movies on the boat my syllabus. I've learned about three different types of machine guns and how to break into a building with a laser watch. I thought I might pick up some tips on how to storm a building, but I've had no luck so far. This movie is equally useless. The hero has biceps the size of a tree trunk and Special Forces training while I have $7,000 and a passport that may or may not get me through border control in Boston. I don't even know how to begin. Sam's marker on the GPS tracker has been stopped for two days, and my GPS marker is gone. My father has discovered my ruse.

To pass the time, I make origami creatures out of last week's newspaper. I have a whole zoo when the clock tells me it's lunchtime. Hunger wins out over my nerves, and I head down to the lounge. Pablo's saving a seat for me.

Aleksey offers me a plate of salmon and round red potatoes. Even my father would approve of the food here, I imagine.

"You missed breakfast," Pablo says. "You sleep okay?"

"Just enjoying my vacation," I say.

He looks annoyed. He should know better than to ask prying questions in front of the others. Luckily, the rest of the men have more than enough to talk about. The ones who can are making plans for their time in Boston. Regulations limit how many of the crew can go ashore.

Pablo finishes his food and gets up to put his plate in the tray with the rest of dishes.

I grab his arm. "See you at dinner?"

His smile lacks the normal bravado. "Yeah, see you at dinner."

Knowing I hurt Pablo makes the afternoon pass even more slowly than the morning. I end up watching yet another action movie. This one's called *The Saint*, about a man who is the master of disguise. Makes me wish I had some makeup to play with, so I could practice some disguises of my own.

A knock on my door interrupts the ending credits.

It's Pablo, holding two trays of food. "Thought you might enjoy a quiet dinner here tonight." He glances at the TV. "Sadly, that's probably the best in our collection of movies."

We eat sitting cross-legged on the bed.

"How was work?" I ask lamely, just to break the silence.

He raises his eyebrows. "Same as everyday. Is that really what you want to talk about?"

"I don't want to talk about anything."

His fork makes a sharp clank as it drops on his plate. "What happened in Algeciras?"

"I told you," I snap. "I missed the boat because I lost track of time eating lunch."

He nudges my sleeve back until the recently healed skin of my wrist is caught in the slanted rays of the evening sun. "And your lunch attacked you?"

I yank my hand away and stretch the sleeve down until it covers my fingers too. "It was that bracelet. The metal was cheap and I was allergic to it."

"The bracelet was on your other wrist."

I'm surprised he noticed. "It's not important. It's better if you don't get involved."

With a shake of his head, he brings our trays to the desk and then sits down across from me again. Gently, slowly, he releases my clenched fingers and lifts my hand until the marks of my imprisonment are visible again. He kisses the sensitive flesh. My eyes close involuntarily. I don't know what Pablo is to me. He is more than a warm body. Less than a future. I don't even have a future—how could he be in it?

He closes my hand in both of his. "My sister was attacked when she was 16. She came home, showered away the evidence, and hid the bruises from us for days." The gravity in his brown eyes traps me. "It took me a long time to understand why. She said she was ashamed. Like somehow she deserved it."

But I did deserve it. The pain I've suffered is nothing compared to the pain I've caused. My secrets didn't seem heavy until he started asking. Now they press on my lungs and fill my stomach to bursting. "He caught me. He handcuffed me to a wall. But I escaped before anything happened. That's what the marks are."

He doesn't believe me, but he doesn't seem angry either. "You think if you tell me any details, I'll make you go to the police."

This does seem like a familiar conversation. "An ocean between us should be enough."

He shakes his head. "You tried that before."

"It's different this time."

"Your Immortal Game," he says quietly. "I remember. I wouldn't make you go to the police." There's a hardness in his eyes I haven't seen before. It's a sharp contrast to his normal jovial, gentle manner. "We didn't with my sister's attacker either."

I hug myself and study this new version of Pablo. I think there's an offer in his statement. "I can make my own revenge." Despite his nosiness, three more days with him doesn't seem like enough. I'm getting greedy with my happiness again.

"What if he follows you back to Boston? He followed you to Spain."

The fact he thinks there's only one man to worry about is a good reminder of why I can't ask for his help. "Then I'll kill him." I didn't mean to tell Pablo that. I sound like a cold-hearted murderess. He will leave me to spend the rest of my nights alone.

He pulls me down to the bed, and I feel this throaty laugh against my ear, his stubble scratching at my cheek. "That's what I thought."

This kiss I feel in a deeper place. Deeper than the places Manuel touched. Before, Pablo and I were two animals seeking warmth; now it feels like we are two creatures with the same instincts.

"I knew I wanted you from the moment I saw you," he says.

"Because I'm pretty," I snap. I am quite possibly the only woman on earth who doesn't like to be told she's beautiful. My father made me that way so I would make a better weapon.

He shakes his head. "Oh, you are pretty. But that's not what I noticed. You carried yourself with a strength, a grace. And I said to myself, that's a woman I'd like to help even if she doesn't need it."

I hope Manuel saw the same thing. I hope his last thought wasn't that he had been betrayed by a pretty lay he picked up at the harbor. I hope his last thought was that he was betrayed by a woman he loved.

Chapter 29

The beeping, roaring, and growling of the machines at the dock is jarring after so many days being cradled by the rhythms of the wind and the ocean. I pretend to be asleep until Pablo slips out. I don't know how to say goodbye to him, so I won't.

Before I get off the boat, I need to block the signal from the RFID tracker in my leg. I take the sheets of tinfoil I stole from the kitchen and wrap them over where the poison pill and the tracker were implanted, then secure the shield with first aid tape I found in the galley. I sound like the tin man when I walk. I use the rest of the tape up covering the foil entirely. It looks like the worst mummy costume ever, but it stops the foil from crackling so much. I'm not exactly stealthy, but it will do.

The Barbie watch I stole from the Harris' has been sitting on the desk for the whole cruise. Time didn't matter when we were at sea. I put the watch on my wrist again.

My father's GPS unit tells me the auxiliary lab is near a small town between Coolidge State Forest and Green Mountain State Forest in Vermont. Figures that Larry wouldn't make it easy on me. A location that rural will be difficult to get to without a car.

Hitchhiking requires too much exposure, and a taxi would attract too much attention. I'll just have to try the bus station and hope for the best. I dress slowly and collect my things in the black duffel bag on the bed. The sheets are rumpled from our last night together. Our very last night.

It's time to go. I swing the heavy bag onto my shoulder and leave the key on the desk for them to find. Lovely, warm sunlight paints the room with bright bands of yellow. I can hear the echoes of Pablo's voice. It's time to go and not look back. I hold my neck muscles rigid and walk out the door, down the stairs.

As I walk by the lounge, Pablo steps out and blocks my path. "I have one last present for you."

I conjure the memory of Manuel's neck wound to remind myself of what happens to those I get too close to. He pries open my free hand and puts a square plastic object in my palm. It's a cell phone. Without asking, he zips open the duffel bag and slips a charger inside.

"I bought the phone off one of the crew. It's prepaid, but it has nearly two hours on it." When he flips it open, one contact is listed on the screen. "Now you have my number and I have yours."

My hand closes around it. I won't give it back. I can't ever call him. "You shouldn't have."

"The ship will be in port for a few days for maintenance and repair work. I'll be touring some of my favorite bars in East Boston. Unless there's somewhere else I need to be?"

I shake my head.

He cups my elbows with his hands. I feel his breath along my hairline just before he kisses me on the forehead. "Anytime, sweetheart. All you have to do is call."

Sweetheart. I wish people would stop using that word.

Chapter 30

This time, I'm not lucky enough to get stuck in a crowd of cruise ship passengers. Border control is nearly empty, except for me and the large black duffel bag digging into my shoulder. The agent in his plexiglass booth eyes the bag suspiciously as he flips open my forged passport. He has crystal blue eyes and hair so short that it's hard to tell the color.

"Name?" he barks.

"Sara Warren."

His smile is about as friendly as a snake's. "And where's home, Ms. Warren?"

"New York."

"And did you have a happy birthday?"

Another test. I pretend like I don't know his tricks. "My birthday isn't until next month?"

"Oh, I see now." He oozes a false friendliness that puts my teeth on edge. "Need to get myself another cup of coffee, I guess. Says here you're declaring a large sum of cash."

I can be just as *nice* as he is. "I was studying abroad. This was my last semester, so I cashed out my bank account."

"What did you study?"

"Spanish."

"¿Cómo terminó el partido entre el Deportivo y Real Madrid?" *What was the score in the game between Deportivo and Real Madrid?*

"No lo sé. He estado en un barco los últimos diez días." *I don't know. For the last 10 days I was on a ship.* I'm glad I'm wearing a hoodie over my t-shirt. He can't see the wet circles forming at my armpits.

"Welcome back home, Ms. Warren."

"Sure."

My legs want to run out of the customs building, but I force myself to walk normally. Still, I don't take a full breath until I'm outside and no one's hand is pulling me back.

I hail a taxi and tell the driver to take me to the bus station. I didn't get seasick on the cruise or Manuel's boat, but within two blocks his careening style has me holding my stomach. He leaves me on a street hemmed in by tall office buildings and shorter colonial buildings made of brick or stone. Rivers of people, mostly in suits, pour out the door of the station.

One look at the bus schedule tells me I'm in the wrong place. All of these bus routes are local. I can feel the cell phone in my pocket. I bet Pablo knows how to drive.

"Stop," I whisper to myself. A businesswoman in her clicking heels and pencil skirt glances at me as she passes.

There are other places to ask for help.

I find the ticket desk. The black woman behind it keeps one hand swinging her gold hoop earring at all times.

"You want to go where?" she asks.

"Rutland, Vermont."

"That's a long trip. I can't even sell you all the tickets."

I will not call Pablo. I will not call Pablo. "Whatever you can do then," I say. "It's very important."

Her expression changes from bored to sympathetic. "Family emergency, huh?"

You could say that. I nod.

Her hands erupt in a blizzard of typing. When the red, manicured nails stop, she turns the monitor to face me. She's showing me a long list of directions on Google Maps. "You'll need to take the orange line towards Forest Hills—that ticket I can sell you. Get off at the fourth stop. Then you'll need to find Back Bay Station, the Amtrak station. Purchase one ticket for the Lake Shore Limited, and that'll get you to the right state. Then you need to get a ticket on the Vermonter line towards St. Albans. You'll have to pick up an Amtrak bus to get from the Cherry Street Transit Station to the Rutland connector."

There's no way I'm going to remember all that.

"Not that it's any of my business," she says. "But it's going to take 20 hours. If you're hoping to get there before someone quits breathing, I'd rent a car." She looks at my unassuming clothes and worn duffel bag. "Worry about paying it back later."

Sam won't quit breathing until I get there. "I'll take the ticket for the orange line, please."

By the sad look on her face, I know she's invented some sort of fiscal tragedy to explain my convoluted travel arrangements. "Here's your ticket." She hands me a square, thick piece of paper with block lettering. It doesn't say anything about the orange line, just a dollar amount. I put it in my pocket next to the cell phone Pablo gave me.

"And if it's not too much trouble, could you print that out?" I point to the screen with the complicated list of directions.

She pats my hand. "I'm not supposed to do things like that, but for you I'll make an exception."

Armed with my ticket and the printout, I take the grungy, spotted concrete steps down to the subway. Fresh wads of discarded gum wait for unsuspecting passengers at the bottom. 14 hours later, I unfold my cramped legs and step into the buzzing fluorescent lights of the Cherry Street Transit Station. Every time I blink, my eyes feel like sandpaper. There are still two bus rides left, but the next bus won't arrive for another seven hours. Nothing about the bus station invites me to wait here. Vending machines are the only source of food. Hard benches line the concrete platform. Even if I wanted to sleep with one eye open, I can't here.

I need a soft bed and a door between the world and me. I find a hotel a few blocks away from the station with signs bragging about the spectacular view of Lake Champlain. I couldn't care less.

The clerk is not happy when I tell her I don't have a credit card for the deposit. I have to pay the deposit in cash. It costs more than the room does. I hold out my passport, remembering the hotel in Màlaga. She looks at me oddly and waves it away.

"We don't need that."

If I'd known that, I wouldn't have registered using the name on my passport.

In my room, I take a quick shower and order a wake up call. I'm so tired that I don't trust myself to figure out the alarm clock. Despite my fatigue, my eyelids are propped open by the problems I know I'll need to solve once I reach Rutland. How to get to the lab, for one. How to get in. What to use as weapons. Finding Sam won't be difficult, but getting past his security will be.

I don't really fall asleep. I get dragged down into unconsciousness by my body but wake an hour later drenched in sweat. The dream, thankfully, fades as soon as I open my eyes. The relentless pattern repeats itself, until the phone jangles and a polite voice tells me it's time to wake up.

Chapter 31

The bus drops me off in Rutland an hour later, around 9 a.m. It's a small town of rolling green hills and white steeple churches. The landscape is in an awkward phase between fall and winter, with skeletal trees whose gnarled limbs make the air seem colder. The only thing open in sight is a coffee shop. There's no one on the sidewalks. A little caffeine couldn't hurt.

For a place that only serves coffee and pastries, the menu has a lot of choices. There's a small shelf of games for people to share. If I had friends, this is the sort of place I would want to meet them.

Never mind. I order the first thing my eyes land on, a latte of some sort.

"I'll have that for you at the end of the counter in just a minute," the barista says.

From the pickup counter, I can see everything she's doing. She moves about her mundane tasks with a practiced grace. She fills a small metal pitcher with cold milk, not spilling a drop. With a deft tilt, she slips the pitcher under a silver probe that sticks out of a large, rectangular machine. There's a loud hiss, almost like the hydraulic machinery on the freighter. I can see tiny bubbles forming in the milk. She leaves the pitcher there until the hissing stops. Then, she combines the milk, a shot of coffee, and splashes of flavoring from tall glass bottles.

I take a table in the back, near a stack of newspapers. The drink in my hand smells like a dessert more than a drink. The whip cream is drizzled with caramel. It tickles my tongue with its sweetness. A blue hatchback with a rusted bumper pulls up in front of the shop. I hide behind the front section of the paper while I sip my coffee, willing the caffeine to give my sleep-deprived brain a brilliant idea.

Instead, the jolt comes from a familiar voice. The voice that threatened Jennifer while I stood on her basement stairs. Larry Broderick, director of the lab. I should have checked myself into a hotel just to have some privacy. I've parked myself in the only coffee shop in town.

I lift the newspaper slightly. Two pairs of legs are standing at the counter. One set of legs is wrapped in a pair of beige khakis. The other set belongs to a woman in a faded skirt and a set of pumps that are one size too small for her feet.

"Black coffee," Larry's voice barks. "Do you want anything?"

"No, thank you," says a quiet, female voice. I don't recognize her.

The two pairs of legs, one nearly hobbling in the uncomfortable shoes, take seats close to me. There are only four tables in the whole shop. I can't hear what they're saying; the machine is hissing again.

The barista finishes her ministrations and sets two cups on the pickup counter. "Black coffee and a white chocolate latte."

"—run a medical facility," Larry says. "We're hiring because we recently lost two of our doctors."

My stomach drops. It must be Harold and Jennifer. Have they been killed? There were holding cells at the old lab. Maybe they're just being held. Jennifer said that they were the most senior members of the team, so Larry might keep them around for what's in their heads. I cling to that hope. When I break into the lab, I will rescue them first.

"Would you mind grabbing those for me?" Larry says.

She hobbles to the counter and back.

"Mr. Broderick, there must be a mistake." Her voice is barely loud enough to hear. "I would love to come work for you, but I'm—uh—not a doctor. I'm a physician's assistant."

"You're very honest." From Larry, it seems like an insult. "I noticed there's quite a long blank on your resume since your last job. You've been looking for work this whole time?"

The faded skirt. The ill-fitting shoes. She's desperate for this job. Hiring people who can't afford to lose their jobs is a good strategy for keeping people in line. I wonder if he hooked Nurse Rita the same way. X-ray vision would be nice right about now. Their table is silent.

"You're a person with values, Rebecca," Larry says. "I can see that. If I may ask, are you loyal as well?"

"Oh, yes," she says. "I think loyalty is very important."

"That'll be fine, just fine," he says. If a shark could talk, it would sound like Larry. "Just one more thing. I need to make sure you're comfortable with the work we do."

He wouldn't say the truth out loud here, right? I turn a page to make it look like I'm actually reading the paper.

"We do use animals in our research," he continues.

The newspaper crackles in my grip. I force myself to unclench my hands.

"Some of the research requires invasive procedures; would you be comfortable with that?" he asks.

"Maybe you could tell me a little more about what your lab studies?"

"I'm afraid I can't. I can't even let you visit the facility until you've signed the non-disclosure agreement. The good news is your background check came up clean."

"That is good news." Even her voice is desperate.

Larry walks her through more questions, making the poor woman more uncomfortable with each one. I squirm with her. He just wants to make sure she's desperate enough to stay after she learns the truth. I wonder if this is how Nurse Rita's interview went.

"Well, Rebecca, I think you're exactly what we're looking for," Larry finally says.

"That's wonderful, Mr. Broderick. When should I start?"

"This is our NDA. Sign it and fax it to this number. Once that's done, I'll have a courier deliver your badge and new hire paperwork."

"If I faxed this today, how soon could I start?"

"You could start tomorrow," Larry says. "You live in Mendon right?"

"We have a farm there." The promise of a paycheck has her sounding more confident already.

"Should be an easy commute for you."

My arms are glad when Larry leaves. I'm on the last page of the front section, but I couldn't tell you a word of what I read.

Just a few minutes before, I was planning to walk to the lab from Rutland. Sure, it would take a day, but there's no reason to hurry into a suicide mission. But now I know that Harold and Jennifer need help, I can't afford to wait. They're alive. They have to be.

Outside, a kid on a bike speeds by, startling an older woman pushing a stroller. A bike. I used an exercise bike for cardio tests at the lab. I could figure it out. It's just about balance, right? And I have plenty of practice with that from dancing.

I gulp the rest of my latte. The barista has her elbows on the counter, caught in a good book. "Excuse me," I say.

"Oh, didn't see you there." She closes the book hastily. "Sorry about that."

"Is there a bike shop close?"

She points to the left. "10 minutes that way. Jeff should be opening up his shop just about now."

It takes me eight minutes. I'm rushing; I don't want to be caught out in the open.

Jeff, I presume, is the man setting up a folding sign out on the sidewalk announcing a 2-for-1 sale on rims. His clothes are what I notice first. His pants only go to his shins. Thick socks hug calves that are absurdly sculpted. The shirt is skintight and garishly patterned with abstract bike wheels. His shoes make a clicking sound as he walks.

He gives me a wide smile. "Just a minute, I need to change out of these clips."

I follow him into the small shop. Bikes hang from nearly every spot on the ceiling. Racks of them line the walls. Shelves of accessories take up what little remaining space there is.

Jeff pulls off the shoes that make clicking sounds and puts on a pair of slippers. Actual fuzzy tan slippers. The pedals on his bike are odd—stems really, more than pedals.

"What can I do you for?" he asks cheerfully.

"I'd like to buy a bike." I look around the tightly packed showroom. I had expected the decision to be simpler.

"Mountain, road, or just casual? Do you want clips like I have, or just pedals?"

"Um, casual?"

"Ah, something for a beginner." From him, it doesn't sound like an insult. "I have a nice basic model that'll run you about 700. 'Course plus helmet and a little bit of gear, it'll run you closer to 900."

"Sure." I'm glad he's going to make this easy.

"Have a look at the catalog here and pick out what you want. It'll take about a week and—"

Larry could be headed back to the lab to order an execution. "I need it today. Now, actually. Do you have a floor model or something I could buy?"

He looks around doubtfully. "Most of the ones I have pre-assembled are higher-end specialized bikes. But..." He wanders around the shop, touching the handlebars like he's reintroducing himself to each one. He stops by a yellow bike with black stripes. "This one might work." He points at my bag. "You, uh, need to haul all that?"

I didn't want to make an impression, but I think I have. "Yes."

"I can install a rack for you. Shouldn't take more than 10 minutes."

"10 minutes would be fine."

"Do you have any cold weather gear in that bag?"

He's starting to sound more nosy than friendly. Perhaps the sleep deprivation is making me paranoid. I wonder if the delay is just a ruse to keep me here. My face must have given me away because he steps back, arms up.

"Sorry, I don't mean to pry. It's just that the weather's supposed to turn this afternoon, and you'll be cold if you don't have any windbreak or insulation layer."

Jeff sells me a map, a bike, a helmet, a rack, two saddlebags, lights for the front and rear, and an assortment of clothing including a face mask. With the mask on, I won't have to dive for the woods every time a car drives by.

Half an hour later and a thousand dollars lighter, I wheel my brand new bike out of the shop. I walk it along the road until there are no more houses in sight. The GPS shows the little red dot, Sam, is only five miles away. My progress is slow at first. I wobble, fall, get bruised, then get back on more times than I can count. Finally, I make it 10 yards without wobbling. Then 20. Then a whole mile. The gravel road is bumpy, reminding me of my bruises with every pebble. I pass through Mendon, the little town where the unfortunate Rebecca lives. From the road, the town is just a gas station, a town hall that seems tired of doing business, and a one-story motel.

A few cars pass, but none give me a second glance. Jeff was right about the weather. The afternoon has turned chilly, and my breath puffs out in white clouds through the holes in the mask. The layers that made me sweat all morning now feel just right.

I stop again to check the little red dot on the GPS. I've actually traveled farther away from Sam. I check the map. There are no other roads that cut through this section of the county. It must be one of those driveways I passed. I'll have to stop at every one. I have no idea what I'm looking for.

The first driveway is marked with a weatherworn 'No Trespassing' sign. A length of rusted chain blocks the driveway. The chain hasn't been moved recently—I can tell because the gravel beneath it is undisturbed.

The second driveway has a sign of a similar vintage, tilted and pockmarked by bullet holes. A shed leans at the same angle as the sign, its graying wood splintering in places. The driveway continues past the shed. A property that looks like it hasn't been used would be a good cover. I can't say for sure this driveway doesn't belong to the lab, but it doesn't look right.

If the next driveway doesn't look like it, I'll turn around. I tell myself that three more times before I find something more promising. The 'No Trespassing' sign is tilted here, but it looks deliberate. The fence post isn't as weathered. I stash my bike in the woods and creep closer, listening carefully for approaching cars. There's a price tag, still lily-white, on the back of the sign. The brush along the sides of the driveway is freshly cleared, some of the cut ends still oozing with sap. All I can see from where I stand is more driveway, curving away into the forest.

There's no way around it—I'll just have to walk down there. In the trees. I hide my bike in the woods, careful to cover it with leaves and brush. I leave the saddlebag with my extra clothes behind. The other saddlebag will come with me. If a guard stumbles over a lost bike and some clothing, it will be a note in a report. If they find a bag with multiple passports and a roll of cash, they'll radio back to the lab immediately.

Walking in the forest with no trail is not easy going. I crawl over fallen trees up to my waist and stub my toes on roots. I swear the smaller branches are deliberately jumping out to scratch at my face.

A car passes, and I freeze. Any move I make will shake the limbs around me. But they won't see me if I stay still. I focus on my purpose to keep my heart calm. I wait until I can't hear the gravel crunching to move on.

I'm not sure how far I've traveled, but it takes a half hour before I see something familiar. No, identical. A tall chain-link fence with softly gleaming razor wire at the top. The lab looks exactly the same, too. An L–shaped building with rounded ends and a small parking lot. From here, I can see several trees with limbs extending over the fence. They changed locations so suddenly that they haven't had time to trim the trees back.

As I go closer, I hear the slight buzz from the electric fence. It's mid-afternoon, but the chill is the same as the evening I escaped. I shiver, even in my warm clothes. Harold and Jennifer might be in there.

I should have planned better. I can get past the fence, but I have no idea how I'm going to get in the lab. I search the saddle-bag I brought with me for anything that I could use as a weapon. There's nothing.

When I was in the lab, sometimes I saw guards propping open the back door, the emergency exit, to smoke. They would disable the alarm from their desk and turn it back on when they were done. Maybe they do that here too.

If I could set up a distraction to lure them away, I might have enough time to slip inside. My watch has a timer. The beeping might be enough to get their attention.

The trees present a dilemma. The branch with the shortest distance to fall is also the thinnest. Some of the leaves at the end are dry and withered, like the branch is sick. It might drop me on the fence instead of over it. I choose the tree with the thickest branch that extends over the fence, even though it will be a longer fall. There's no good place to hide my bag on the ground. I bring it up with me and hang it on a twig, hidden by the changing foliage. I ease myself onto the branch, moving one inch at a time. It will be a long fall—15 feet or so.

Stuntwomen do this all the time. Vogue profiled one once. There's a trick to it, if I can just remember.

I'm about to break the cover of the leaves when the emergency exit opens. I freeze. I can't risk climbing down. As long as whoever it is doesn't look up, I'll be okay.

Two men in uniforms prop the door open. The taller one turns over a box of cigarettes and taps it twice against his palm before opening the plastic wrapper. The shorter one has the lighter. My legs, folded into a precarious crouch, start to protest.

"They have the director squirming, don't they?" the taller one says.

The shorter one smiles, revealing a row of uneven teeth. "With all the security those VIP's brought with them, we should have been able to take the day off."

Extra security. Just my luck.

For a few drags of their cigarettes, the two men savor the thought of Larry squirming. The taller one glances sideways inside the door as if he's worried about who might overhear them. "If they find her, I'm taking off."

The shorter one isn't nearly as confident. "You mean go AWOL?"

The taller one nods. "I overheard the doctors they have in the holding cells talking."

Harold and Jennifer are alive. I close my eyes in relief and nearly lose my perch.

"That crazy guy who volunteered for the gene therapy, they say he's the trigger," the taller one continues. "And if they bring her in the same building... I don't care if the director thinks it's safe."

"Yeah, easy for him to say. He's already vaccinated. The new batch of vaccine isn't ready yet."

"That Larry guy is fuckin' crazy. Sends all the vaccinated guards out into the field to look for her and leave the new guys here."

"But AWOL?" the shorter one asks. He tries to take a drag of his cigarette calmly and fails.

"I'm going to tell the others too," boasts the taller one.

A germ of an idea plants itself in my head. If I can just get close to Sam undetected, none of the guards will dare interrupt us.

The shorter one nearly drops his cigarette. "You want to organize a mutiny? You heard Larry's plan for the doctors who helped Sarina. He's only keeping them alive in case he needs to use them to bring her in."

So they're safe for the moment. Until Larry either catches up with me or loses his patience.

"If everyone goes AWOL, they can't discipline all of us."

They move on to complaining about the food, then the living quarters, and then the shortage of good bars in Rutland. The only muscles in my legs that don't ache now are the ones that have fallen asleep from staying crouched for so long. Their cigarettes run out before their complaints. The shorter one throws the stub of his cigarette against the fence. It sparks against the silver wires before falling into the leaves. I watch the red embers fade to black as the door shuts.

I inch myself out onto the branch again. The fall looks much farther from this perspective. Extra security certainly doesn't help my chances. And maybe I shouldn't rush in, like I wanted to. One night, I tell myself, to come up with a better plan. I can backtrack to Mendon, stay at that little motel. The gas station might have something I can use for a weapon. At this point, even a plastic fork would improve my odds.

Chapter 32

A short bike ride takes me back to Mendon and the motel, which is a string of five rooms attached to a manager's office. The long shadows of the late afternoon sun highlight the cracked sidewalk and the weeds slowly breaking up the parking lot. A breeze kicks up, cooling the sweat on my face. The manager's office is locked, even though the hours listed on the door says it should be open. As the wind settles, a white piece of paper taped to the window whispers against the glass. The note says to check in at the gas station next door.

I was hoping to minimize the number of people that saw me. I wonder if my lodging choices would be better in Rutland. It's only a few miles away, easy enough with my bike. Except that Rutland is where the guards talked about drinking on their night off. And where Larry stopped for coffee. No, it's safer here. There's only one car at the pumps of the gas station, a blue hatchback with a rusted bumper. I saw it outside the coffee shop earlier.

It could be Larry.

I hear liquid sloshing on the other side of the concrete column. The driver must be grabbing the window cleaner. There's nowhere to hide in the patch of short weeds that separates the motel parking lot from the gas station. Before I can decide what to do, Rebecca steps out from behind the column. My odd clothes disguised me on the bicycle, but they make me conspicuous here. She smiles politely and returns her attention to the gas pump.

This is bad. Very bad.

I often heard the guards complaining about what they sarcastically referred to as the yearbook. It's a book kept locked up in the director's office that has the names and pictures of everyone in the lab. There's only one copy. All employees are expected to memorize the faces and names attached to them. The badges employees carry at the lab don't have any writing or pictures, so they can't be traced back to the lab if they are lost. When Rebecca shows up for work tomorrow, she will be shown the yearbook. She'll recognize me. Then Larry will know I'm here. I'll have to get into the lab tonight, or not at all.

Rebecca hums softly and sticks the nozzle into her gas tank. I turn toward the gas station, hoping there's a bathroom I can hide in until she drives away. Turning back to the hotel now will only look suspicious. I hear the nozzle click and shut itself off as I walk toward the door.

Out of the corner of my eye, I see Rebecca reach into the car and grab a manila envelope. She hugs it to her chest with a smile. It must the paperwork from the lab that Larry said would come by courier. Inside the gas station, a stocky woman with a name tag that reads 'Wanda' guards rows of cigarette packs and lottery tickets. She tells me the bathrooms are outside.

Great. I duck into the aisle with the chips and try to slouch out of sight as Rebecca enters. She motions for Wanda to lean over the speckled counter. "I got that job," Rebecca whispers. "At that lab that just opened. I'm not supposed to tell anyone, but I'm just so excited." She blinks back something that I think are tears. "We'll be able to keep the house."

Rebecca's confession earns her a hug from Wanda.

"They even gave me my badge." She pulls out a plain white plastic card that looks identical to the ones Harold and Jennifer used to carry around all the time in the lab. I stare at the hair dye and toiletries next to the chips while Rebecca gets a second hug. Maybe I won't have to break into the lab tonight after all.

Wanda and Rebecca are discussing some medical problem of Wanda's now, completely oblivious to my presence.

Rebecca turns to leave. I straighten up so I will look more official. I'm too young to be anyone she interviewed with, but I might pass as a secretary. She's halfway to her car. Now she's opening the door.

I hear Pablo's voice urging me on.

"Rebecca?" I say. My tone comes out falsely sweet, with the insincere politeness of someone in charge.

She freezes, like prey sensing a threat. "Yes?"

"I'm with the lab," I say. "I'm Larry's secretary. I was going to call you after I finished my bike ride, but since I ran into you—"

"You probably overheard," she says, scared now. "I'm so sorry I mentioned the lab. I know I shouldn't talk about it, but it's been such a hard few months, and the bank calls every day, and..." She sniffs, about to cry.

"A minor mistake," I say. "I'm sure it won't happen again."

She nods slowly. "So I still have a job?"

"Oh, of course. Our little secret. What I needed to talk to you about was your background check. There's been a mix-up with your paperwork. I'll need to take your badge until we get it cleared up."

She looks like she might cry again.

"It's a paperwork thing," I assure her. "Nothing for you to worry about." Nurse Rita's second favorite complaint was all the paperwork at the lab. Her first, of course, was me.

Hesitantly, Rebecca holds out her badge. I try not to look eager as I take it. "So I can't start tomorrow?"

"I'm afraid not. Someone checked the wrong box on one of the forms, and now... Well, I won't bore you with the details. But in the meantime, we have to follow procedure."

"Of course," she says, eyes downcast.

"Someone will contact you soon and send a new badge over."

She doesn't look any less upset. She might call someone at the lab just to ask for reassurances. "We're very excited to have you on board though," I say quickly. "And since this is our mistake, you'll still be paid for tomorrow."

This seems to settle her nerves. Her handshake is firm and dry. "Thank you, thank you, Ms.—I never caught your name?"

Shit. "You can call me Ellen."

I keep the handshake going for a second longer than I should to memorize her face. Her cheekbones, low and prominent. Her nose, long and straight. Her eyes, smaller than mine and farther apart. Her eyelashes are longer, though it could be the mascara she has painted on.

Too fast, she's gone, mumbling more thank you's.

In the gas station I pick up a bottle of hair dye and one of everything in the cosmetics aisle. The expiration dates aren't promising. For dinner I buy cheddar sour cream potato chips and mini-donuts. After so many years of strictly healthy food, I have some making up to do.

Wanda raises her eyebrows at my purchases. I don't offer any explanations. By tomorrow afternoon, I will either be dead or gone.

While she's ringing everything up, I remember that I need more foil and first aid tape too. The day's exertions have nearly sweated the sheets of foil loose. The can of roach killer is also tempting as a weapon, but the metal detectors at the lab would catch it. Unlike everything else in the store, the roach killer appears freshly stocked. I wonder that says about my accommodations for the night.

"Who do I talk to about rooms at the hotel?" I ask.

"You're looking at the owner, the proprietor, and the maid."

"One room then," I say. "Two nights." I don't want her finding evidence of my transformation until after I'm long gone.

She reaches under the counter and produces a key. A scratched keychain with '5' in gold lettering is attached. She doesn't blink when I pay for the room and the deposit in cash. It makes me wonder what types of people pass through here.

"I'll be working the counter here until I find a new full-timer," she says. "So you know where to find me if you need anything."

I do need something I can't buy here. None of the clothes I have are suitable for a first day at a new job as a physician's assistant. "Is there a clothing store close?"

She looks even more curious. When I don't offer an explanation, she points down a small road that runs past the gas station and bisects the main highway. "There's a thrift store down that road a piece. It closes soon, though."

"Thanks."

I carry the bulging bag of makeup and junk food to my room, then hop on my bike to find the thrift store. Wanda's directions are good. The building is a squat, beige structure in the middle of a scrubby lot. One bored clerk lounges at the sole checkout counter, barely looking up when I enter. The selection is bare. This is probably what Rebecca had to choose from too. Finally, I unearth navy pants and a matching blazer that were the height of fashion in the late nineties. The stiff fabric adds pounds to my figure. Good.

A nasally voice over the loudspeaker announces that the store will close in five minutes. The clerk is looking directly at me. I dig through the blouses quickly, settling on the one with stains that won't show when I have the blazer on.

The cars on the road all have their headlights on as I bike back to the motel. The room is cleaner than I expected, but there's nothing fancy here. I have to carry the bedside lamp into the bathroom just to get enough light to work on my transformation into Rebecca. I follow the packages on the hair dye package exactly, and I still ruin two hand towels.

The makeup takes longer. The cosmetics I had in the lab were of higher quality. The stuff at the gas station was cheap to start with, and most of it has sat on the shelf a while. The first step is to add a few years to my face. I add shadows to my cheeks and underneath my eyes. I use dark brown eye shadow to add subtle lines to my forehead, around the eyes. A coat of foundation blends them in nicely.

A few more artful shadows give the illusion of lower cheekbones. The long eyelashes are easy to accomplish with mascara. Making my eyes appear smaller is trickier. I have to exaggerate my nose and cheekbones. Some strokes of blue eye shadow tone down the green in my eyes. It's a good first try.

I wash my face and start over. After some practice, my disguise is respectable. I fall asleep thinking of Harold and Jennifer, hoping nothing happens to them before I get there.

Chapter 33

I wake up before my alarm. The pillowcase is smeared with eye shadow and foundation, even though I scrubbed my face. I don't remember tossing and turning. I guess last night's rest is only good in comparison to how I've slept lately.

There's no point in rushing. I never saw any of the medical staff in before 8 a.m. Most of them didn't arrive until 9. The guards at the auxiliary lab are all new. They'll only know my face from pictures. My disguise isn't likely to fool the medical staff; they saw me up close every day. That means I need to arrive late for Rebecca's first day of work. Hopefully by the end of the day, a tardy employee will be the least of Larry's problems.

I spread out everything I have on the bed to examine my options for weapons. The entrance has a metal detector, which rules out a knife or a gun. If I even knew how to get one. The tired, once-white bag that Jennifer gave me has cords that could be used for strangulation, but I don't have the strength to overpower the guards. A well-placed strike with the pen on the nightstand might be lethal, but that's beyond my skills.

As I disqualify each item, I move it to a different pile on the bed. Eventually, the only thing left is the picture Harold gave me. His and Jennifer's smiles waver between happy and mocking in my fragile state of mind. *Do you really think you can rescue us?* they seem to ask. I can almost hear Jennifer's bitter voice telling me I'm the closest thing they have to a daughter.

I need to think like my father. There are four types of weapons: conventional, biological, nuclear and chemical. Conventional is out. Biological weapons kill too slowly. Nuclear, ditto, unless I had some sort of explosive. That leaves chemical.

None of the dangerous chemicals at the gas station were small enough to fit in my pocket. Most of them were in metal aerosol cans. But I did buy a travel-size bottle of hairspray. There's a way to make a cheap pepper spray using ground chilies and water. I saw it on a gardening program once.

I'll just have to make it in a concentration suitable for human-sized slugs.

At the gas station, I have my choice of chili powder or hot sauce. I choose hot sauce. The mixture makes my eyes tear when I test it in the bathroom. I can only afford one test, or I'll arrive at the lab with red eyes.

Time to get dressed and do my makeup. The stiff rustling of the navy pants covers the crinkling of the foil around my upper legs. When I'm done, I'm a passable imitation of a woman 10 years older and 30 pounds heavier. I put on my helmet carefully to avoid rubbing off the morning's work. The saddlebags are already secure on the bike rack.

There are no more tasks to delay me.

I brush my hand against the phone Pablo gave me, snug in my pocket, knowing I should leave it behind.

I think of poor Rebecca nervously waiting for good news in the house she can't afford. My remaining cash is much more than I need.

There's no notepad, but the Bible on the nightstand has a blank page. I tear it out. I'm beyond redemption anyway. I leave one green brick of cash on the bed with a note: *For your friend Rebecca.* Maybe Wanda will take one of the bills for the towels I ruined. Maybe I've misjudged her and she'll take all of them.

The ride to the lab feels too short. I have been traveling for weeks, and it comes down to this: two rubber wheels on a gravel road. I ditch the bike a mile before the driveway, so no guards will find it, and walk the long driveway up to the lab

My heart hammers in my chest when I reach the gate. It's not the possibility of dying. I can't even imagine what I'll do if I survive this. It's the possibility of failing halfway. Of getting in, not dying, and never getting out again.

Rebecca wouldn't feel any of these things. I swipe her badge clumsily at the gate sensor. Machinery grinds. I square my shoulders and walk across the newly paved parking lot. The front door opens easily. I don't know why I was expecting it to stop me. I can hear the foil wrapped around my legs crinkle as I walk. But I can also hear the swish of my pant legs, the swirling air of the ventilation system, and a foot lightly tapping on the floor. Fluorescent lights hum above a maintenance closet next to the guard's desk. The guard behind the desk is watching me carefully.

Here goes nothing. I remind myself the guard doesn't know my voice. All he knows of Sarina is a photograph he'd have to pull from memory.

"I'm Rebecca, the new hire." I smile so hard my foundation must be cracking. I hold out my hand. That's the socially correct thing to do, right? The name embroidered on his fatigues tells me his name is Palmer.

"Not many people arrive on foot," he says. When he speaks, I can see the points of his canine teeth. He has large brown eyes that are about as welcoming as barbed wire. The set of his jaw reminds me of the pit bulls rescued from fighting rings I've seen on television. The top dogs who are well fed, criss-crossed with scars, and absolutely obedient.

"A friend dropped me off at the driveway. My car had to go into the shop. What a day for it to break down, huh?"

He shakes my hand mechanically, then consults a list in a book. As I expected, the book has no pictures. "Rebecca Harrington," he says. "The director said to give you this packet. Also, you'll need to see Dan to set up your biometrics. All of the rooms for our research subjects are protected with retina scanners."

The subjects. I was a subject. I wonder if Sam realizes he's a prisoner.

My first task of the day is to get to Harold and Jenny. Once the lab realizes I'm here, they'll lock everything down.

"I'm supposed to check on the prisoners in the holding cells today," I say. "Can you tell me where they are?"

He gestures without looking up from his magazine. "Through the double doors and to the left."

I walk past the imposing metal detectors, hoping the thin layer of aluminum foil around my legs won't set them off. Before I put Rebecca's card up to the lock, I look through the narrow windows to make sure no one who will recognize me is in the hallway. Nurse Rita is there, eyes focused on a chart in her hand. I pretend to look in my purse for something until she enters an office. I wave the card over the lock, one eye on the door Nurse Rita disappeared into. The millisecond before the lock beeps feels like an eternity.

There's another hallway on the left, just like the guard said. I duck into it just as I hear a door open behind me. Breathe slower, I tell myself. *Calm down.*

I was never allowed in this part of the old lab. I walk tentatively down the long corridor. There are no rooms here, and no other hallways. Just one door at the end, with a reinforced window. Through the wires, I can see a guard with his feet up on the desk. He's nursing a bottle of soda, giving more of his attention to his television than the door.

I hide my homemade pepper spray in my hand. One shot to the eyes should be enough to get his gun. I open the door like I'm meant to be there, but it just jerks in the frame. Locked. The guard looks up. I give him a friendly smile and wave. He lifts his feet off the desk like it's a chore, then I hear a click as he motions for me to come in.

The sounds of a couple screaming at each other on a daytime talk show fill the room. There are two cells, each with toilets and a slot for food to be pushed through the bars. In the one closest to the guard, Harold is lounging on the bottom bunk, his leg still in a cast. Jennifer sleeps on the level above him. They look as if they haven't showered in a couple days, but otherwise they seem all right. I'm not too late. When I see the person in the next cell, my hand clenches so hard I nearly pepper spray myself.

It's my father. He hasn't seen me yet. I turn my back to the cells quickly.

The guard leans forward to adjust the volume on the television, like I'm interrupting his real work. "Yes?"

My voice catches in my throat. Harold will recognize me the second I speak, but he won't give me up. Who knows what my father has planned. He knows the lab will do anything to keep me here.

"Miss?" the guard asks.

I tell myself it doesn't matter. My father's presence doesn't change the plan. "I'm the new hire. I'm here to do a health check on the prisoners." Even though I know I shouldn't, I risk a glance over my shoulder. Harold is alert now, watching me carefully. My father is also watching, wearing his best predatory smile.

"One cell at a time," the guard says. "And I'll need you to sign in." When he reaches for a binder with signatures in it, I bring my little plastic bottle up. The soft hiss of the spray is followed instantly by the guard's swearing. The blowback leaves me coughing. I go for his weapon before my lungs recover, lunging into the cloud still hanging in the air.

It stings like being burned. The gun blurs as my eyes tear. My hands close around the black grip and yank. The holster stops me. Despite his red eyes and near-constant cough, the guard's hand close over mine.

"Sarina," my father says. "I knew you would come."

The guard releases my hands and reaches for a metallic box sitting on his desk, much like the one Martin had. I fumble for the snap and release his weapon, then back away. He hovers his hand over the kill button. "You shoot me and you die anyway. Drop the gun."

It's all too familiar. My throat closes over my threats.

"Fine," the guard says, and he lets his hand drop on the button. He looks confused when nothing happens., exactly like Martin did. I'd like to avoid shooting him. I won't give my father the satisfaction of seeing me kill.

"Do exactly as I say, and I'll let you live." I have no idea how I'm going to keep him quiet. I must sound more confident than I feel, because he doesn't protest. "Put your handcuffs on the desk." Guards in prison always have handcuffs, right?

He puts a bundle of plastic zip ties next to the signature book. The ink is running from my pepper spray. My father clucks disapprovingly in the background.

"Tie your wrists to the chair. One wrist to each armrest."

He finishes the second wrist by pulling on the zip tie with his teeth. It's only then I set down the gun. I zip tie his ankles to the base of the chair and make a gag from his belt and his socks.

"Our chances are better if you kill him," my father says.

I search through the guard's desk for keys. "I'm not going anywhere with you." I should have asked before I gagged him.

"The locks are computer-controlled," Harold says. Jennifer sits up and hops to the floor.

I move the mouse on the guard's computer and, sure enough, a diagram of the cells pops up with buttons for unlocking and locking the doors. With one click, the door on Harold and Jennifer's cell opens outward silently.

Jennifer jumps down from her bunk and hugs me, then stands back and shakes her head. "You shouldn't have come."

"I told you she would," my father says. "Clever how you got away in Spain. I followed that bracelet all the way to Reykjavik before I figured out it wasn't you."

"I've heard enough from you over the past week," Harold snaps. "We're leaving you here for Larry."

I take the guard's RFID badge and give it to Jennifer. "This will get you out the back door. From there, you can…" They can what? Climb the electric fence with one person in a cast?

Jennifer's hand clamps down on my arm. "You're coming with us."

"You don't know her like you think you do," my father says to them. "She didn't come here to rescue you."

Harold rolls his eyes.

My father's accusation makes my words tumble out. "I didn't know that Larry had you locked up. Until yesterday."

"It doesn't matter what you came here for," Jennifer says. "What matters is that you leave here with us."

My father's mocking laugh grates on my nerves. "You still think you belong with people like them, Sarina?"

I remind myself that I may have come here for Sam, but I put the rescue mission first. "Save your breath. I'm not letting you out." The strength in my voice doesn't match the unsteadiness in my legs.

"Let me out?" He laughs again. He fiddles with the something near the lock, a bit of string that's only visible if you look closely. The door swings open. "I broke the lock days ago. I was just waiting for you."

Jennifer puts herself in between us like a sentry. "You fooled me once, old man. You won't fool me again. Get into our cell or I'll shoot you myself."

Harold goes to the door and peeks out the window. "Shift change is soon. We need to go."

I'm transfixed by my father's green eyes, so much like mine. They have a knowing, merry, malicious twinkle. He predicted I would come here. I wonder if he knows me better than I give him credit for.

"You belong with me, Sarina," my father says. "See how easily you outsmarted Larry? He never expected you would come here. You won't save yourself by killing Sam. You'll just make yourself more valuable. If you want your freedom, you'll work with me. We'll found a new society. You won't have to follow anyone else's rules ever again."

I push Jennifer out of the way and point the gun at my father's heart. My finger won't pull the trigger. A shot will bring the guards. Killing him means I don't get Sam, and leaving Sam alive means my father wins.

"No, it's not that you want, is it?" My father steps closer. I stumble back against the desk.

Harold looks down the hall again. "Don't let the bastard in your head. We've been listening to this bullshit for days."

"You want another boy toy?" my father asks. "Or a cute little nuclear family in a dollhouse?"

Every muscle in my body is frozen with a disgusting revelation. I'm tempted by the simplicity of the vision he offers. I could be a dark princess under an evil king. It would be so much easier for a person like me to not care about what happened to others. All the pain I felt over the past few weeks, all the guilt I've carried for years, could go away.

"With my friends, with my money, we can buy whatever you want," he says. "I can buy 10 of those dumps like the one the Harrises had."

It wasn't a dump. It was a place where people were loved.

"I could buy you—no, even better—make you a baby sister."

I see Rose's head lying peacefully on the table, a contradiction to her startled green eyes. I don't need a gun to kill him. I lunge at my father, letting the gun clatter to the floor behind me. His head cracks against the concrete. I use my elbows, knees, and fists to smash at whatever I can reach. Fine, wet sprays of blood cover my arms and hands. His lip splits open. His eye swells. He laughs. I don't stop.

He's still grinning, even with his teeth coated in blood. I grab his ears and slam his against the concrete. I will keep going until that damn smile leaves his face. Until he's dead and cold.

I feel a hand rest gently on my shoulder. "Sarina," Harold says. "He's not fighting you."

I propel myself back, arms windmilling, as if my father's touch were infectious. My outfit is covered in the evidence of my rage. I am my father's daughter. A look at him confirms my savagery. A fountain of blood streams from his nose. Bruises cover his arms where I kneeled on them. One of his teeth is resting by the wall.

He pushes himself up to his elbows. "You should be proud, Sarina. I knew you had it in you."

Harold's eyes narrow. He's leaning against the wall, holding the gun. In his other hand, he has the guard's soda bottle. My father puts the picture together too late. Harold sticks the gun into the neck of the bottle and shoots my father in the heart. The bottle dulls the sound of the shot. Tiny droplets of the brown liquid cover my father's body. What's left in the bottle drips and foams along the exploded plastic edges. The room smells sweet —sickeningly so—and I nearly gag.

I open my mouth to scream at Harold. Jennifer glues a hand over my mouth and wraps me in a backward hug. Even biting and kicking doesn't make her let go.

Harold is back at his post by the door. "No one's coming. There's nothing on the radio. I think the soundproofing covered the shot."

I feel Jennifer's nod against my shoulder. "I guess we can thank Larry for one thing."

That's why the guard's TV seemed so loud when I came in. I *could* have shot my father if they'd just told me. My heart stutters, and I know I have to stop fighting her. She releases me a minute later.

"Why didn't you let me finish him?" I hiss at Harold.

"You would have regretted it," he says.

I won't tell him that he's right. "Get out of here while you still can. You said the shift change was soon."

Jennifer checks the clock. "In five minutes. You're coming with us." She sounds positively parental.

I won't leave until Sam is dead. "You need someone to distract the guard at the front desk," I point out. "They're not going to let you walk out."

Jennifer purses her lips. "And you'll follow us."

I hope my nod is convincing. I take the gun from Harold. "I'll get the guard away from the door long enough for you to get out. Are your car keys here?"

She doesn't quite believe me, but she can't argue with the logic. "My purse is in the guard's desk somewhere."

While she searches, I take silver box that will trigger the poison pill. Only the guard sees me, and he can't say anything.

"Give me two minutes," I say. "Then go to the front."

"We'll wait for you at the end of the driveway," Jennifer says.

If I'm going to convince her, I'll have to make this look real. I lean my head close to hers and whisper as if the guard shouldn't overhear us. "Go two driveways to the east. There's a shed there where you can hide the car. It's only a half-mile. I'll meet you there."

"We're going to wait for you," Harold says. "And if you don't show up, we're coming back."

I bite my lip. "You won't have to, I promise." Once the lab goes into lockdown, they won't have a choice. No one will be able to get in or out.

The guard's radio squawks, announcing his replacement is on his way. I nod one last time at the closest thing I have to parents, then walk to the front desk with my heart beating too fast.

Palmer is still on duty. His eyes widen at the state of my clothing.

I giggle like I'm embarrassed. "I spilled a whole unit of blood from the fridge." They always kept several in case something went wrong with surgery. "Rita sent me for cleaning supplies. Can you let me into the maintenance closet?"

They're never supposed to leave their post when they're on shift. He glances at the parking lot and then behind him at the hallway. For the moment, no one is coming. He frowns, but carries a bristling ring of keys toward me. I wait until both of his hands are busy, one turning the key and one turning the handle, before I put the gun at his back.

"Hands on your head." That's what they say in the movies. I didn't think to bring the plastic ties from the other guard. I'll find something in the closet.

He obeys stiffly. He'll fight me the first chance he gets.

I take his gun and his radio. "Inside the closet." It's dark, but all the rooms at the lab have motion-detecting switches. The door shuts behind me. In the split second after the closet goes pitch black, I realize I've miscalculated. The light isn't turning on. Palmer slams me against the door with one hand, his other hand at my back as he's fumbling for the door handle. I can't let him get out, but I was bluffing about the gun. Harold and Jennifer will never get out if I bring the rest of the guards—and their guns—to the front door.

Palmer won't have any qualms about shooting me, though. I throw both guns, his and mine, as far away as I can. From the thump and the clatter, I think they fall behind a shelf. The door opens a fraction under Palmer's efforts. I kick it back. He puts both hands on my waist and tries to pull me away. The soles of the cheap pumps I found at the consignment slip against the floor. I wiggle them off and dig my heels in, searching for hand-holds in the pitch-black. Grease slips under my fingernails as I grab at the hinges. My other hand finds a shelf. It sways in my grip and threatens to fall.

My opponent releases me to steady it; he knows it would block the door. Five minutes. I just need to give them five minutes. As long as it takes for them to get to the door and out of the parking lot. Palmer gives up on trying to move me and starts hammering my gut with his fists. I count the seconds, wondering how long I can hold out as a punching bag. He takes a timeout, two panting breaths, before starting on the next round. Now his knuckles are landing on bruises as they form. I double over in pain, held up only by his blows. I have to find a weapon. I can feel the round, plastic necks of bottles—nothing heavy enough to do any damage. My free hand could get the pepper spray, but my eyes are still itching from my encounter with it earlier. In such close quarters, it will incapacitate us both.

A fist in my stomach empties my lungs. The radio I clipped on my belt bruises my hip as I'm pushed against the door. The heavy brick of a radio. It comes off my belt with a snap. I aim my strikes at the warm breath against my shoulder. The back of my hand grazes just under his chin. He gasps in pain and steps back, coughing. I hammer at every shadow that moves, following the sound of his coughs.

"If that's how you want it," he mutters.

I have no idea what he means until I see the gleam of metal lit by an indicator on the radio. A knife. Now I'm dodging the shadows instead of attacking them. I bounce off the shelves that line the walls, listening for the whoosh of his arm. He grabs me by the hair, yanking my head back. My eyes have nearly adjusted to the dimness.

Just in time to see the whites of his eyes as he holds the knife to my throat.

He tilts my head back further, until my muscles scream. "There are two ways this ends, with you dead or with you captured. Take your pick."

That's an easy choice. I drop down, feeling chunks of hair rip from my skill. I can't go forward or backward, so I scamper to the side. The knife slashes in my direction, then I hear swearing and a shelf rattling. His arm is stuck.

I grab as high up as I can on the shelf and pull. Plastic bottles of chemicals bounce and roll as the shelf crashes to the floor. An eerie quiet follows. He moans softly, and the shelf creaks as he tries to move. I paw at the wall by the door until I find a light switch. Beneath a mound of paper towels and bleach bottles and glass cleaner, I see his head moving slightly. I clear the pile with sweeps of my bruised arms. It's the second time I've wanted to puke today.

He's impaled himself with the knife between two ribs. I can't tell if the wound is fatal.

"I'm sorry," I stutter.

The guard's eyebrows lift in surprise.

I find two mop heads and press them against his wound. He may live, as long as I don't remove the knife. Air cools streaks of his blood on my right thigh. A swipe of his knife ripped through the foil shielding the poison pill. At least the shield on the tracker is still intact.

The radio on the floor crackles to life with a voice I don't recognize. "All units, all units, facility is in lockdown. Dr. Wocek is dead. The other prisoners have escaped. Sarina is on premises. I repeat, Sarina is on premises. The kill button is inoperable."

It sounds like the mic is being taken away; then there's another voice on the radio. "Take her alive if you can, boys," Larry says.

I see the dull black handle of one of the guns underneath a pile of bathroom soap. There's no time to look for the other one. The guard we tied up at the cells will report that I headed back to the lobby. Soon, they will find the wounded Palmer. Maybe he'll live.

I turn off his radio, then clip it to my belt. His RFID badge will be useful too. I leave the closet door open so they will find him sooner.

I've watched them do lockdown drills before. All non-military personnel are supposed to stay wherever they are. Half of the men will be sent to secure the perimeter while the other half will be searching for me. In civilian garb, I'll stick out like a sore thumb.

Through the front door, I can see a car waiting just beyond the front gate. It must be Harold and Jennifer. They'll have no choice but to leave now.

I head back to the hallway. A stampede of military boots is coming from the holding cells. I duck into the first office I find. It's empty. If I wait for the footsteps to go to the lobby, maybe I can make it to the main lab area before they backtrack.

A rustle of fabric and the scrape of a wheel make me turn, gun in hand. It's Nurse Rita. She looks at my gun, my torn jeans with slivers of foil hanging out, and the silver box on her desk. Another kill switch. I wonder if my aim is good enough to kill her while she reaches for it.

My finger hesitates on the trigger as Palmer's moans echo in my ears. There has to be another way. "How did Larry keep you here?"

Her upright arms waver in surprise. "What?"

"I overheard him interviewing the new girl at the coffee shop. And I know how he made Jennifer stay. What about you?"

The double doors to the lobby slam shut. I should just kill her. The soldiers will search every office in this hallway in a few minutes. Her lip trembles, but she doesn't speak.

I lower the gun. "Please." I don't want to hate her anymore. The emotion weighs too much. "I want to know."

"My son was diagnosed with MS 18 years ago." She folds her hands carefully in front of her stomach. "My husband couldn't handle it, so he left me to deal with it on my own."

"Larry knew your son would always be vulnerable."

She glances at the kill button again, then nods. "That's how it works around here. Larry has a file on everyone. Sometimes, it's blackmail material; sometimes, it's a loved one."

I think of Palmer bleeding in the closet and wonder what dark deed in his past led him to this place. "When I was kept here, I didn't know how Larry used people."

"Well, now you do." She looks between our respective weapons and unclasps her hands. "What are you going to do with me?"

"I'm here for Sam and Larry. No one else."

"And I'm collateral damage?"

I shake my head. "Only if you want to be."

"You think I can help you."

I toss the guard's radio on the desk. "Is this lab laid out like the original?"

She nods slowly.

"Tell them you saw me in one of the operating rooms." That will send the guards as away from the subject's quarters as possible. "Or don't, and I'll have to shoot you."

Nurse Rita gives a very convincing performance on the radio. We both duck as we hear the guards run past.

"Now I need you to get me into Sam's quarters," I say.

She hesitates. Sending the guards to the operating rooms will only buy me a few minutes.

"If I kill Sam, that kills the project. You'll be done. Larry will be disgraced."

"Keep the gun out and I'll help you," she says.

"What?"

"If the guards find us, you're on your own." That's Nurse Rita, always the sentimental one.

I open the door a crack, scanning for any signs of life. There are none. I put my gun in Rita's back, and we run toward the main lab area. Soon, we are running side-by-side and I'm faced with the glass cages that haunted my nightmares.

Everything is exactly the same, except my gym area has been turned into quarters for Sam. He's reading a paper on his bed, unconcerned about the blaring alarms.

There's distant commotion in the operating rooms. Nurse Rita holds her face up the retinal scanner on Sam's cell. The lock clicks open. She holds her arms up, like I've pointed the gun at her. I follow her eyes behind me and see guards running toward us. She has to play the part of hostage. I move my finger to the outside of the trigger guard, and aim the gun at her as I step into Sam's glass cage.

"Good luck," she whispers, before the door locks me in.

Sam calmly folds the paper and sets it down on the bed. "Did Father send you?"

My 'brother' is delusional. "He's dead."

"How—"

"I killed him." It's close enough to the truth. I want Sam to die afraid. Manuel did.

His face crumples. "Y-you're here to kill me too."

I search myself for compassion and find none. "That's right."

Sam cowers on his bed. He looks so pitiful, it seems like cruelty to kill him. Until I see the glint in his eye. He's playing me like my father did.

I raise the gun. Sam runs to the glass wall. The guards who eagerly ran toward me earlier are now keeping a safe distance. Some are even sitting down in the observation area. "Come get her!" Sam yells. "She has a gun." As if the guards can't see that.

"None of the guards have been vaccinated," I say. "They won't listen to you."

Sam looks scared for real this time. A man not wearing fatigues strides in from the operating wing. The rhythm of his footsteps is familiar. This must be Larry. His face is smashed like a pug's, and his mouth is pursed like he tastes something sour. I expected a man with his inflated ego to be wearing a suit, but instead he's wearing cargo pants with a gun holstered at his waist. Like he fancies himself a man of action.

"Go get her!" he tells the milling group of soldiers. Some waver, some don't. None come any closer. Larry looks between the mutinous soldiers and me. His gun is useless as long as I'm in here. The glass walls are bulletproof. If he wants to kill me, he'll have to come inside. Without backup. "You," he stabs a finger at the closest guard. "Go get masks from one of the operating rooms."

The guard obeys, but he's not hurrying. It's a good decision. Masks are only partially effective. I doubt Larry will tell his troops that.

With a disgusted look, Larry leaves his pack behind and comes up to the glass. "There's nowhere to go, Sarina. Leave Sam alone, and come out like a good girl."

He's right, of course. About having nowhere to go. I knew that when I walked in this morning my chances of leaving were slim. Still, I feel a twinge of grief when I realize I will never see Pablo again. Larry hasn't figured out that survival isn't my goal. Of course he wouldn't; I doubt there's any cause Larry would sacrifice himself for.

I line up Sam's chest and pull the trigger. The shot swings wild as the gun kicks back, nearly hitting me in the forehead. Martin's gun was lighter.

Sam weaves as he runs at me. I scramble back, tripping over his chair, still firing. The recoil doesn't get any easier to control. I fire until the clip is empty, and I've only nicked him in the shoulder. I throw the gun away and grab the lamp from his desk. Sam circles me, unafraid. He's enjoying the game.

Never mind. Use the time to take inventory, I tell myself. I still have the pepper spray, but that's hardly lethal. The kill button is only good against me. Unless they kept to the schedule and Sam has his implants.

I lunge at him. He protects his face with one arm and with the other catches me in the ribs, hard. I swing the lamp at his upper thigh, where his incisions would be. His cry of pain tells me they are still tender.

While he's recovering, I put his bed between us and bring the kill button out of my pocket. The plastic cover clicks open. Sam freezes. Just do it, I tell myself. Do it *now*. But my hand doesn't move. I'm not worthy of this world, but I will miss it.

Larry slams his fists against the glass in frustration. "Unlock the door!" he screams. He doesn't care about backup anymore.

The door swings open. I press down on the red button. Just as I feel a hard pinch in my leg, I see a familiar figure pushing through the guards. It's Jennifer. Arms grab at her, but she yells something and they let her through. My leg goes numb beneath the incision; I fall painfully on my hip. The numbness spreads a little farther up my leg with each beat of my heart.

Sam is down too, clutching at his leg as if he could stop the poison from spreading. The sight makes me smile. Larry may still be alive, but I won.

It's three more heartbeats before Jennifer reaches me. I wonder why Larry doesn't stop her. My hip is numb now. I will the poison to reach my spine faster. She has a needle in her hand. A very large needle. She plunges the silver tip into my chest, and I feel it pierce my heart. Then my heart stops.

When I imagined Jennifer stopping my heart, it was always on the operating table, and out of malice. Malice would be easier to bear. I will spend the last seconds of my life watching my good deed go to waste. She strokes my hair just once. Her quiet tears wet her cheeks. As my vision goes black, I see two guards in masks leaning over us, pulling her away, and her cries become sobs and screams.

Chapter 34

When I wake up in a hospital room, my first thought is that I'm back at the lab. Then I see Harold in a chair next to my bed. And the window, with bright sunshine streaming in. The door to the room is open, and I can see people walking by. No one's wearing an army uniform. The ID badges hanging at their waists have pictures, not like the ones at the lab. A patient leaning on a walker crosses in front of the doorway. It's a real hospital, for real people.

"Sarina, you're up," Harold says.

He seems awfully calm. "Jenny, the coffee can wait," he calls into the hallway. "She's awake."

Jennifer appears in the doorway, unharmed. She takes a chair on the other side of my bed. "It's good to see your eyes open, sweetheart."

I shift uncomfortably. This is wrong. I should be dead. Did the poison not work? Did Sam survive too? How am I free if Sam is alive? How am I free at all? "What happened?" I manage with a scratchy voice.

They look at each other and laugh. "A lot," Jennifer says. "Have some water." She fills a small paper cup.

I push it away. "I saw them take you."

Harold takes the cup and holds it to my lips. "Drink. You're safe. We're safe. We can explain everything later."

I sip the water. My throat is grateful even as my mind whirs impatiently. It feels like five minutes ago, I was lying on the floor watching Jennifer get recaptured. "Please, just tell me now."

Jennifer reaches for Harold's hand across the bed. Their clasped hands are warm on my leg. "I was locked up after you blacked out. He wanted to execute me himself, but he didn't get to it right away because of everything else. I think he liked the idea of making me wait." The smile drops from her face. She squeezes Harold's hand.

"I went for help," he says. "There were a few journalists working on the story of your father's escape. Between them and the local cops, Larry was forced to release her."

"He's alive, then," I say. I know I shouldn't wish him dead, but I do. Larry made the continuation of my father's dreams possible. If not for Larry and his gang of thugs, I would have been cured. The Harrises and Manuel wouldn't have suffered for my sake.

Harold shakes his head. "Larry died in his prison cell. They're calling it suicide, but with his friends? Who knows."

It's a fitting end for him, even if I didn't get the honors. "Sam is dead?"

"Sam is dead," Jennifer says. "You got him, just like you wanted." She almost sounds disappointed.

"You want him alive?" I ask, a little too sharply.

She releases Harold's hand and covers mine. "No, I didn't want you to—" She fidgets with the thin blanket. "I didn't want you to have to kill him. Even if he deserved it. Do you understand?"

"No. I don't regret it." Not much anyway.

"We wanted you to come with us so we could protect you," Harold says. "You've never had anyone to protect you. It wasn't fair."

Unwelcome tears sting my eyes. "I want to know everything that happened after we split up."

Jennifer and Harold exchange a look, frowning. "Are you sure you don't want to rest?" she asks. "We have all the time in the world."

I shake my head. "How did I get here? And how did you get back in the lab? And…" There are so many questions to ask, I don't even know where to start.

"I saw you grab the kill button from the guard's desk," Jennifer says. "I knew you weren't going to follow us. So after I helped Harold get to the car, I came back. The lobby was still empty."

I must have been fighting Palmer in the closet that whole time.

"I was searching for you in the operating wing when Larry ordered the lockdown."

"None of the medical staff stopped you?" I asked.

Jennifer smiles a little. "I had my gun in the car. I brought it with me. I'm sure they reported me, but the priority was finding you."

It makes sense I wouldn't have heard about Jennifer being inside. I kept the radio off except when Rita was sending the guards to the wrong side of the lab.

"Anyway," Jennifer continues, "I knew you might be stupid enough to use the kill switch and I couldn't find you right away so I went to the operating wing to prepare a syringe with a potassium solution. Like they use in open-heart surgery."

Stupid? I thought I was being brave and noble.

"I managed to hide in a supplies closet while they were searching, and then you were spotted in Sam's quarters. At that point, they weren't paying much attention to anything else, so I was able to follow them. When I saw you hit the kill switch, I ran to you as fast as I could."

I remember how the guards grabbed for her and then let go. "You told them you could save me if they let you through."

"The poison is neurotoxin that spreads via the circulatory system, but it breaks down quickly to avoid detection. I knew if I stopped your heart, we might be able to prevent any permanent damage."

I wiggle my toes, relieved to see the sheets move over both my feet.

Harold pats my arm. "Yes, you seem to be completely re-covered. I'm not sure what they did, but judging by the operating room setup when the police forced their way in, they probably induced a coma after they restarted your heart."

"They induced a coma to help me heal?" I ask.

"More likely, the coma was to keep you from escaping again," Harold says. "You were more resourceful than Larry anticipated."

That answers a few questions. But it doesn't explain how I got here. "So you found me when the police forced their way in?"

"Have a little more water," Jennifer insists.

The water does feel good. I finish the half-full pitcher.

"We don't know how you got here," Harold says. "You weren't in the lab when it was shut down."

Jennifer fidgets with the sheets again. "Larry told me you were 'put down.' I saw the pentobarbital IV in the operating wing when they released me. It is fatal in high enough doses. We didn't know what had happened, but I couldn't—" She recomposes herself with a deep breath. "We thought maybe whoever had been given the order couldn't do it, maybe they dropped you off somewhere half-conscious."

"Everyone in the lab hated me except for you two."

Jennifer blinks, surprised. "Is that what you think? It wasn't like that at all. You know how hard Larry worked to reduce turnover. Most of us had been there since you were young, long enough to watch you grow up. They kept their distance to protect themselves. Martin and Larry... That was different. You were a threat to them."

I try to digest this new bit of information as Jennifer keeps talking.

"So we called all the nearby hospitals inquiring about Jane Does, and that's how we found you here, Hartford General."

There are loud voices down the hall. One of the voices sounds like Pablo's. I must be hearing things.

"I'm here about Janine Harris," he says, obviously frustrated.

"We don't have anyone named Janine Harris, sir," says the nurse stiffly.

"Someone called me and said they dropped her off here two days ago."

"There was a Jane Doe dropped off then. She didn't have any ID."

I had the phone Pablo gave me when I was recaptured. I told him my last name was Harris. But the lab wouldn't have called Pablo, would they? It was stupid of me to bring it at all, now that I think about it. The lab might have tracked him down.

"Third room on the left," says the nurse. "Visiting hours are..." By the way she trails off, I know Pablo is walking here already. I recognize the cadence of his steps. Harold is up, guarding the door before I can tell them Pablo is a friend. Even with his leg in a cast, Harold looks formidable.

"I'm here for Janine," Pablo says. "Let me in."

"Janine?" Harold asks.

"The fake passport, sweetie," Jennifer says, getting up.

"Fake passport?" Pablo asks.

"I don't know who sent you, but I'm not just going to let you in," Harold says. "Why don't we start with your name and how you know her?"

"Pablo. I'm her... boyfriend, I guess."

Harold's posture changes from wary to aggressive. "Her boyfriend's dead. Try again." My father must have told Harold about Manuel.

"You're confused. I don't normally hit men in casts, but I'll make an exception if you don't get out of my way."

"There are two of us to get through," Jennifer says.

I try to make my voice heard over the argument at the door, but my throat is too parched to carry. There are other ways to make noise. I take the pitcher of water and bang it against the tray. Harold turns to look at me.

"Let him in," I say.

Pablo pushes past my guardians and folds me into a hug. I've missed him more than I want to admit.

"I wanted to get here sooner," Pablo says. "But I couldn't get off until we stopped in Charleston. Some woman called me from your number, didn't even give her name. She said she was supposed to kill you, but instead she was dropping you off here. She had a really gravelly voice, like she smoked too much."

"Rita," Harold, Jennifer, and I say together.

"She must have snuck you out and dropped you off here instead of following her orders," Jennifer says

"Rita? Snuck out?" asks Pablo. "What the hell happened to you? And you two." He gestures at Harold and Jennifer. "You're the ones from the picture she had. The ones who aren't her parents."

"The picture?" It's Jennifer's turn to look confused.

"They're…" I'm not sure exactly how to start. Pablo is holding my hand like it's the most natural thing in the world. And it is. "It's a long story," I say finally. But this time, I'm going to tell him everything.

My name is Sarina.

My breath is poison.

I was not born out of love.

Acknowledgements

When the idea for this book crawled into my head (and refused to leave), I had no idea how many friendships would be forged or strengthened along the way. My longtime friend, Bridget Kromhout, read the early draft and gave me encouragement (and some edits). A new friend, Chris Gales, lovingly matched the draft with an editor, Olivia Ngai. My fellow writers on Critique Circle (Carol Ervin, Lindy Moon, Katherine Lato, and Sky, among others) went through two drafts with me and kept me honest. My uncle, an anesthesiologist, patiently answered all my medical questions. Collectively, this group has been my best cheerleaders and my best critics. I am grateful to them all.

I also owe thanks to a couple strangers. BeeJavier created the cover art. The builders of Calibre deserve a shout-out as well, for an excellent program that saved me hours of heartache.